DEATH IS THE ISSUE

JANET HARWARD

Janet Harward lives in the Midlands with her husband and two daughters. Her first novel, *Murder on The English Riviera*, was published in 1995, and was followed in 1996 by *The Teddy Bear Murders*, the first Josephine Blake mystery, *In Memory of Murder*, the second Josephine Blake mystery and *Echoes of Death*, the third in the series.

Death Is The Issue is the latest in the Josephine Blake series.

Janet Harward

DEATH IS
THE ISSUE

O'Neill Publishing

First published in Great Britain by O'Neill Publishing, 1999.

Copyright © Janet Harward 1999

A CIP catalogue record for this book is available from the British Library.

ISBN: 09525161-4-4

9 8 7 6 5 4 3 2 1

Book design and typography by DP Fact and Fiction.
Printed and bound in Great Britain by Caledonian International Book Manufacturing, Bishopbriggs, Glasgow.

DISCLAIMER

This book is set in Birmingham in the Midlands and Torbay in Devon. Most district names are genuine. Some places are fictional. The characters and situations are entirely imaginary and bear no relation to any real person or happening. All of the locations, businesses or buildings are mentioned in a purely fictional capacity.

DEDICATION

For Sandy, 'man's best friend,' and certainly mine.

And to the memory of Marcel Cassauwers, who was a fine man, and will be greatly missed by all who knew him.

ACKNOWLEDGEMENTS

The Author wishes to thank:

Dr P. R. Acland of the West Midlands Pathology
Department.

Dave Earl of the West Midlands Police.

Jonathan Marshall for his help in typing this
book.

James Blackie P.I. for his insight into the world of
the private investigator.

DEATH IS THE ISSUE

Chapter 1

SHE GRASPED HER FATHER'S HAND with tiny fingers and laughed as they paddled in the sea.

Then, suddenly a strange force came between them that started to pull him away.

"Don't go Daddy. Don't go—"

A dark cloud enveloped his body and he vanished.

She was being pushed along on a trolley, with people running beside her. Everyone was in a hurry, and they were dashing about.

Voices, there were so many voices.

"Quick, O3's free. Is Doctor Rand here yet?"

"Yes, he's just scrubbing up."

"Good, there's not much time."

What's all this commotion about? Why is everyone so agitated? I just want to go and see Dad. Josephine thought. She felt calm and serene.

And then there was darkness.

She was no longer small, as she sat at her father's bedside watching him take his last breath of life before slipping away peacefully. Then she heard a strange, evil voice in her ear.

"Jack's here. Do you want to join your father?" He stood over her, the knife in his hand dripping with blood.

"Yes, I do. I want to go with him."

"Well you can't. You're going to live!"

She was being sucked down a long dark tunnel, her father at one end, beckoning to her, and familiar faces at the other, although she couldn't put a name to any of them. They were all calling to her in the dark swirling channel and she was confused and crying. Her father's voice said,

"You must go back, my dear little Jo. It's not your time yet."

"But I don't want to, Daddy. I want to be with you."

"Go back my child. Go back."

She opened her eyes and strained into the blackness—something advanced in the shadows. As she tried to move, the pain in her chest was excruciating, and her back was clammy with perspiration.

Fear—Fear—I must get away from him.

As light flooded the room a woman in blue came up to her and said in a soft sweet voice

"There, there, it's alright Josephine, you've been having a nightmare."

"Where am I?" she asked, as she looked round the strange clinical room.

"You're in hospital, you've been unconscious for quite some time. I'll get the doctor."

"Don't leave me," Josephine said as she grasped the nurse's hand, "I don't want to be alone, in case he comes back."

"Don't worry." The nurse said kindly as she pressed the red button at the side of the bed.

Some minutes later, a man entered the room, and

introduced himself as Doctor Mason. He was in his late thirties, with auburn hair, and pale freckled skin. As he smiled at her his green eyes looked tired and sore.

"It's nice to have you back with us, Mrs Blake, you've been unconscious for some time."

"How long?" she asked.

"You came out of your coma about four days ago," he started to explain. "Up until then you were in Intensive Care, but the last three days you've drifted in and out of a disturbed and agitated sleep. I'm afraid that you've had hallucinations, possibly a side effect of the drugs we've been administering."

"Are you telling me I'm going mad?"

"Certainly not; I think considering the ordeal you've been through, both emotionally and physically, you're a remarkably sane woman," he said, as he patted her hand and smiled.

"In fact, it's the staff round here that are ready for the loony bin," the nurse joked.

"Is it any wonder we're all bonkers with the hours we have to work," the doctor agreed.

Josephine was glad that these two had been on duty when she had come round. They had curbed her fear, by joking with her.

As the doctor was checking her blood pressure and pulse, she winced in pain.

"I'll give you something for that," he told her.

Her throat was very dry. "I'd love a cup of tea," she announced.

"I'll see to that right away," the nurse said as she

left the room.

"I don't suppose you're the one who saw me when I came in, are you?" she enquired. "Only everything's so muzzy and I feel confused."

"In time you'll feel more adjusted, especially when you start eating properly—you've been fed intravenously with a drip. As to your first question, it was Mr Rand, one of our top consultants who operated on you. He's doing his rounds later today," he said, as he glanced at his watch.

"What time is it now?" Josephine asked.

"Three thirty in the morning," he replied yawning." And I'm still on duty till eight o'clock."

As the nurse entered the room with the tea in a plastic cup and a straw, she said

"Your daughter and husband have been several times, and also a colleague, a Doctor Blythe, but you've always been asleep. They'll be pleased to know you're now fully awake. In fact, Doctor Blythe has spent several days in the hospital while you were unconscious. I sent him home at about eleven o'clock last night, as he looked exhausted, but I have all the telephone numbers if you want to contact them."

Dear Andrew. He must have been so worried, Josephine thought as she sipped her tea through the plastic straw.

"Should I ring your husband?" the nurse asked.

"Andrew—oh no—it's—"

"Are you OK?" the nurse asked.

"Yes—er—Tom is my ex-husband. We're only

16

recently divorced."

"Oh I see—still, he did seem concerned about you and your daughter."

"Can you ring them before you go off duty? I don't want to wake them in the middle of the night."

"Yes, I'll see to that for you."

"Oh, and will you ring Doctor Blythe first, only he's a good friend," Josephine told her.

"Of course, I understand." the nurse said with a twinkle in her eye.

Josephine suddenly remembered why she was in hospital.

"Do I have a guard outside my door?" she asked.

"No, why ever should you. You're quite safe here."

Josephine's heart started to pound, and her chest ached.

"Don't you see? If he knows I'm here, he'll come and get me again!" She became very agitated.

"I'll get something to calm you down."

"I don't want anything," she protested.

Some minutes later Josephine was sleeping peacefully due to a Valium injection the doctor had given her.

When she stirred at nine o'clock, Andrew was sitting by the side of her bed, holding her hand. She opened her eyes slowly, and it was a few seconds before his face came into focus. Although

17

he was smiling, his eyes were full of tears and he looked tired and drawn.

"Oh, my darling Jo. I thought I was going to lose you." He squeezed her hand as he looked into her eyes. "I knew the real danger was over when you came out of the coma, but you kept slipping in and out of consciousness, and you weren't aware anyone was here. Jessica's been worried sick and believe it or not, Tom's visited several times."

"I need to sit up," she said wincing in pain. He helped her up gently and made her more comfortable by adjusting the pillows at the back of her head. Her face suddenly went taut and she looked afraid. "Did they get him. Is he safely locked away?"

"Don't you remember?" Andrew asked gently as he stroked her hair.

"Some things I can recall. I remember him stabbing me with the knife, but then it's all so muddled."

"He slit his own throat in front of you," Andrew told her.

Josephine suddenly had a flashback to the night she had to fight for her life with the copycat Jack the Ripper killer who had pursued her so relentlessly.

"It's all over now Jo, he's dead," Andrew told her.

"Oh thank God for that! I kept thinking he was coming to get me in here. The nightmares were so real."

"I'd have never let any harm come to you. If he hadn't committed suicide, I'd have killed him myself!"

"Strong words, from a forensic psychologist," Josephine said lightly, feeling an immense relief at what he had just told her.

"When you're strong enough to leave hospital, I'm taking you away for a holiday. A friend of mine has a villa on the Costa del Sol that we can have. It's still warm even at this time of the year and the sun will do you good."

"It sounds wonderful," she sighed "But I'm so weak and frail, I'd be a burden to you."

Andrew's tender expression turned to one of both anger and hurt.

"Don't ever let me hear you say that again. I love you Jo, and you'll never be a burden. It might take time, I know, but with the right care we'll have you fit and well again, and that's all that matters. As long as we're together, we have all the time in the world. Just look to the future now. Don't look back."

The consultant breezed into the room, followed by three junior doctors and a nurse. Mr Rand was in his early sixties with dark hair that was parted down one side. He wore a smartly cut pinstripe suit and waistcoat with a bright yellow spotted bow tie.

"Nice to see you back in the land of the living, my dear. And how are we today?"

Josephine was just about to answer him when he continued talking.

"Now, Mrs Blake here was a very lucky woman, for two reasons. A—The stab wounds just narrowly missed one of the main arteries leading to the heart. And B—I was available to operate on her when she was admitted."

Obviously, modesty isn't one of his virtues, Josephine thought to herself.

He picked up the chart at the bottom of the bed.

"Mm—pulse and blood pressure are fine, slight temperature, but nothing to worry about. I see you were able to manage some breakfast today. That's good."

"When do you think I'll be well enough to leave?" Josephine asked him.

"You're still very weak and have lost a lot of blood, so we had to give you a transfusion. Still, you're relatively young and were fit and healthy beforehand; I'd say about a week, if you behave yourself, and do as you're told."

If the man standing before her hadn't brought her back from the brink of death, due to his skills as a surgeon, she'd have been quite annoyed at him talking to her as if she were a child, but decided under the circumstances to make allowances.

"And when do you think I'll be able to go back to work?" she asked.

He turned to his group.

"Mrs Blake here, is a policewoman."

"A Detective Inspector, actually," Josephine

corrected him.

"Yes quite, quite, and you've been through an emotional ordeal, as well as a physical one. Obviously that's not my field, but I'd like you to have some counselling with our clinical psychologist."

She was just about to object, when her thoughts went back to the terrible nightmares she'd experienced, and despite the fact Josephine was a very logical and level headed person, she did feel she'd had a close encounter with the 'other side'.

"Yes—I think I'd like to talk to someone."

"Splendid, splendid!" he replied.

"You haven't answered my first question," she added.

"What was that my dear?"

"When I'd be able to go back to work."

"Possibly in a couple of months time, though I don't see why you want to go back to police work—it's so dangerous."

"It's my profession, and it's what I do best. Surely someone in your position can understand that." One of the young doctors gave a little snigger.

"Quite, well, it's your decision, I'm just here to patch you up." He removed his fob watch from his waistcoat pocket, "Goodness me, is that the time?" he declared like the rabbit in Alice In Wonderland. "Well, must get on with the rounds, come along." He turned briskly and left the room and the rest of them followed him obediently. The nurse was the last to leave.

"I don't think I've heard anyone get the better of him before," she said smiling as she closed the door behind her.

It was about three o'clock in the afternoon, when Jessica crept into her mother's room carrying a bunch of freesias in one hand and grapes in the other. Josephine was fast asleep.

"Mum—mum," Jessica whispered gently in her ear.

Josephine slowly opened her eyes.

"Hello darling, it's lovely to see you."

Jessica looked at her mother, her face so pale and thin. "Oh mum, I really thought I'd lost you!" Jessica burst into tears. She rested her head on the pillow as Josephine stroked her hair.

"Don't cry love. I hope you've got me for a good while yet."

After a few minutes, when Jessica had stopped crying she wiped her eyes.

"Help me to sit up will you," Josephine said. When she was comfortable Jessica gave her the flowers. "Oh freesias, I've always loved the smell."

"I've brought you some grapes as well, although I don't know if you're allowed to eat them."

"I'm on a light diet at the moment," Josephine told her. "By the way, have you got a mirror on you?" Jessica mooched through her bag and pulled out a small compact mirror, which she handed to her.

As Josephine looked at her reflection, she gasped "Oh my God. I look such a mess, so pale and drawn! To think Andrew's seen me like this!"

"Don't worry mum, you look fine," Jessica tried to reassure her.

"Don't lie, I look a wreck and you know it. You'll have to leave me some of your make-up and next time you visit bring me some things from home."

Jessica took her make-up bag out and handed it to her mother "See if there's anything you want in there."

Josephine took out a foundation, blusher, and mascara. "Jessica, what a terrible colour!" she said as she pushed up a purple lipstick.

"It's the latest colour."

"It may look okay on your young skin, but it will make me look like one of Dracula's victims. Mind you, I probably do already."

"There's a shop in the hospital grounds, do you want me to go and see if they sell make-up?" Jessica asked.

"Yes, you know the sort of thing I wear, peach, coral, something like that, and get me a hair brush, and some body spray."

Jessica stood up.

"I won't be long," she said picking up her bag. "Oh by the way, Dad's waiting outside, he'd like to see you."

"I'm amazed Marion let him visit," she said a little bitterly.

"Don't be like that mum, he's been just as

worried and concerned as anyone."

"I know, I'm sorry, send him in on your way out."

"Don't you want to put some make-up on first?" Jessica asked.

"No, your dad's seen me without my face on before."

Jessica left and a few minutes later Tom came into the room. He walked up to Josephine and gave her a peck on the cheek.

"It's good to see you sitting up, we've all been so worried."

Jessica warmed to Tom, and realised her criticism of him to Jessica had been unfair. She'd been married to him for over twenty years, and despite the fact they were now divorced and both involved in other relationships, she still cared for him. It was impossible to feel any different when you'd spent so much of your life with one person.

"How are you, feeling?"

"I'm in a bit of pain and I feel weak, but according to my consultant, there's no permanent damage. Anyway, how's Marion?" she asked.

"She's fine, sends her regards and hopes you have a speedy recovery."

I bet she does! Josephine thought.

"I know we've got separate lives now Jo, but when I thought I was going to lose you it was awful, I didn't realise until then just how much I cared. I don't suppose there's any chance that we might…"

Josephine stopped him before he went any further.

24

"Look Tom, it's understandable that you were upset, we had been married for a long time. If you'd have been badly injured and I thought you wouldn't survive, I'd feel exactly the same."

"Then is there any possibility we can…" He didn't finish his sentence.

"No Tom, it's water under the bridge and there's no turning back. You're the father of my child and I still care, but we have to move on. We hadn't got on over the last few years, all we did was argue, and you're happy with Marion aren't you?"

He didn't answer for a few moments "Yes—I think—yes I am."

"And I'm happy with Andrew," she announced.

"Do you intend to marry him?" Tom enquired.

"God, don't talk about marriage! All I can say at this moment is he cares about me, and he's been there when times were bad. Who knows if we'll be together in six or twelve months time? Having come so close to death I don't want to make plans any more, I just want to take one day at a time."

He looked sad and dejected as he sat at the side of her bed. Josephine reached out and touched his hand "Listen Tom, I'm glad we're friends for Jessica's sake. We need to make sure her future is secure when she leaves University."

"I suppose you're right, in fact you always bloody well are," he said laughing.

Jessica returned. It felt good to see her mother and father were friends, even though she had no illusions that they would ever be a couple again.

She handed Josephine a carrier bag "There you are, mum. There's a few things in there that'll make you look better."

"I think the only thing that would improve my looks at the moment is a face lift," Josephine said as she took the bag from her daughter.

Chapter 2

THREE WEEKS LATER.

JOSEPHINE LAY BACK on the lounger, and felt the warm sun on her face. The villa where they were staying was situated on a hill that overlooked the Mediterranean. It felt good to be alive and virtually free from pain, as long as she remembered to take the drugs at regular intervals. Her close to death experience had made her a more philosophical person. She had come to terms with her own mortality, and realised, as people do from time to time, that she was only on this earth for a relatively short time. She thought of all the things that she'd wanted to do. Somehow she'd never found the time, due to both the pressures of her job and of life in general. It's only the things we never get round to doing that we regret. She hadn't kept in touch with some of her family and friends who lived in the Midlands. There had been so much she had wanted to tell her father when he was alive, but had never had the chance. Now it was too late. Although, due to her strange experiences while she was desperately ill, she felt that someday it might be possible.

She watched Andrew as he swam in the pool; he looked fit and tanned. *My Dear Andrew, my hope, my salvation!*

He had reached her just in time before the serial killer had the chance to finally finish her off, although he had almost achieved his goal before slitting his own throat. That scene would haunt Josephine for the rest of her days, but thanks to Andrew she was trying to come to terms with what had happened. He had boosted her confidence when she was at an all time low, made certain she took all the drugs that the hospital had prescribed, and when she had no appetite, he had enticed her to eat by preparing her favourite meals. Thanks to his tender loving care, she was regaining her health. As he finished swimming one more length of the pool, he climbed out and wrapped a towel around him as he kissed Josephine on the tip of her nose.

"Andrew, you're dripping water all over me" she said laughing.

"Why don't you have a swim?" he suggested.

"Mm—I think I might," she said getting slowly up from the sun lounger.

'Mind you don't overdo it, though."

"I shouldn't think I've the strength," she replied.

Later that evening they were having a meal in a lovely Spanish taverna that was situated at the far end of the beach. They discovered it one day as they were exploring the coves. It was mainly frequented by the locals, as it was off the main tourist track. This was their third visit in less than a week as Andrew and Josephine had become friendly with Carlos the owner. This evening on his recommendation they were having grilled sardines with a salad tossed in olive oil. They'd usually order a carafe of dry white wine and Carlos would always give his customers a complimentary starter which consisted of hot crusty bread, black olives, and a dish of his home made garlic mayonnaise, which Josephine adored. She usually ate so much before her main meal arrived that she often couldn't finish the second course.

After the meal they walked along the beach, as they did most evenings. Josephine looked out over the moonlit sea and said,

"It's a pity we have to go back, I feel I could stay here forever."

"You've changed your tune, you said a few days ago, that you were missing Jessica, and saying that you couldn't wait for the, doctor to sign you off, so you could go back to work."

"I know, I know," she agreed "But I'm settling in now. I feel sure I could get used to this way of life."

"Well there's not much chance of that unless you win the lottery, and I've never seen you buy a ticket," Andrew remarked.

"I've never believed in gambling, the way I look at it, it's just the odds of life. No-one wants to think they'll be the one to die of some disease or get smashed up on the roads but they always want to be the one who wins the pools or the lottery, the odds are the same."

"Very profound words," Andrew said teasingly, "But I must admit I do see your point."

As they walked on a little further, he asked "Are you sure you want to return to police work after what's happened?"

"It's the only thing I'm good at, and I just can't

see myself doing anything else." She paused for a few moments and then said, "I'll tell you what I'd like to do Andrew. I'd like to go back to Birmingham for a few days. See my family before I go back to work. I haven't been in the city since I was in my twenties. I just don't know where the years have gone..."

"But you've seen your Aunt's sister—I can remember you saying she was coming down to Devon for a holiday," Andrew said.

"Oh yes, I've seen Auntie Win, but none of the others."

"Well I'm afraid I can't see why you want to go back, even for a few days. It's noisy, overcrowded, and dirty."

"How would you know?" she asked angrily.

"Because I was there last year for a conference, you haven't been there for over twenty years. It's changed so much," he informed her.

"What place hasn't? Anyway you're talking about the place I was born and spent the first half of my life. It's where my roots are. I love Devon, and I can't see myself living anywhere else, but I need to go back home, if only for a short time."

"Well it's your decision," Andrew began, "And if you really feel the need to return, then you must go with your instinct, but I'd have thought it was far from the ideal place to recuperate."

Chapter 3

"TRANSFER?" Chief Inspector Cunningham looked shocked. "Are you sure? You've been through an emotional and physical ordeal—are you certain you've thought this through properly?"

"I can assure you sir," Josephine began, "I've thought of nothing else. I don't expect you to understand my reasons. I think that only someone who'd been as close to death as I have could relate to the way I feel. If it hadn't been for Andrew Blythe and the skill of the surgeons I wouldn't be standing here having this conversation with you."

"Yes... quite. But, I mean, Josephine. You have your family and friends here. What about Jessica? A girl needs her mother!" The chief was trying to act the part of a concerned friend who had her interests at heart. He was in no danger of collecting an Oscar for his performance.

"I'll miss Bill and the team, there's no denying that. But I'm only asking for six months—it's not as if I want it to be permanent. Jessica's been at University for the past three years—I'm sure in that time she's learnt to cope without me."

"It won't be like here in the West Midlands, you know. There's more crime in the cities, and Birmingham is no exception. It's a pressure cooker. Pollution, race problems, drugs, major crimes, even some terrorism. I'd have thought after what you've been through, the stress and strain of policing a major city would be the last thing you'd want!"

"I take your point, but it *was* in sleepy old Devon that I was nearly killed by a serial killer, sir—the third of my acquaintance. Birmingham is where I was born, and I still have family there. And I want to go home, for a while."

"It's changed since the sixties you know. Some of it for the better, but some for the worse."

"I daresay it has, sir. Perhaps I'll hate it; perhaps I'll love it. But I'll never know unless I go. If the knife had hit me a little higher I'd never have had the chance to find out which."

Cunningham knew Josephine well enough to realise that when her mind was made up about something there was little sense in arguing. He prepared to give in gracefully.

"Six months you say. Okay, I'll see what I can arrange, and I'll let you know when I have something definite."

Josephine had decided not to mention her decision to anyone at work, until she was certain of the outcome of her request. It was a further week before she was called back into his office to find that he'd got her a six-month secondment to the Major Investigation Unit in central Birmingham.

"You'll be working under Chief Detective Inspector Robert Lyle. I've met him before and he seems like a decent sort, if a bit of an old woman."

"Thank you sir, I appreciate what you've done for me," she said, smiling.

"Well, I know from investigations past that when you're set on something…" He shrugged, wryly. "Just make sure you come back to us in one piece when you're finished, DI Blake, as I wouldn't want to lose you. What would we do with our next serial killer? Tell Lyle we'll be counting the days."

Josephine left his office feeling a sense of contentment. Over the years she'd found Cunningham sparing with praise, and she'd felt flattered at his clear desire to keep her. It was obvious that he, at least, wasn't worried that her brush with death would effect her efficiency as a copper. She only wished that she had the same confidence in herself. Perhaps her sojourn in Birmingham would restore it.

"Now look here, Josephine, I won't have you staying in police accommodation, you must stay with us."

Her late father's sister, affectionately known as Auntie Win, was obviously not going to take no for an answer.

"Arthur is so looking forward to seeing you, and we've plenty of room. In fact we could arrange a little get together, family reunion, you know the sort of thing."

"Look here Auntie Win, I don't want you to go to any trouble," Josephine told her when she had finally managed to get a word in edgeways.

"Nonsense, you know we love a knees up. It's a pity little Jessica isn't coming with you."

"Little Jessica is taller than me now," Josephine informed her.

After a further fifteen minutes on the phone Josephine agreed to stay there for the first two weeks or so. She said she would then move into police singles accommodation, which would be provided. She went on to explain that due to the hours she worked, she could be contacted any time day or night, and that it wouldn't be practical. When the arrangements were finally settled, Josephine put down the receiver feeling completely exhausted.

Explaining her decision to Jessica was no problem, but then Josephine had never thought it would be. Jessica had recently finished the degree, and was now staying at home at Josephine's house in Babbacombe. Jessica had written letters and had sent CVs off for several positions, and was just waiting for replies. Having supported Jessica while she was studying, both financially and emotionally, Josephine hoped that eventually her daughter would find a career that suited her.

"I think it's a great idea," Jessica said. "It's a pity I can't come with you, there are some great clubs in Birmingham, but I have to stay here in case I get anything positive on the job front. I've also got one or two interviews in the pipeline. Still, you'll need me here to look after the house. I was thinking of asking Sally to come and stay, if that's alright with you."

"That's fine by me, but just don't get asking everyone around. I don't want to come home and find the house wrecked," Josephine replied.

The one person she was dreading telling was Andrew. She felt so much in his debt, although he would never have wished her to feel that way. After her divorce from Tom, her confidence had been at an all-time low. Then Andrew came along, wined and dined her, made her laugh when she wanted to cry, and had shown what she considered to be genuine love and affection, despite the fact she had been very wary of men at that time in her life. Ultimately, he had arrived just in the nick of time, as she was being slashed by the serial killer. Along with the surgeon's skill he had been partly responsible for saving her life.

She decided to ask him over for dinner on Friday evening, as she knew Jessica would be out with friends. She'd prepared a special menu of all his favourite foods. Avocado and prawns to start, rib-eye steak in a red wine and mushroom sauce, and raspberries and cream to follow, not forgetting his favourite cheese, Stilton, that he would enjoy with a glass of tawny port.

As he uncorked a bottle of wine, he glanced into the dining-room area. The table looked exquisite. She had used all the best china, lit the candles, and made a small centrepiece with fresh flowers.

"That looks wonderful," he observed. "What's the occasion?"

"Nothing in particular, I just wanted to spoil

you," she said without turning around as she stirred the sauce on the hob.

"Cut the crap Josephine, I'm not a complete imbecile!" he said bitterly.

She put down the wooden spoon and turned to face him.

"I... Err..." Before she had time to speak, he said, "I know all about it."

"Who from?"

"Does it really matter how I found out? The point is, why am I the last to know?" he demanded. "I suppose you were just going to walk out of my life without saying a word."

"There was no problem telling everyone else about the transfer because it didn't really bother me what they thought. You were the last to find out because I didn't know how I was going to explain. That's why I asked you to dinner."

"So all this," he said as he waved his hand towards the table, "Was to soften me up."

"Yes... no... Oh look, Andrew... can you pour me a drink, I really need one."

He poured her a large glass of red wine, while she turned the gas down, hoping the meal wouldn't spoil. She went into the lounge and sat down.

"Look, it's because I care, that I found it so difficult to tell you."

"I thought things were fine between us," he began.

"They are, as far as I'm concerned," she replied.

"So why ask for a transfer?"

"Come on, you're a forensic psychologist. I thought you understood the human mind," she said a little sarcastically.

"I do."

"So you must understand, after what I've been through, I value life and relationships more than I did in the past."

"Obviously that doesn't include ours," he snapped.

"You mean more to me than anyone. I couldn't have got through any of this without you," she said tenderly.

"So now I've served my purpose, but you feel obliged to be kind, because you feel indebted to me. Is that the case?"

"Look I was born in the Midlands, I spent my youth there. I just wanted to go back for a few months, to see old family and friends. I never really kept in touch, and life's short."

"You could have stayed for a couple of weeks, there was no need to move up there," he suggested.

"I know that, but I thought it would be a challenge, to do a stint in a Major Investigation Unit in a big city."

"Well, with the workload I've got at the moment. I doubt I'll be able to get to see you, but you probably don't want me there anyway," he said in a childish manner.

Considering Andrew Blythe was an eminent psychologist, his actions and words didn't justify his status. He was a man in love, and wasn't acting in a rational manner.

"Listen Andrew, I care about you because of who you are. Okay, so you helped me through a bad stage when Tom left, and you saved my life. I suppose you have done more for me in the relatively short time we've been together than some have done in many years of marriage. Even after saying all that, I'm with you because I want to be, not because I feel I have any obligation. How can you repay someone who's done that much? It would be impossible, so I am not even going to try. All I can offer is my love."

Andrew was touched by Josephine's declaration of her feelings, and secretly he did understand her need to see her family and for a tempting career change. The professional side of him could appreciate her position. It was the emotional side that wasn't so logical.

"Okay, I suppose our relationship is strong enough to withstand a six month separation," he admitted.

"I know it can," she replied positively, "And I hope that you'll be able to come and visit me some weekends despite your work commitments.

He pulled her towards him. "Don't worry, I'll be calling on you now and again to see you're behaving yourself," he said, smiling. He kissed her tenderly.

DS Bill Hughes sat on the edge of Josephine's desk

as she cleared away her last few belongings.

"I heard you put in a word for me with the chief about me being acting DI while you're away, and he's agreed."

"I'm sure you'll do an excellent job," she replied.

"There's only one problem really," Bill started.

"What's that?"

"Who will I have to criticise and make fun of while you're away?"

"I'm sure you'll find some poor sod, Bill," she told him.

"Yes, but can I call round and see them when I fancy a good nosh-up, and want to have a good moan about Joyce, when she's getting on my nerves?"

"No… I don't suppose you'll find anyone else *that* daft," she said, digging him in the ribs.

"I've heard you can't beat the Balti houses in Birmingham, they reckon. They do a brilliant curry. Don't be surprised if I pop up and see you one weekend. We'll have a few drinks and you can show me the sights."

"That's if I know where they are. I've heard it's changed a lot since the last time I was there. You know you're welcome to come—it'd be nice to see a friendly face. I don't know what sort of reception I'm going to get from the force there. It's the only thing I'm really worried about—do you think they'll accept me?"

"Of course they will, you idiot—you're a star! How many people on their force have put the kind of villains you've netted out of action? That's settled then—expect me for curry and a tour of the concrete jungle," he said, grinning. "I suppose your Auntie Win won't mind putting me up?"

Bill could never be described as the shy retiring type! He'd worked with Josephine for almost five years, and at the beginning there had been friction between them, as he hadn't taken kindly to the idea of a female boss. Over the years he'd come to admire and respect her, despite the fact that he didn't always agree with her somewhat gentle approach when interviewing suspects.

"A bit of space at last!" he said, as she finished clearing away. "Your office is much better than that pigeon hole I have to work in!"

Josephine suddenly felt very emotional, and her eyes filled with tears. She bit her lip and said "Don't get too comfortable—I'll be back in six months time."

She opened her office door with one hand as she supported the cardboard box that held her things in the other. Bill sat back in the chair—her chair—and put his feet up on the table.

"Don't forget to sort out those curry houses, so when I come up you can take me to the best ones… oh and by the way, ma'am…"

"Yes?" she said, turning.

"I'll miss you."

"Me too, Bill," she muttered, and left the office quickly, knowing that if she'd stayed a moment longer she'd have broken down in tears.

40

"I'll miss this view," Josephine sighed as she looked out of her lounge window to the sea.

"Still, never mind, think of all the tower blocks and high-rise monstrosities you've got to look forward to," Andrew replied sarcastically.

Josephine didn't answer. Andrew had been making various similar jibes over the last week or so. She turned her attention to Jessica, who was in the kitchen. "So, can we go through these things once more?"

"If we must," Jessica sighed.

"All the bills are paid by direct debit from the bank. The freezer's full, so you'll just have to do a small shop each week."

"No problem," Jessica replied.

"Now remember, no smoking in the lounge, try to vacuum at least twice a week and just keep the place reasonably tidy. The window cleaner comes every three weeks and I've left the money with Arthur next door... Now let me think. Is there any thing else?"

"I'll just look on this small list you've left me," Jessica said, pointing to an oversize sheet of paper that was pinned to the corkboard on the wall. "Although it's permanently imprinted on my brain, we've been through it so many times. I may have to sue for mental cruelty!"

"Right, I think that's it then," Josephine said, looking around the room as if she'd forgotten something. "I've given you Auntie Win's number and I'll let you know what the department's number is when I find out. Now, was there anything else…?"

"Mum, you're moving to Birmingham for six months, not the moon. You can drive back here in a few hours. Will you please go!" Jessica pleaded, "I'll be fine!"

Josephine accepted Andrew's offer of a lift up to the Midlands, as she hated motorway driving. It would give them a chance to be together a little longer and he would get to meet her family when they arrived.

Chapter 4

AUNTIE WIN GREETED Josephine with open arms. She was a large robust woman in her late sixties, with white permed hair and a florid complexion. She'd always reminded Josephine of a farmer's wife, although she'd had a life-long aversion to anything resembling the countryside and had hardly ventured out of the city.

Her husband was the complete opposite; he was small and slim, with very dark hair. At nearly seventy, not a single grey hair showed on his head. This wasn't due to any genetic predisposition, but rather to the over-liberal application of hair dye, giving his slicked back hair a slightly unreal appearance.

"So *this* is your young man!" Auntie Win said, beaming at Andrew. "Can't you persuade her to stay here, instead of the police accommodation?"

"I'm afraid, Auntie Win—if I can call you that— I couldn't persuade her to stay in Devon, so I think you're asking the wrong person."

"She was always stubborn as a little girl, she was," she agreed.

"I'm sure you could both do with a drink," Arthur intervened, winking slyly at Josephine. He ushered them both into the lounge and poured two glasses of wine. "I'm sure they must be hungry, Win," he said, looking at his wife.

"Of course! Whatever am I thinking of!" she exclaimed, as she bustled off to the kitchen to check on her cooking.

Despite all their attempts, Andrew couldn't be persuaded to stay the night and travel back the following morning. Josephine and he couldn't get a moment alone to say goodbye, despite Arthur's attempts to get his wife out of the way.

Andrew just gave Josephine a quick peck on the cheek as he got into his car, and simply said "Take care, I'll ring you," although the look in his eyes spoke volumes.

Chapter 5

AS SHE ENTERED Police Headquarters at Lloyd House in Birmingham, the first thing that struck Josephine was the size of the building. The reception area was like a vast set from a science fiction movie, with its large glass panels and steel doors.

She was shown up to the fifth floor, where Chief Inspector Robert Lyle was waiting to greet her. The first thing Josephine noticed was his height, he was five foot nine at the most, and was quite stocky. Because his mousy brown hair was receding slightly, it emphasised his round fat face. As he smiled at Josephine, she noticed a large gap between his front teeth. For some reason she took a sudden dislike to the man, even though she knew it was unprofessional to feel that way.

"DI Blake, I'd like to welcome you to the West Midlands Police, and introduce you to the team you'll be working with at the Major Investigations Unit." DS David Rankin, a young blonde man in his early thirties, stepped forward to shake her hand. Then she was introduced to DC Katie Lloyd, who appeared to be about the same age as her own daughter. She wore trousers and a shirt, had very short hair that looked almost shaven and her face didn't have a trace of make-up on it. If she hadn't been so well endowed, she could easily have been mistaken for a man. Finally, a young man of about thirty with red hair and pale freckled skin introduced himself as DC Mike Freeman.

"It's nice to meet you, ma'am," he said as he shook

her hand. Josephine's impression of him was that he was very polite, and a little shy. Her past experience of young male DCs was that the majority of them were usually over confident and sometimes abrupt.

When the introductions were over Robert Lyle began.

"Now I want you all, to give DI Blake here as much help as you can while she's settling in. Of course we all appreciate you may find it difficult adjusting to city policing. We do things a little differently here than in Devon."

"Really?" Josephine remarked. "Surely, police procedure is more or less the same to some extent, no matter what part of the country. Torquay is quite a busy resort, and we do have a fair share of murders and you're obviously aware of our drug problems, as we have so many that are smuggled in on boats around the area and we've had difficulties with foreign students especially in term time."

"I can appreciate that, ma'am," DS David Rankin intervened," but the crime rate in Birmingham is considerably higher and we do have a fair share of race related crimes and violent deaths being a major city."

"DI Blake has far more experience than we have in that field, as she's an expert on serial killers, but I'm sure there's no need for me to elaborate, as you've all read her case history," Robert Lyle said in her defence.

Josephine thought that perhaps she had been a little too hasty in forming a negative opinion about the man, when he continued.

"She's recently been very badly injured as you all know, so I feel she'll need time to—" He didn't have the chance to finish his sentence.

"I don't need treating with kid gloves," Josephine announced. "If I hadn't been passed as fit by the police doctor I wouldn't be standing here now and if I had the slightest doubt I couldn't cope, I wouldn't have asked for a transfer." She knew in her heart that although she was physically fit, she didn't feel that confident about her mental and emotional state. Her nights were still haunted by recurrent nightmares about her ordeal. She didn't want to start on the wrong foot with her new team or the chief so she decided to change the subject as she asked about the cases they were working on at that moment in time. DS Rankin spent the next fifteen minutes or so bringing her up to date with their present work load, after which the chief suggested they all go down to the canteen for lunch.

Just as the team left the room, the chief took her arm.

"I know you were quite high profile in the Torbay police department, but this is my patch and personally I don't think you'll be able to cope."

Josephine pushed his hand off her arm.

"Well, I'll just have to prove you wrong, won't I?" she said before marching down the corridor.

She sat in the police canteen drinking coffee, Josephine wasn't a coffee lover, but the tea was so awful she had no alternative. She slowly turned the spoon round and round the cup.

Wherever I go, I seem to cause waves.

Why are people so aggressive? Perhaps they do resent me moving in on their patch, but it's only for a matter of months. We're all on the earth for such a relatively short time. What's the point of all this friction?

Just at that moment, DC Katie Lloyd came up to her.

"Do you mind if I join you, ma'am?"

"Not at all," she replied. Katie sat down opposite her and demolished a large fry up and two rounds of bread, a meal Josephine could never have managed to consume. But then Katie was a big girl and probably needed it to sustain her.

"If you don't mind me saying," she began, as she drank from her mug of tea. "You were remarkably calm, ma'am."

"I suppose you know what happened to me in my last post," Josephine remarked.

"Yeah!" Katie smiled. "According to the grapevine, you fought him off as good as any man!"

"He still managed to injure me pretty badly though," Josephine informed her.

"Still, in my opinion it was 'one for the women'".

"Well, I don't know about that, but because I almost died, I've a different outlook on things now. Life's too short to be constantly bickering."

"Well as far as I know, no-one here has had such an experience. They don't mind what they say, or who it offends. They resent women, and they're probably jealous of you."

48

"That's a bit harsh, isn't it?" Josephine replied.

"Whenever I bring my girlfriend Sam to any of the police gigs, they always shun us."

"I take it from that remark you're gay, Katie."

"Yes, and proud of the fact. Do you have a problem with that ma'am?" she said with a tinge of aggression in her voice.

"None whatsoever. I've always believed in 'live and let live'. As long as it doesn't interfere with your work, I'm not interested. I'll judge you on the sort of person you are and how you do your job. Your sex life doesn't bother me in the slightest," Josephine answered.

"Well, it's nice to know you're on my side."

"I'm not on your or anyone else's side, Katie, but I'll tell you this. I don't like this notion of yours about hating men. There are good and bad men. Some are male chauvinists, and they really believe the sick concept that 'If you had a real man for one night, you wouldn't be a lesbian.' But there are some decent men both in and out of the force. Hatred is a waste of energy that could be channelled into your work. I say what I feel, and it's always worked well for me in the past with my team of officers. Ignore any remarks about your sexual preferences, and don't rise to the bait. If you get on with your job and do it well, you'll be admired and respected for that."

The young DC was silent for a few moments and then said,

"I can see what you say makes sense, but it's going to be hard to ignore the jibes."

"Nothing's ever easy that's worth achieving,"

Josephine stated.

"Do you know ma'am, I'm really glad they picked me for your team."

Well at least I've got someone in my corner Josephine thought to herself.

Josephine sat in the passenger seat as DS Rankin drove through the city. As they approached Broad Street, she instantly recognised Baskerville House, the large council building on her right; it was no different from how she remembered it from her youth, though possibly a little cleaner, but she was amazed at the other changes. The new buildings were gigantic, and towered above her like huge spacecraft made of steel and smoked glass.

"If my memory serves me well there used to be an Expresso coffee bar here," she said as she pointed to a space next to the register office.

"It was demolished a few years ago, ma'am," Rankin informed her.

Josephine recalled sitting there with friends during her lunch breaks from work, drinking frothy coffee and listening to Ike and Tina Turner on the jukebox. As they drove further on past the Symphony Hall, Rankin pointed out all the new buildings.

"God, it's changed so much, if it wasn't for the odd landmarks here and there I very much doubt if I'd have recognised the place," Josephine remarked.

"It's a multi-million pound development now, and they've refurbished the canals and built loads of new pubs, clubs and restaurants."

At Josephine's request, Rankin parked the car and they got out to walk. As they strolled along, Josephine thought it all rather odd and strange. There was the occasional building that had remained unchanged since the sixties, but these were surrounded by huge skyscrapers.

"This gets packed in the evenings, it's a real jet-setting place with all the pubs and clubs, I often bring my girlfriends here."

The few things that Josephine had found out about Rankin since she'd arrived was that he spent a fortune on getting his hair cut and highlighted at a top salon and regularly worked out in a health centre with a solarium. Hence his golden tan, despite the fact it was still officially winter.

"Yes, I can see this would probably be your scene. In my day there were only about three nightclubs in this area," she told him.

"I don't suppose this is *your* scene, ma'am," Rankin added.

"I'm not a complete country bumpkin, you know sergeant. Torquay is full of clubs and restaurants, it's more metropolitan than some sea-side resorts, but I suppose you think I'm too old to be part of the club scene."

"No, not really, ma'am," Rankin lied, "It's just that men can get away with a lot more. I feel I always fit in no matter what the venue. If course I don't always let them know I'm a copper. That would be asking for trouble," he boasted.

Josephine looked over at her sergeant. *He's handsome*

51

there's no denying that she thought. *But doesn't he know it. He certainly believes he's a 'man about town' and I bet he spends a fortune on designer clothes.*

Josephine just couldn't understand the obsession younger people had with designer clothes. They would pay extortionate amounts just to have brand names visibly displayed on garments.

The sky was grey and it had just started to rain.

"Shall we make our way back to the car, ma'am?" Rankin suggested.

"Yes, I think we'd better," Josephine agreed as she pulled up her coat collar, shivering slightly.

"I bet you miss the good weather," Rankin remarked.

"It's not abroad you know," she joked "but I must admit we do get more sun in South Devon and it's a lot warmer even in winter. It's done nothing but rain since I've arrived, I'm amazed you've got such a good colour."

"It's all down to a sunbed," he admitted "I find all the girls like a tanned body."

From that moment on, Josephine was of the opinion that her sergeant was totally obsessed with his appearance as well as being pompous and chauvinistic. All she could hope was that his shallow attitude didn't spill over to his job.

Chapter 6

MICHAEL STEVENSON and Lewis Brown stood at the side of the canal, in Thimblemill Lane, Aston. They wore green waders and waterproof coats.

"I'm really excited about raising this sunken narrowboat for the museum," Lewis stated.

"I know, I thought we'd never get the funds we needed. I had to twist one or two arms, before they finally agreed." Michael added.

"Mind you, we did get a good price from this salvage company," Lewis said.

"Yes, he's a decent bloke Joe, the owner. He knows I'll always put any work his way."

Joe walked towards them; he also wore waders and a bright yellow fluorescent jacket. He had a very strong Irish brogue, which occasionally made it difficult to understand him.

"Bejesus, it's a pity it wasn't a metal barge, it would have been a lot easier. We could've just slid a chain beneath it and lifted it out of the water with a crane. It'll need treating like a wee woman as it's wooden," Joe said.

"It's not a barge, it's a narrowboat," Michael corrected him. "Anyway just be careful Joe, it needs preserving you'll have to treat her with kid gloves."

"Are you sure you've got enough men?" Lewis asked, as he looked a few yards down the canal where four workmen were standing. "I told you I could've arranged for some volunteers from the museum, being enthusiasts they would have taken particular care," Lewis added.

"I can't be doing with too many outsiders, my men know their job. Patrick, you go down to the nearest lock and start running the water through," he shouted to one of his men. Lewis Brown looked nervous and agitated.

"Just relax," Michael told him. "He knows what he's doing."

Sometime later as the water level became lower, the sides of the canal were more visible as the boat started to rise. The two men looked on anxiously as the boat slowly emerged from the water. Being enthusiasts, this event was probably as exciting to them as watching the birth of a child. This boat was their 'baby'. When the water was below the gunwales Michael said,

"Right, we need to cover the holes and gashes with plastic to stop the water seeping in." He walked around the boat with Lewis as they carefully inspected each area.

"My men can do that for you," Joe offered.

"No—we'd rather do this part ourselves."

"Please yourself," Joe said shrugging his shoulders. When the holes were all covered, they started to pump the remainder of the water out of the boat.

"She appears to be in a much better condition than we could have hoped for," Lewis said like an excited schoolboy. "I can't wait to get her towed back."

Joe boarded the boat and pushed open the doors of the small cabin.

"Don't stand on there. Get off you idiot you'll damage it. I thought you said he knew what he was doing." Lewis said to his colleague.

Joe ignored his request and just stood there, staring into the cabin.

"What the hell's wrong! Will you get back on the towpath!" Michael shouted.

"JESUS, MARY, AND JOSEPH!" Joe exclaimed. "What the hell's that?" The two men tried to look round him, but Joe was partly obscuring their view. He got off the boat in a daze, and his face was as white as a sheet.

"There's a bloody monster in there!" he uttered.

"How many pints of Guinness has he had?" Lewis asked.

"None, to my knowledge," Michael replied. He leant forward, looked into the dark chamber and there sat what appeared to be a man's body. It looked like something from a horror film. Parts of the body were covered with a jelly-like gunge and parts were exposed bone. They all stared in disbelief at the hideous creature. The two men had a dreadful sense of foreboding; it was as if they had opened some sacred Egyptian tomb and would be cursed by the mummy.

Michael Stevenson got out his mobile phone and dialled 999, while his colleague Lewis knelt down on the side of the towpath and vomited in the water.

Josephine Blake sat at her office desk and looked out of the window. Her only view was the smoked windows of the tall office block opposite. As she stared at the grey depressing looking building and the dark rainclouds, she yearned to be back home in Devon. Closing her eyes, she imagined herself to be walking along the beach, with the salty sea air blowing in her face and the sound of seagulls above her. The daydream was suddenly interrupted by the chief's voice as he barged into her office without knocking; Sergeant Rankin stood behind him.

"What do you mean, he thinks it's a body. Doesn't he know?" he demanded.

"Well, no, sir. He said it looked like some sort of monster. I suppose as it was found on a sunken boat the water has disfigured the corpse."

"Fill DI Blake here in with the details and get over there right away," he said as he left the office without acknowledging Josephine.

"Since the chief obviously thinks it's unnecessary to speak to me, what's the position?" she asked.

"A call has just come in ma'am, from some men that think they've found a body on a sunken narrowboat," he informed her.

"Right, do we have the location?"

"Yes ma'am, although it's a bit difficult to get there, but I have the directions." DS Rankin replied.

"Right, let's get the SOCO team there and the police doctor, though I doubt we need him to certify death, and we'll also need the forensic pathologist;

who is he by the way?" she asked.

"Doctor Mortimer," he informed her.

Josephine thought back to Brian Morrison who was the attending forensic pathologist in Devon. She had had a good working relationship with him and wondered what Doctor Mortimer would be like.

"Do you think we'll need police divers?" she asked Rankin.

"I don't think so, the boat has been raised."

"Right, get hold of two DCs and let's get moving, and also arrange for some other officers to be there, in case any of the public turn up."

They headed out of the city about a mile or so to the Aston area, and passed a newly built police station as they travelled along the Lichfield Road to Thimblemill Lane that led down to the canals. "We can't drive any further, we need to walk along the towpath to lock number eleven," Rankin informed her.

"I hope the others managed to find it, it's a bit off the beaten track," Josephine remarked. As they got on to the towpath, about three hundred yards or so ahead they could see a boat and people in bright yellow fluorescent jackets. The first boat they reached appeared perfectly dry and in good condition, the raised boat was some yards behind.

As they walked along a little further, Michael Stevenson and Lewis Brown came up to meet them. "I was the one who phoned you," Stevenson told Rankin, obviously thinking Rankin was in charge.

"I'm DI Blake," Josephine began. "And this is DS Rankin. Can you tell me what's happened?"

"We were raising this sunken boat to take back to the museum, when we found it inside," Lewis said.

"I could do with a bloody drink," Joe uttered.

"Who's this?" she asked.

"This is Joe O'Neill, he and his team were hired to raise the boat," Lewis replied.

"I think we'll go and have a look at the body, although we can't go on board until forensics and the SOCO's arrive." Since they'd only had to travel two miles to the scene of the crime from the city, they had been the first to arrive. It was now about 3:30 in the afternoon, and due to the fact it was a dull day and it had rained several times, the light was very poor. Josephine stood on the edge of the towpath and stretched her neck forward in an attempt to look into the cabin at the partly decomposed corpse.

"It looks bloody terrible doesn't it?" Lewis declared.

"That's probably because it's been underwater for some time," she turned to the sergeant. "There's not a lot we can do until they all arrive, but I don't want anyone to leave as I need to speak them all later. Is that your barge?" she asked.

"It's our narrowboat, actually," Stevenson corrected her. "We brought it down here in order to tow the sunken boat back to the museum after it was raised."

"Well, I'd like you all to wait on the boat till we're ready to speak to you a little later."

"Surely, there's no need for me and my men to stay is there?" Joe O'Neill asked.

"When I say all of you, that's what I mean," Josephine replied sharply. The six men boarded the boat just as Doctor Mortimer and the SOCO team arrived.

The doctor came up to Josephine and shook her hand firmly

"DI Blake?"

"Yes, that's correct," she replied, a little taken aback that he knew who she was.

"A bit depressing round here, don't you think? Nothing like Devon," Doctor Mortimer remarked.

"Yes, you could say that," Josephine agreed.

"I've got a weekend cottage in Barnstaple, Mrs Mortimer and I try to get down there as often as my work allows. Anyway, enough of this chatter, let's see what we have here." He put on his protective clothing as he said "I'd give you a suit as well, only the cabin area appears so small I think there'll only be room on board for me and my assistant."

"I'll leave it to you then," Josephine replied.

When they were kitted out in their protective clothing, Doctor Mortimer and the young man went on board. His assistant held a very large and powerful battery operated light, which he shone into the cabin. Josephine did manage for a moment or so to get a glimpse of the inside. It was like going on a ghost train at the fairground when suddenly a monster's face would light up for a few minutes and then disappear.

The first thing the doctor noticed was that the hands were tied with orange nylon rope. The corpse was in an upright sitting position and the feet had detached themselves from the body, but were still in the victim's boots. Parts of the corpse were covered in a thick soapy clay. Other sections of the cadaver showed protruding bones. Doctor Mortimer started to talk into his small cassette about his findings, while his assistant took photographs from several angles. When this was completed, he turned to him and said,

"Give the Inspector a suit and ask her to come on board."

Several minutes later, Josephine stooped down as she entered the small cabin, now she could see why the people who had found the body had been so horrified.

"It's awful, part skeleton, and part flesh, if you could call it flesh," she said a little shakily.

"It's a condition medically known as adipocere, which occurs when bodies have been in the water for a considerable time, though I can go into this in more detail with you when we get the remains back to the morgue. Briefly, the fats of the body turn into a soapy clay, which is fairly crumbly, so great care must be taken when the corpse is moved," he enlightened her. "The parts of the body that are most fleshy like the upper arms, buttocks, and thighs etcetera consist of this soapy clay. But as you can see, where there is little or no fat, there is just the skeleton showing." He pointed to a hand where all the fingers were exposed as bare bone. "As you can see his feet are no longer attached to his body."

"Do you think they were cut off?" Josephine enquired.

"No, as there is little or no flesh around the human ankle area, they have separated themselves, but the skeleton of the foot has remained in the boots."

"Any idea how long he's been down here?" she asked.

"Impossible to tell at this stage, it could be one, five, or even ten years. When a body has got to this state it's very difficult; still, let's hope we discover more after further extensive examinations."

"Thanks Doctor Mortimer, I think I've seen enough, I'll get off now."

"I don't blame you my dear, dreadful stench, don't you think? Anyway I'll be in touch later," Mortimer told her.

As the SOCO team got on with their task and the area was being cordoned off with tape, Josephine turned to her sergeant and said,

"It's a rather remote spot here, which in a way is good for us, as we don't have the public crowding round like they normally do."

"Yes but at the same time I doubt if we'll get any information or sightings of the victim if not many people come down here," Rankin replied.

On the other side of the canal, they noticed a youth cycling down the towpath on his bike.

"I think I spoke too soon, I suppose he'll go and tell his friends and they'll all be back here to take a look at the show," Rankin said.

"Right, let's go and speak to these lot on the boat. Tell DCs Lloyd and Freeman to assist Doctor Mortimer, as he may need help in transferring the remains of the body to his vehicle, as it's parked some distance away," Josephine turned to another DC that was standing nearby "I'd like you to take statements from the team of workers, while DS Rankin and I speak to the two men responsible for getting the boat raised."

As Josephine and Rankin boarded the boat, O'Neill's team were all drinking tea out of large thick mugs.

"Right Mr O'Neill, my DC is outside waiting to talk to you and your men if you'd go to see him," Rankin began. O'Neill got up rather grudgingly, obviously not wanting to leave the warmth and comfort of the boat. When they'd gone the sergeant and Josephine sat down on the narrow bench.

"Would you like some tea?" Lewis asked.

"Yes, thank you, but we'll need to get all the information down first. Now, your full names," Rankin asked as he got out his notepad and pen.

"I'm Michael Stevenson, and this is Lewis Brown."

"Now you say you were raising the boat for the museum," she began.

"Yes, we were very excited about the prospect till this happened," Lewis said, depressingly.

"What can you tell me about the boat?" she directed her question to Stevenson. "I don't profess to know anything about the boats or canals, even though I spent the first twenty odd years of my life in Birmingham," she admitted.

"The boat we were raising is known as a Joey," he began. "It was originally used as a trade boat and would carry most goods, coal, wood, even perishables, to factories around Birmingham."

"Do they still operate?" Rankin asked.

"No, most of them were made redundant in the late fifties and early sixties. I'd say this particular boat has been here since about 1960."

"Mm, thirty-nine years is a long time," Josephine reflected.

"If it had been metal, she would have been a lot easier to raise; being constructed of wood we have to take a lot of care so that she isn't damaged further," Stevenson informed her.

"Would the driver have lived on the boat?" Josephine enquired.

"No, the Joey boats have very small cabins, they consist of just a stove and a bench, to be used during the day. The Butty is a larger type of boat that would be used by families, and the cabin area would be bigger to accommodate beds."

"So when did you actually discover the body?" Rankin intervened, as far as he was concerned they'd had enough education about different types of boats for one day!

"When we were pumping out the water from inside. It was Joe who spotted it," Lewis answered.

"After the boat had been raised, what would have happened then?" Rankin continued.

"Once we'd covered any holes and gashes, she would have been slowly towed by our boat back to the museum."

"Do you have any ideas on why the body may have been on there?" Josephine asked them.

"My God! No!" Lewis uttered, raising his voice slightly.

"I don't suppose it's the original owner, after all this time?" Josephine suggested.

"I couldn't say but there is a list of registration numbers which can be traced back to the original owner," Michael Stevenson informed them.

"We don't know how long the body has been there, I'm amazed it's even in the condition it is," Josephine remarked.

"Being in the cabin area with the door shut, it would have been like a chamber which could have protected it to a certain degree," Lewis added.

"Right, I think that's all for now," Josephine said "Sergeant Rankin here will give you our number in case there's any information you may think of in the future, and we'd also like your addresses and telephone numbers, should we need to contact you."

"When will we be able to move the boat?" Lewis asked.

"I'd say it would be quite some time, as the Forensic team need to examine it thoroughly," Josephine replied.

"I hope they don't damage it in any way, as the wood is quite fragile."

"I'm sure they'll be careful, but it's inevitable there will be some damage, so I can't honestly guarantee what condition the boat will be in when it's eventually moved," Josephine replied.

"Are there many of these boats left?" DS Rankin enquired.

"There are some sunken boats in derelict arms dotted around the waterways both in and around the Birmingham area, but this one was in a remarkably good condition compared to the others. The only shock was it came with a tenant!"

When she arrived back at the Major Investigations Unit Josephine's spirits were raised. Despite the wet murky weather, and the fact that she had just encountered some rather gruesome remains, which had always affected her to a certain extent, she was glad of the opportunity to get her teeth into a case. That's if it was a case. Although the fact that the hands were tied did suggest foul play. She had been doing some rather tedious paperwork, helping to tie up loose ends on the cases that her team had been working on since she'd arrived, but had high hopes that this one, would be her baby.

An hour or so later she was in the chief's office,

giving him what little information they had to date. "Apparently the boat's been there since the late fifties or early sixties, although obviously the corpse hasn't been in the boat that length of time. As soon as I get the report from the forensic pathologist, we'll hopefully have a better idea how long it's been there."

"Probably just some old drunk or tramp, had one too many and fell in," the chief suggested lethargically. "If that's the position, we don't want to waste too much time and manpower that could be used on more important cases."

God! He's worse than Chief Inspector Cunningham was back in Devon, Josephine thought. *He'd always be on about the funds and budget he was restricted to, but that was usually when we were in the throes of an important murder enquiry, and the force were having to do extra hours overtime. This case hasn't even got up and running and he's watching the purse strings.*

"The one thing we do know," Josephine began, "Is that his hands were tied, which suggests some sort of foul play."

"Well, get back to me, when we know more." He looked down at a form in front of him as he picked up his pen and began to write. It was obvious he no longer wished to discuss it with Josephine. She left the office with the opinion that he was a very arrogant and unreasonable man.

As they were driving to the morgue Josephine

turned to DS Rankin,

"Is the chief always so obsessed with budget and wasting manpower?"

"What do you mean?" he asked.

"Well, he gave me the impression that he didn't think this case warranted much manpower, and I feel that was ludicrous at this stage, when we don't really know what it entails."

"His superiors are always on his back about the amount his department is spending. Yet, when something goes wrong because we don't have enough men on the job, he gets it in the neck. The chief really can't win," Rankin said in his defence. "If I may point out, ma'am, the policing of the second city is somewhat different to Torbay," he added sarcastically.

"I am quite aware of that sergeant, and I did in fact go through the figures for this department, and the funds are not enough to cover the policing required. That applies to divisions all over the country. You're obviously aware of my last case. A serial killer in a seaside resort is no picnic, I can assure you. I not only had my superiors but also the Torbay Council on my back, to get the case solved as quickly as possible. Their biggest worry being that it would affect tourism, which is their major form of income. We had to employ the services of many professionals, including a Jack the Ripper expert, and those sort of people don't come cheap. I've gone cap in hand to my chief many times, to literally beg for extra manpower, but it's always been worth it in the finish."

"Er—I can see that it would be, ma'am, I'm sorry—I didn't mean any—"

"Don't insult my intelligence," Josephine interrupted him. "I know exactly what you meant, but it's of no consequence. I hope, in time, you realise all this sarcasm and backbiting is a waste of time. The only thing I want you to channel your energy into is finding the cause of death of the body we're about to see."

Ten minutes later the car pulled up outside the Pathology Department.

As they entered the examination room, a young woman wearing a white coat approached them. "Can I help you?" she asked.

"DI Blake and DS Rankin to see Doctor Mortimer," the sergeant stated.

"Oh, he's still working on the corpse. I'm not sure he's completed his report yet—" she sounded a little vague.

"We've received a call from this department asking us to come and see Doctor Mortimer," the sergeant said abruptly.

"If you'd like to wait in his office I'll go and speak to him. It's at the far end on the left," she said as she turned and pointed down the corridor.

Josephine was annoyed, it was obvious there was a communication problem between the staff, and she was tempted to criticise the department to DS Rankin, but decided to say nothing, as he already looked slightly embarrassed and irritated. "They do have a heavy work load as they also do reports and examinations on road accident victims," he said in Doctor Mortimer's defence.

Josephine thought how busy and congested the roads in the city were, and she'd lost count of the amount of ambulances she'd seen speeding through the streets of Birmingham with their blue lights flashing. In the summer months, Torquay traffic had been heavy, due to the influx of tourists, but it was nothing compared to what she'd seen in this major city.

They could hear voices down the corridor that became louder as he approached. "He might be a University graduate, but he's bloody useless at relaying messages. I distinctly said, I was waiting for the anthropologist's report," he finished his sentence as he entered the office. His green gown looked a little tight across his rather ample stomach, and his white hair dishevelled; he looked very much the professor with his small steel rimmed glasses that rested on the bridge of his nose.

He smiled at Josephine when he entered the room.

"I do apologise for keeping you waiting. I'm afraid there's been a bit of a mix-up. Although I do have some findings for you, I did want to consult a friend of mine, Doctor Waring. He's an expert anthropologist who can determine the age of a corpse from the bones; unfortunately my new assistant got rather confused."

Despite the mix-up, Josephine felt it was

impossible to be angry with the man that stood before her. The impression of Doctor Mortimer she had formed when they had first met by the canal had not changed. She rather liked this man, who reminded her of a slightly eccentric uncle who had passed away some years earlier. She felt as if she could talk to him like a member of her own family, but decided to take a more professional, yet friendly approach.

"These things happen, but now we're here, I suggest we get on and you give us what information you can, and then we can have the anthropologist's report as soon as he's examined the body."

"Certainly, if you'd like to go with Miss Wright here, she'll give you the protective clothing and then we can view the body or at least what's left of it."

Several minutes later they were standing over the remains. The body was partly skeletonised and the other parts of the corpse were covered in a soapy substance. It resembled something from a horror movie, and Josephine's repulsion showed in her face.

"Not a pretty sight is he?" Doctor Mortimer stated.

"It looks worse now in these bright fluorescent lights than it did in the cabin of the boat," she remarked.

"As I explained earlier," he began "this condition is medically known as adipocere. The fatty contents of the body such as the thighs, cheeks, buttocks and so on, as you can see, have turned into a substance like crumbly clay. This is due to submersion in water for a considerable amount of time. The hands, wrists and ankles, and so on, where there is little or no fat are in a skeletonised state. Luckily the adipocere relatively preserves the architecture of the face."

"Do we know the cause of death?" Rankin enquired.

"I've examined the skull in detail and these crescent shaped indentations," they both looked as he pointed to the marks on the head, "And depressed fractures suggest he was struck several times, and I would say the weapon used was a hammer."

"Are you sure?" Josephine asked.

"As certain as I can be; I've seen it many times before. A hammer gives a characteristic split in the skin, and the rounded end doesn't come down completely flat, that's why the indentations are more pronounced on one side. Anyway, my lab assistant has taken a full set of pictures, including the skull, so you can take them back with you."

"So you don't think he drowned," Rankin proposed.

"No, I don't, after careful examination, there's nothing to suggest that."

"According to the men that were raising the boat, it was completely submerged in water," Josephine told Mortimer.

"That may be true, but I can tell you he didn't drown. The small cabin area would act as a sort of

71

vacuum chamber, which has preserved the body to a certain degree."

"So is it possible he was murdered and then put on the boat?" Josephine asked.

"You're the detective, you tell me. Even if the blows to the head weren't the absolute cause of death, they were certainly heavy enough to have caused unconsciousness and possibly deep coma. I've measured the length of the torso, head, and length of bones, and I can tell you he was about five feet and ten inches in height. Although when he's examined by the anthropologist he may be slightly more accurate, but I doubt it would be much more than an inch or so either way. There's also a small cut on his left femur at the top of his leg, since the thigh area of the leg is usually quite fleshy. He's been stabbed quite viciously in this area for the knife to have marked the bone."

"According to the men from the Black Country Museum the boat's been there since the late fifties or early sixties, I don't suppose the body's been there that long," Josephine hinted.

"Goodness me, no. Even the preserving qualities of that small cabin wouldn't have conserved or protected it for that length of time," he replied.

"Well, can you give me a rough idea of how long the body's been there?"

"I can't be accurate but I'd say at a guess no longer than five years, although until the anthropologist does further examinations it's difficult to tell; off the record I'd say between eighteen months and five years, but don't get quoting me."

"There were no items of any sort on the body, so we're going to have to find the identity, which will be no picnic," DS Rankin said lethargically.

"Any idea of the victim's age?" Josephine asked.

"No, and that's precisely why I need the anthropologist to look at the body. They are experts on determining the age just by examining the bones. One thing I can tell you, however, is that given the length and weight of the bones, plus the fact the wisdom teeth are fully formed, it's an adult male, but that's all I can determine at present."

Josephine felt frustrated and a little disappointed, but she knew the doctor could not commit himself until further examinations had been carried out, yet she felt impatient.

"Look, off the record, if you had to hazard a guess, what would you say?"

Doctor Mortimer rubbed his chin as he surveyed the remains.

"Well it's partly guess work and perhaps partly instinct, over the years when you've examined as many bodies as I have, you get a gut feeling. I'd say between thirty-five and fifty, but don't quote me."

"I won't, Doctor Mortimer," Josephine reassured him.

"Call me Charles," he said smiling.

"Well thanks Charles, if you can contact me as soon as the body has been examined by the other expert—"

"I will, and I shall do it personally, that way I'll

know you'll get the correct message."

As they were leaving the building Rankin said "I think he's rather smitten with you."

"What makes you think that sergeant?"

"Well I've known him quite some time and I had no idea his Christian name was Charles, let alone been asked to refer to him by it."

"That's the effect I have on people," Josephine said playfully as they got into the car.

Chapter 7

THE FOLLOWING DAY, Josephine assembled the team in the incident room for a briefing. Chief Inspector Robert Lyle was present, and he'd assigned another two officers to the case, saying they would only be available until they were needed elsewhere. Nevertheless, Josephine was thankful for the additional manpower, if only for a short length of time. Just before the meeting began, the chief took her to one side and said,

"I'd normally be working with you on a major incident like this. I can't see why we should put a great priority on it, due to the time he's been deceased. I've a heavy workload at the moment, working on the current budget, so I've decided to leave this case to you and DS Rankin. Just fill me in on any major developments, and I expect to see written reports on each stage of the investigation."

"That goes without saying, sir. You'll be kept up to the minute with any progress made."

"Right then DI Blake, I suggest you get on with the briefing."

Josephine was pleased that he had given her a free hand, so to speak but she didn't know the reason why.

Was it due to the fact she'd dealt with far more complicated, gruesome murders and serial killers in the past? Did he genuinely think that with her expertise and experience this case would be relatively simple? Or had he simply got too much on his plate, and couldn't be bothered to get involved, laying the responsibility solely on her shoulders? She knew how much routine financial administration was at the heart of the modern police force, unknown to the public.

But then, she thought, *the public wants to think of their coppers catching villains, not filling out a spreadsheet. Maybe secretly he wants me to slip up? No, I must snap out of this negative attitude. I've been given the case, and I'll cope.*

She walked over to the pinboard, feeling resolute and determined. On one half of the board was detailed pictures of the corpse taken by Doctor Mortimer's assistant and on the other side a set of photos from the SOCO team.

These were in chronological order, re-creating the scene, showing the canal bank where the submerged boat had been raised. Both the raised boat that had contained the corpse and the one from the museum that was to be used to tow the sunken boat were shown. There were also pictures of the opposite side of the canal, where two factories stood about eight hundred yards apart, one derelict, the other still operating.

Several detailed pictures were taken of the boat and the cabin area where the corpse was found.

"Now if I can have your attention, everyone, I'd like to begin," Josephine said loudly. "According to the forensic pathologist, Doctor Mortimer, these blows to the head were rendered with a hammer," she said pointing to a picture of the victim's skull.

"He's more or less certain, as these crescent shaped marks are very characteristic with that particular weapon. So I'd say from that fact alone, we have a murder case. He hazarded a guess at the victim's age, although he was loath to do so. He believes him to be between thirty and fifty years old, though I must stress there is no scientific evidence at this time to support this."

She walked away from the board round to the back of the desk and continued.

"The major problem we have at the moment is the body could have been on the boat between two to five years. If we had a more accurate or specific time, we could have checked through the missing persons files for a particular year, as it is, there's not a lot to go on. Although the body will be re-examined by an anthropologist, so hopefully, we can expect more information. The boat on which the body was discovered is a wooden trade boat, known as a Joey. One man would operate it and the small cabin area would contain just a bench and a stove. We don't think he was actually killed in the cabin area, since it's only big enough for one person.

"I suppose it's always possible he was killed on the top of the boat and then put into the cabin? Although until we have the report back from forensics, there's nothing to support that theory," DS Rankin added. He then turned to DC Katie Lloyd.

"You can chase the report from forensics to see

if there are any traces of blood or damage that might suggest a struggle."

"The main problem we have at the moment," Josephine continued "Is that although the boat has been in the disused arm since some time in the early sixties, which is over thirty years ago, we don't know when it actually sank. We need to speak again to the men who were raising the boat to get more information. Let's assume for a moment that it's been underwater for the last five years or so. It's then possible he was murdered on the nearby towpath, and then his body was put into the boat."

"I don't suppose the boat was far enough underwater for diving equipment to be needed?" DC Freeman enquired.

"No, it was only a matter of two or three feet below. It would still have been awkward for the killer to manoeuvre the body into the sunken cabin, but he'd have got away with just wearing waders," the sergeant replied.

"Surely it'd take two men to get the body down into the cabin?" another DC commented.

"Yes, that's a valid point. It's possible the killer had an accomplice," Rankin conceded.

"That's feasible. Although most murderers are so desperate to dispose of or conceal their victim's body, they often find extra strength and stamina due to a rise in their adrenaline," Josephine added.

"One thing I do believe, ma'am," Rankin began "It seems a lucky coincidence for the assassin, if he killed his victim on the towpath, that there happened to be a sunken boat nearby for him to use to hide the body. If the victim was killed elsewhere it would have hard to transfer the body without being noticed. The killer must have known the boat was there, so it's possible he lives locally. If the boat had been completely submerged he'd have had to know of its existence."

"That's a good and valid point sergeant," Josephine said. "Maybe he managed to entice his victim to that particular spot before attacking him, although I do appreciate this could be pure conjecture. If it *did* occur five years ago, obviously no-one came forward at the time. It may be difficult, if not impossible, to trace any witnesses."

"We'll go through the missing persons list for the last five years, although it's a long shot. Something may show up, though it's possible the victim wasn't local," Rankin added. "The clothes were badly damaged, and there was nothing discovered on the body to give us even the slightest clue of his identity. Most people have something on them—loose change, a watch, credit cards—and yet the SOCOs found nothing when they searched the boat."

"I suppose he could have been robbed, sir," Katie Lloyd suggested.

"He could have been a tramp, or a down and out, since he had nothing of value on him," Josephine suggested. "So, if he had no family he wouldn't have been reported missing."

"I doubt that," Rankin said sharply.

"We know so little about our victim, I don't think we can eliminate any possibilities, sergeant," Josephine replied.

DS Rankin shrugged his shoulders like a moody schoolboy, and didn't answer.

"To recap on everyone's assignments," Josephine began, "DC Lloyd, you're chasing the Forensic report. DS Rankin, you and DC Freeman can check through the missing persons records, concentrate on the Birmingham area to start with, and you two, I don't know your names."

The young men stepped forward.

"DC Rogers and Macmillan, ma'am."

"I want you two, to investigate that stretch of canal. Despite the length of time it's possible someone may have remembered something. Talk to the local residents and the employees of the factory."

"Will do, ma'am," they both replied.

She turned to DS Rankin and said

"We'll need to visit the Black Country Museum to speak to Stevenson and Brown again and to get more information about the boat."

After the meeting had finished, Josephine made her way back to the office. The building was so large all the corridors reminded her of a giant maze. The incident room that they had been using was situated on the fifth floor and Josephine's office was on the second. As she entered the lift, the desk sergeant from the reception area was just about to step out.

"Oh, ma'am, do you have your mobile turned

off?"

Josephine reached into her pocket.

"Yes, I always turn it off during a briefing," she replied.

"Only there's a message for you from Doctor Blythe, he's been trying to get hold of you for some time."

Her heart missed a beat.

"Oh right, thanks sergeant."

"He wouldn't leave his number, said you'd got it."

"Yes—I have, thank you."

They went down on the lift together and she got out on her floor. As soon as she was in the office, she rang Andrew's number.

His secretary answered.

"He's with someone, but asked me to put you straight through when you called even if he was busy. So if you can hold for just a moment..." Half a minute or so later Andrew's voice came on the line.

"I think I'd have more luck trying to contact the Queen. Your mobile's been turned off and the switchboard there is chaotic. They keep me waiting for what seems like an eternity, and then say they can't locate you."

"I'm sorry darling, but I'm glad you kept trying, it's so good to hear your voice," Josephine felt like crying. "Your secretary said you had someone with you."

"It was Peter, he's just left. Very tactful chap old

81

Pete, he knew I'd been trying to get hold of you, so he made an excuse and left. He'll contact me later, we were just going through some case notes."

"You could always ring me at Auntie Win's, though I'll be moving into the singles police accommodation next week."

"I don't know what the hell you're doing there anyway!"

"Don't start Andrew, we've been through this before."

Andrew was tempted to moan at Josephine, but it was such a relief to finally contact her he thought *I mustn't waste what little time we have to talk.*

"Anything exciting happened?" he asked.

"It was a bit mundane to begin with, but we've found a body in a sunken barge that we're trying to identify. Everything points to it being a murder case."

"There are lots of canals and barges in Birmingham aren't there?"

"Yes but one thing I've learnt, the enthusiasts like you to refer to them as narrowboats, they get quite insulted if you refer to them as barges."

"Really?" Andrew said, bored and having no interest in canal lore at all. "How are you feeling anyway, I hope you're looking after yourself."

"Auntie Win's looking after me. She's feeding me up with lots of roast beef, Yorkshire pud, and her speciality is home made faggots and peas. At this rate I'll be putting on so much weight, you won't fancy me anymore!"

Andrew laughed "Nonsense! You were too thin! I like a woman with something to grab on to."

"You'll certainly have that, if she keeps feeding me like this. The problem is, when she's prepared it I feel I can't refuse, and I must admit she's a good cook. Anyway, I've missed you. Any chance of you coming up to the city?"

"Not for a few weeks I'm afraid, I've got so much work, but you may get a visit from Bill."

"How's he coping as acting DI?" she enquired.

"Fine, I think, he hasn't mentioned the job, just keeps on about visiting you and having a Balti, he tells me Birmingham's famous for them."

"There are loads of curry houses here and I've heard they're very good, although I haven't sampled one yet."

"I don't suppose you've had the chance with all that home cooking. Anyway, at this rate you'll probably see Bill before me."

"I'd much rather you came up to see me, still, Bill does make me laugh, and I can catch up on all the news from the station. He's better than any woman when it comes to finding out everyone's gossip."

Josephine heard a buzz on Andrew's phone.

"I've got to go, Anne has just come on the line to remind me I've an appointment with a patient at twelve thirty."

Josephine glanced at her watch; it was 11:45.

"You'd better get a move on then. I'll try and make sure my phone's turned on in future."

"Better still, you ring me."

"I will, I promise, take care, I love you," she said tenderly.

He didn't answer in the way he normally did but just said,

"I'll be in touch, look after yourself Jo, don't get overdoing it," and then he hung up.

As she slumped down in her chair Josephine felt more like a vulnerable teenager who had been rejected by her boyfriend than a mature Detective Inspector.

I wanted you to say I love you and miss you darling, Andrew, and you didn't say any of those things she thought dismally.

It didn't register that the fact he'd been trying to get her for days showed that he cared. Her eyes started to fill with tears, when suddenly the phone on her desk started to ring. She thought it was Andrew ringing back and she snatched the receiver.

"Switchboard here, I've got Doctor Mortimer from Pathology on the phone, ma'am," an abrupt female voice told her.

"Oh yes, put him through please."

"Hello, Charles here."

"Hi, have you got the anthropologist's report?" she asked.

"Not yet I'm afraid, he hasn't had time to examine the body yet as he's extremely busy, but he's promised he'll be here in the next day or so—actually the reason I called you is I've been conducting a more detailed examination of the

84

victim's teeth. He's got a few fillings but the remainder are badly decayed."

"Could that have occurred while he was encased in the boat?" Josephine asked.

"No, when a person is dead there's usually no further decay to their teeth," he informed her.

"I don't understand, is that important?" Josephine asked vaguely.

"It appears there was a time in his life when he looked after his teeth and then suddenly stopped. I'd say he hadn't visited a dentist for at least ten years."

"Maybe he couldn't afford the charges," Josephine said lightly.

"If he was on the dole he'd get his dental treatment free, but he obviously didn't bother to go," Mortimer remarked.

"I had a notion that he might be a tramp or a down and out," she told him.

"Quite possibly, it's surprising the amount of tramps and wino's who once held down jobs and lived in houses with their families. Then something happens, and they lose everything and end up on the streets. This man obviously visited a dentist at some stage in his life. I suppose I could have waited to give you this information when I had the other results, but I thought it might be important."

"Thank you Doctor—er, Charles. I'm glad you let me know, it's nice someone wants to help me."

"Aren't you getting co-operation from your team?" he asked.

"Well, yes—I am but—oh I don't know, I feel some of them resent me, just turning up out of the blue and taking on the investigation."

"Well then, knock them into shape my dear, because no-one else will do it for you. I for one have every faith in your ability, and I'm here if you ever need to chat," he said kindly.

"Thanks Charles, it's good to know I've got someone in my corner."

Chapter 8

RAYMOND O'CONNOR lay in bed in his lavish room. The thick green and gold brocade bedspread felt heavy on his thin frail body. He was connected to a drip and monitor, attended by a young agency nurse in a crisp white uniform. There was a knock on the door, and an attractive looking dark-haired man in his late thirties entered the room.

"You can take a break now, nurse. I need to speak to my father. Make yourself some tea and a sandwich. You'll find what you need in the kitchen.

"Thank you sir," she replied, and left the room.

"How are you feeling today?" the young man asked.

"The same," his father replied, lethargically.

"This idea of yours, to trace Annette. I think it's ludicrous, you know," he said, with a gentleness in his voice. "They'll never find her."

"You might be right, James, but I have to try. I need to make my peace with her," his father explained.

"I don't see why. She doesn't give a damn about you—never has. Four years, and not a word from her!" he spat the words out angrily.

"When she left I wasn't ill. I'm sure that if she knew there was so little time left, she'd come home. If not for good, at least to see me," the old man said, sadly.

"I'm the one that's looked after you, not her. Annette's only ever cared for number one!"

"Then why has she never contacted me for money? She must know I'd help her! She left in just the clothes she was wearing. She could be anywhere. I just hope she's alright."

"After what she's done? She's never been right in the head, and you know it. Good riddance, that's what I say. She's evil," James declared.

"I don't know how you can talk about your own sister that way. She's your flesh and blood! It doesn't matter what she's done, she's still my child and your sibling, and each day I live in hope that the private investigator will find her before it's too late."

"As far as I'm concerned it's simply a waste of time and money."

"What else can I do with it? I can't eat or drink properly; I have no pleasures left in life. I'd give everything I own just to see her again," the old man said, with tears in his eyes.

"Then you're as mad as she is," his son told him.

"Just go away, James. You didn't come to enquire about my health; you just want to persuade me to halt the investigation. Which I don't intend to do. Now go away. I'm tired. I need to sleep," Raymond O'Connor said, as he closed his eyes.

"Stubborn old sod!" James muttered under his breath as he left the room.

Chapter 9

JOSEPHINE HAD CONTACTED the Black Country Museum to talk to the people who were responsible for the raising of the sunken narrowboat, to arrange an appointment.

She was informed she needed to speak to the Director, Mr Dougal, and that he would arrange for the two men who had discovered the body to be present at the interview.

Since she wasn't conversant with the roads and motorways in the area, as they had changed so much in the time she'd been away, DS Rankin had offered to drive. Josephine accepted, as she was totally bewildered with the maze of ring roads, flyovers, and new motorways that had sprung up over the last few years.

During their journey to the Black Country, Josephine looked over at the young, handsome, and yet somewhat unapproachable man who sat beside her, and suddenly realised how much she had missed her old sergeant, Bill Hughes. Bill had never been the ideal colleague and they'd definitely had their fair share of ups and downs. But Bill was a similar age to Josephine, and despite the fact he could be a tease and a bit chauvinistic at times, Josephine still felt she could say anything to him. Any grievances either of them had were brought out into the open. If they had a difficult case, they would go to the pub when they were off duty and discuss their ideas and hunches with one another.

She closed her eyes and reminisced. They would sit in the cliff gardens of her local, and look out to sea eating crusty crab sandwiches and drinking cider. She was never afraid to tell him about any idea or notion of a particular case no matter how far fetched or improbable it seemed at the time.

Suddenly, she was brought back to reality with a large jolt as Rankin braked sharply.

"Bloody idiot!" he shouted. "I've a good mind to book him. Did you see how he just pulled out in front of me?"

"I didn't actually, I'd closed my eyes for a moment or two," she replied. The sergeant tutted and moaned for the next five minutes.

Josephine felt that lots of people never confided in those close to them, and sometimes even if they cared for a particular person, had difficulty in showing their true feelings until it was too late. Although she felt nothing emotional towards her colleague, they did have to work together, and she sensed a certain animosity and resentment from him.

She decided not to broach the subject while he was driving after his encounter with the careless motorist, but when he pulled up in the car park at the museum she said,

"There's one or two things I'd like to go over with you, David." He looked a little surprised that she'd referred to him by his Christian name.

"Should we perhaps wait until we have some information from the museum?" he suggested.

"It's not concerning the case," she informed him.

"Oh, right—ma'am," he said dubiously, as he thought she was going to mention the incident on the road.

"I know you regard me as an outsider, and a bit of a country bumpkin," she started. "I had an excellent working relationship with my DS in Devon. I don't expect us to have the same sort of rapport, but we're working on a murder enquiry and I want you to respect me, even if you don't like me."

He opened his mouth to speak, but Josephine continued talking.

"I would like us to get on as colleagues even if we can't be friends. I've always believed in being straight and fair with all my officers, and I expect the same in return. I shall only be here for a matter of months, so I suggest that during that time you try to make an effort. Do I make myself clear?"

"Yes ma'am—certainly." He tried to sound professional, although he was quite taken aback by her very forthright approach.

"Right, let's go in, we mustn't keep them waiting," she said.

After walking through the reception area, which contained several exhibits and models of narrowboats in large glass cases, they were shown to the Director's office. He came forward to shake their hands and introduced himself.

"I'm DI Blake and this is DS Rankin," Josephine told him.

"You've already met Mr Michael Stevenson—unfortunately, Mr Lewis Brown cannot attend, as he is suffering from a bout of flu. Though I'm sure if you need to speak to him at a later date, it can be arranged." Mr Dougal informed her.

"That may not be necessary, I'm sure yourself and Mr Stevenson will be able to give us any information we require."

"A dreadful business, by all accounts. I suppose he drowned?" Mr Dougal muttered.

"It's being treated as a murder enquiry," the sergeant enlightened him.

"Oh—I see—I wasn't sure—"

"To be perfectly candid, despite the fact I lived in Birmingham many years ago, I know nothing about the canals, so if you could explain in detail why the boat was being raised."

"In the Birmingham and surrounding areas, boats have been left in disused arms. This one as you've probably been informed was a day boat known as a Joey, and was used to transfer goods to and from the cities."

"Why did you decide to raise this particular boat?" DS Rankin asked.

"It was of a certain historical value, and also had been left in a British Waterways arm, against a privately owned one, so we didn't have the problem of chasing the owner's permission. Some boats are metal, but despite the fact this one was wooden it was in quite good condition," Stevenson informed them. "We had to lower the water level from the nearest lock, and then the sides of the canal became more visible. As the water ran out of the boat, we would look for any holes or gashes and cover them with plastic before bringing it back to the museum. Unfortunately, as you know we never got that far."

"I can't understand why it's been there for such a long time. Would the owner of the boat not have to be contacted before it was moved?" Josephine asked.

"Since the boat was left in a disused arm, that wasn't obstructing anyone, the owner would not be chased to move it," the Director informed her.

"When the boats are on the top of the water, we can clearly see the name and number. In this case, as you know it was the *Pied Piper* and the number was 025659. They are always six digit numbers that begin with a zero. Since the boat was underwater, we couldn't see the markings or the licence number until it was raised."

"Now you do have the information, have you traced the owner?"

"I checked our computer originally for details of the licence, but had no luck, so I've gone through the old records. Certain information was transferred to the computers, but not all I'm afraid. So, I contacted our head office at Watford. They have lists that go back much further than ours. It was registered to a Mr Joe Ledbrooke, I have his address, although it's been some years ago, so even if he's still alive, he may have moved house," he said, as he handed Josephine a piece of paper with all the details on.

"What I'd like to know, is if the boat has been there since say 1960, when would it have sank, and what would cause that to happen?" Josephine enquired.

"I'll let Mr Stevenson answer that, as he's the expert in that field."

"It's unlikely it's been underwater for more than five years," he started to explain. "If it had been any longer, the condition of the boat would have been such that it wouldn't warrant raising it for the museum."

"That does tie in with the forensic pathologist's estimation of the body being in the cabin area between two to five years," Rankin commented.

"Sometimes a hole can occur if it has been hit by another boat, which in this case is unlikely due to its position. Being a wooden boat it could have sat on the surface of the water for the last thirty odd years. Water would have seeped through the planking leading to it springing a leak. Perhaps it just started rotting in a sensitive area and then it slowly started to submerge," Stevenson told them.

"We believe the body was put into the cabin area while it was underwater. So obviously the murderer knew the boat was there," Josephine said.

"A local person would probably have known of its existence, and there's a large number of canal walkers. It's not a very picturesque stretch of canal; it's not like a canalside in the country. The only things of interest you'd see there would be winos, tramps, and the factories. Quite a depressing site unless you're interested in social reform or industrial architecture!" DS Rankin announced. "Unless it was someone who walked along the canal to their workplace, it's someone who knows the layout of the canal system, and possibly even how far underwater the boat was positioned. We can't be certain until we get the reports back from forensics whether or not the victim was killed on the boat. I think that's unlikely. I'd guess it was just a convenient place for the killer to hide the body. If you hadn't decided to raise the boat the body could have lain undiscovered for many more years," he continued.

"I think it's feasible that a boat owner could have known of the boat's existence, and in that case the crime could have been committed some distance away. In fact, anywhere. The body could have been transported on the boat, moored alongside the sunken narrowboat, and the body transferred," Josephine suggested.

Michael Stevenson pondered for a few moments. "Mmm, yes. I do believe that's possible. It would be a messy job transferring the body, but it's feasible. It'd be fairly safe—it's a legal requirement that people register their boats, but at night you'd be safe in assuming it would be hard to recognise one narrowboat from another. And in all honesty most narrowboats wouldn't travel past 7:00 p. m., so it's unlikely anyone would spot you."

"People living on narrowboats live a silent and

unobtrusive existence. The average man and woman don't even think of them, let alone that there's a substantial moving population on the canals. They're not all on the electoral register; they don't use mains gas or electricity and don't even have a milkman call. A small number of people moved onto boats to avoid the poll tax when it was introduced. It's a perfect lifestyle for someone who wants to disappear for any reason, and could easily cloak our killer," Stevenson continued.

"I've never thought of it like that," Josephine said. "Even travelling can be done unobserved. A ten-mile journey on the canals is far removed from a motorway—no speed limits, roadworks, speed cameras or police. In other words very little chance of unwanted recognition. And even if you travelled by day, a cagoule with the hood up and a scarf is fairly standard gear. No-one would think it might disguise a killer."

"That's just reminded me of a stint I once did with another department," Rankin said. "One of the older officers told me it was rumoured at the time of the Great Train Robbery that some of the money was transported by canal boat. Whether there's any truth in that, I suppose we'll never know. But that was when there were still a few working barges in the country. Not like now."

On that note Josephine decided to conclude the interview, after thanking them for their co-operation. She handed over a card with their contact numbers on it to Dougal, in case any further evidence came to light.

"Just in case anything else occurs to you—don't hesitate to contact us," she said.

On the return journey, Rankin drove with more care and less speed. Josephine was both surprised and relieved. She had never been a good car passenger, and only really felt relaxed when she was behind the wheel. Even so, she wasn't really anxious to navigate her way around the congested roads of the city.

They passed through a predominantly Asian inner city district that was abundant with shops of all kinds, some specialising in selling food, cloth, carpets and others that seemed to sell everything under the sun. The area was run-down and a little grim, but bustling with shoppers and tradespeople.

"This has changed since I was last here. What are the crime figures in areas like this?" she asked Rankin.

"There's always problems in areas where most of the people are poor," he said. "Some drugs, obviously. Not as much street crime—muggings, car crime—as you might think. Most of the villains have got the wits to thieve in areas that are more prosperous or the town centre. The majority of people here are just the same mix, as law-abiding and avoiding as anywhere else. The truth is they're more likely to get nicked here because they can't afford the kind of protection your middle-class villain can."

"Is that a bit of politics, sergeant?"

"Might be, ma'am. If you want to fix the problems in areas like this you need to invest in education and jobs. It's hard to blame kids who are going straight to the dole, or whose suitability for a job rests on the colour of their skin, for trying to bypass the system. Mind you, I reckon Brum's less racist than most places. I was stationed up North for a bit."

"We have a drugs problem in Torquay. I've had to clear up the aftermath of a war between rival dealers. The main dealer was shot dead in the war."

"One less on the streets then," Rankin observed.

"My sentiments exactly. Still it's hard to come to terms with guns in the streets of Torquay. Perhaps our worlds aren't as far apart as you imagine."

"You may be right," he conceded. "I doubt there's many areas left that are crime free. Often the countryside is worse than the city. People don't realise the amount of self-regulation that cities have. Some lad might be a hard nut in his area, but the first time he ventures into the city centre for some fun, he finds there's a few professional hard men, and often comes to his senses. In the country they often *are* the toughest in their area, and no-one intervenes until they've done something really bad. Cities get a bad rap because of the population density. Also, we do actually *police* the cities. Where are you most likely to get arrested for drunk driving, city or country, you tell me."

"I take your point, sergeant."

"You know, ma'am, I feel we may have got off to a bad start. I do tend to be a little too judgmental, well, according to an ex-girlfriend, that is."

"Women are seldom wrong, you know, sergeant," Josephine said, as she began to laugh.

Would you like to go for lunch, before we go back to the station?" he asked.

"A peace offering?"

"If you like."

"You're on. I'll leave the choice of venue to you."

Some twenty or so minutes later, they were sitting at a table in a small licensed Mexican restaurant.

"I'll have to admit to ignorance of any Mexican food except for chilli," Josephine said, a little sceptically, as she perused the menu.

"I'll order for you if you like, ma'am," Rankin suggested.

"With pleasure…"

He ordered a starter of tortillas with guacamole and salsa dips. Josephine found the guacamole delicious and felt quite full even before the main course arrived.

"The next dish is fajitas, basically tortilla bread that you fill," he told her.

The waiter brought a large dish of tortillas, with more dips, and placed it next to a large sizzling tray of chicken cut into strips, with big chunks of peppers and onions seasoned with herbs and spices. It looked colourful and inviting.

"Just follow me," he said. He took a tortilla and filled it with a selection from the tray, adding some of each of the dips as he did so. He rolled the tortilla up, and then lifted it to his mouth and bit into it. As he did so the juices escaped and ran down his chin. He quickly grabbed a napkin and wiped his face with it.

"I must warn you, ma'am, it's delicious, but messy," he muttered with his mouth half full.

Josephine attempted to recreate his concoction, which she found to be an adventurous, if not slightly primitive, way of eating. Nevertheless, it was a gastronomic experience. As she wiped her mouth with the napkin and finished her wine, she said,

"That was different and delicious. Thank you sergeant, you must let me pay half."

"Not likely. You're on my beat now, ma'am—my treat."

She sat back in her seat, running her fingers through her hair.

"When we get back to the unit I'd like you to check Joe Ledbrooke's address. You never know what the computer might turn up for us. I've learnt more about workings of the canal system today than I thought was possible. I felt quite ashamed, being a Birmingham lass, to know so little about them. Although, thinking back, I can remember lots of hippies hanging about on boats that were moored by a pub in the city I used to go to as a teenager."

"That would have been The Narrowboat, ma'am—it's a Firkin pub now. I'm surprised you can remember that. I know all the pubs, clubs and restaurants around Brindleyplace and Broad Street—that's because I frequent them all in both my professional and personal capacities," he said, grinning.

He was still trying to impress her with his man about town image, and yet Josephine was warming to him. There would always be personality clashes between officers in every police force, yet Josephine felt she needed some rapport with her staff and fellow officers. Police work was stressful and complicated enough, without any added pressures.

"We'll need to contact forensics to see if they've got any more information, and you can check our files, just in case there are similar cased listed."

"I'll run a computer search, although I doubt we'll find anything. After all, it's not exactly your run of the mill killing. Bodies in sunken boats. I think someone would have remembered anything similar, and mentioned it by now," Rankin replied.

When they arrived back at the station, the forensics report was on Josephine's desk.

"When did this arrive?" she asked DC Katie Lloyd.

"Not long after you'd left for the museum with the DS, ma'am. We weren't sure whether to contact you on your mobile or wait till your return."

As the DC left the office, Josephine read the report.

The first section just confirmed that no jewellery or personal effects were found on the corpse or the boat. However, they'd found a manufacturer's label on one article of clothing, the trousers. The name was that of an old, but reputable chain of tailor's shops that had for the most part faded into obscurity. The rise of the chain stores selling off the peg suits and fashion wear had spelled the end for them. These days only professionals such as solicitors and consultants tended to invest in tailored suits of quality. The suit trousers had a forty-four inch waist. A large belt with a buckle had been found on the victim, although it had no particular markings. The feet that were separated from the body were encased in a cheap brand of boots that were found under many brand names in markets and discount stores.

As she continued to read the account, she saw that the only damage to the boat was due to standard wear and tear over the years. The dents and holes she had seen in it were perfectly normal, and there was nothing to suggest that there had been a violent struggle on board. The gashes had not been made with a weapon of any sort. This tended to confirm the conclusion of Josephine and her team that the killing had been done elsewhere, and the body then hidden on the boat.

She sat at her desk feeling a little depressed and disappointed by the inconclusive report. She'd hoped that some small, apparently insignificant fact would have been turned up by the examination. An R McAllister had signed off the report. She picked up the phone and dialled the forensic department's number. When they answered, she asked to be put through to the extension at the top of the report.

About a minute elapsed before anyone responded.

"Path Lab."

"Hello. DI Blake here. I've just received a report from Doctor McAllister, and I'd like to speak to him if that's possible."

"I'm afraid he's busy at the moment. Can I help at all?" the man's voice replied.

"I'm also busy, but it's crucial I speak to him. When will he be free?" she asked, sharply.

"He's just completing a series of tests in the lab, so it could take half an hour or so."

"Could you ask him to ring me when he's finished, please."

"Does he have your number?"

Josephine gave the man the main switchboard and her extension number before replacing the receiver.

She suddenly felt agitated, and yet an hour ago she had been in quite a genial mood. She sat down, closed her eyes, and began to massage her temples. *It must be the time of the month*, she thought. *Or I'm missing Andrew and Devon more than I'd like to admit.*

Her menstrual cycle had become irregular over the last few months. The consultant had told her to expect some change due to the trauma and her injuries, although Josephine suspected it could be the onset of the menopause.

About twenty minutes later the phone rang.

"Doctor McAllister here, can I speak to DI Blake?"

"Speaking."

"My assistant tells me that you need to speak to me urgently."

Josephine felt a little guilty. Perhaps she had exaggerated the importance of her call.

"Well... It wasn't of vital importance, but nevertheless thank you for returning my call so promptly," she replied, in a slightly apologetic tone. "I've read your report on the narrowboat murder, and it really just confirms our belief that the killing took place elsewhere. I was rather hoping for something in the way of a lead."

"We can only report on our findings, and not concoct information that's not there, Inspector," he replied, sharply.

"And you're certain you've checked everything—there's nothing you might have missed?" As soon as she'd finished, she regretted her words.

"I can assure you our department is thorough and professional; however, if you want a second opinion..." She could tell from the tone of his voice that he was becoming more exasperated.

"No, that won't be necessary. Just let me know if you find anything else."

"That goes without saying, Inspector Blake," he replied and then hung up.

Chapter 10

ALTHOUGH JOSEPHINE was very fond of Auntie Win, that evening Win's chatter annoyed and agitated her. She felt a little guilty at not being able to finish the lamb and potato hotpot Win had made for her supper. Auntie Win looked dismally at the remains in her dish.

"You don't eat enough my girl," a phrase she had used since Josephine was a child. Win was still in the habit of treating her as if she was a slip of a girl, despite the passing of over forty years.

"Don't worry," Arthur began, "I'll finish it." He stretched over and poured the remaining food into his bowl.

"And *you* eat too much," Win announced, staring at his paunch.

"It was delicious," Josephine said, "But I went to a Mexican restaurant for lunch, and I'm afraid I rather stuffed myself on some wonderful dishes I'd never tasted before."

"Ugh! Foreign muck! You can't beat good home cooking," muttered Auntie Win as she made her way to the kitchen.

"When are you moving into the singles quarters?" Arthur asked as he devoured a large spoonful of lamb and carrots.

"Sometime next week," she replied.

"I bet you can't wait," he grinned, "At least you'll get some peace."

"Oh don't say that! I know Win can be a bit of a

nag at times, but I love you both dearly."

Some ten minutes later Win returned from the kitchen empty-handed.

"Where's the apple pie?" her husband enquired.

"I've decided it'll keep until tomorrow in the fridge," Josephine was relieved, as it would have been an effort to have eaten even a small portion.

"There's no point wasting good food!"

"I was looking forward to my pudding," Arthur said, disappointedly.

"It won't harm you to go without the odd pudding with that," she said, poking his large stomach and laughing. She seemed in a better mood. "I've decided to have a little family get-together this weekend, before you move out," she informed Josephine.

"There's really no need... I..."

"Nonsense!" Win interrupted. There's your cousins Susan and Mark, Uncle Ray and the children, to name but a few, and they'd all love to see you."

Josephine had fond memories of her cousins. She was an only child, and they had often played together when they were small. When they'd reached their teenage years, they'd gone to clubs and discos together. She recalled how Mark had always fancied himself as a John Lennon lookalike back in the late sixties, and he'd wear round steel rimmed glasses with his black leather cap. Josephine would go to the hippie markets with Susan to buy hot pants and flares, not forgetting the huge flowered earrings, which they both adored. They would parade themselves like two proud peacocks at the clubs and discos showing off their new gear! Her thoughts of that wonderful era were interrupted by Auntie Win's voice.

"Are you alright, dear?"

"Oh… yes. I was just thinking back to when we all went clubbing together. It'll be good to see them again."

"That's settled then. I'll start ringing round and making a list of what will be needed for the buffet. You can organise the drinks," she said, looking in Arthur's direction. "Now, where did I put that address book?" she left the room, muttering to herself.

"I'm glad you agreed," Arthur said, as he reached over the table and squeezed her hand. "At least it'll keep her out of our hair for a few hours. Now, where's that remote? There's a good match on Sky Sports about now."

The following morning the long-awaited call came through from Doctor Mortimer, informing Josephine that the forensic anthropologist Doctor Anthony Waring would be coming to examine the corpse.

"He should be starting about eleven o'clock, he's an excellent chap is old Tony, best in his field," Doctor Mortimer began. "If you can get here at about twelve-thirty, we can discuss his findings."

"Right, I'll be there with DS Rankin," Josephine replied.

Doctor Mortimer and Doctor Anthony Waring were in autopsy room three, as it was fitted out with extra ventilation. The age of the corpse and its putrefaction made the examination even more unpleasant than usual. They were wearing green surgical scrubs, plastic goggles and latex gloves, with respiratory equipment on standby. Over the years, Doctor Mortimer had come to the conclusion that no amount of extraction equipment or disinfectant could hide the smell of death.

"It's far cleaner than when it came in, but a bit of a mess with the adipocere," he told his colleague.

"I can imagine. Still, I see the water has preserved it to a remarkable extent, no doubt due the lack of a strong current. We have the whole skeleton despite the feet being separated," Doctor Waring replied. "Long hair for a man, eh?"

"Yes. A sample has been bagged and sent for analysis."

"There doesn't seem to be a problem with race. Light hair and what's left of the skin appears fair," Waring noticed.

He went on to examine the arms. "The humerus is fully formed, and the legs. The head of the femur and all the long bones are fully matured. X-rays have verified this, and, as stated in the autopsy report, the wisdom teeth are fully erupted. I see no arthritic change in the joints, yet the teeth look well worn. So we'd have to say early middle age." He noticed a slight smile on Doctor Mortimer's face as he looked up.

"I made a guess at the age, and it wasn't far off the mark," he explained.

His assistant entered the room.

"Sorry to disturb you sir, DI Blake and DS Rankin have arrived. Do you want them to wait in your office?"

"No, suit them up and let's get them in here. DI Blake seemed to feel the case was urgent. I'm sure she'd be interested in Doctor Waring's examination," he said.

Several minutes later, Josephine and Rankin entered the room, both of them visibly paling at the smell. Doctor Mortimer made the introductions, after which Doctor Waring said,

"You don't really need me you know. Mortimer here was pretty close in his estimation of age. Still, I might find a little extra information for you." He turned to Josephine. "He's a male, all bones fully formed and not yet arthritic, so we could say he's probably forty to fifty or thereabouts. Height five foot ten inches, Caucasian.

"Could you hazard a guess at his weight before death?"

"It's difficult to say after a few years have passed. The size of the bones can be a guide, although you can get small-boned people who are obese. This skeleton has a medium bone structure, so he'd probably have been between eleven and thirteen stone in weight. Why do you ask?"

"He was wearing size forty-four waist trousers, obviously too big for him as they were tied up with a belt," Josephine replied. "We think he was probably a down and out, due to the clothing and the length of his hair. He'd have got the trousers from a jumble sale or charity, or even stolen them. They were a good make, part of a suit and tailor-made for someone."

"I follow your reasoning, Inspector. For this man to have had a forty-four inch waist he, or the original owner of the trousers, would have had to be between eighteen to twenty stone. I doubt very much whether this man was ever that size. If he were that heavy we'd have seen more problems with the knee joints—heavier men cause more damage to the joints earlier in life." He turned back to the remains. "After examining the indentation on the skull I agree with Doctor Mortimer. The victim received several strong blows to the head with a hammer or similar implement. See these crescent shaped indentations?" He pointed to the horror that was the head. DS Rankin moved backwards.

"This was the cause of death. But this is very interesting," he pointed to the arm. "These marks on the right wrist. I've examined them closely with a microscope. I think they were made with a knife. Knife marks have a definite pattern to them. This isn't a flesh wound—it goes deep into the bone, as if the assailant was trying to sever the hand. The knife used was too small to do this—our man would have needed an axe or saw. So he had to give up."

"Do you think this was done after the victim was dead?" DS Rankin asked.

"Dead or unconscious, or presumably the victim would have had something to say about it. He'd have had to be in a coma at least. Anything less and the pain would have roused him, and even an enfeebled man is a difficult man to dismember. The cuts are not defence cuts, and they concentrate on one site, so I'd say he was unconscious.

"There's one other thing I've found. At the top of the left leg there is a cut at the top of the femur. I'm quite surprised that it has penetrated through to the bone, as the thigh is a very fleshy part of the body. The knife must have been plunged in with tremendous force. It's possible the assailant was trying to sever one of the main arteries in the groin, although the blood loss would have been so severe that the murderer would have been, in effect, spray-painted with blood. The alternative is that for some reason the killer was trying to sever the victim's penis, and that the victim was trying to defend himself and the knife was deflected into his thigh. I've no conclusive proof of this; it's pure conjecture on my part. I will say that whoever delivered the blow was either unusually strong—it's a difficult angle to exert any strength at—or was in a profound fit of rage."

"Thank you Doctor," Josephine said, "You've

given us a better insight into the killing and the possibilities surrounding it. Thank you for your time and expertise."

"He seems to know his stuff," Rankin remarked, as they drove back to the station.

"I agree. He's competent and skilled, but more importantly he knows how to use his abilities to imagine the circumstances of a crime. So, we have a possible method of killing. But we're still no closer to the identity of the victim, or why he was murdered," Josephine replied.

Chapter 11

DC KATIE LLOYD handed out photocopies of both the Path Lab and forensics reports to the team of officers assembled in the incident room.

Josephine stood up to address them.

"To summarise findings to date; Long-haired, white male, aged between forty and fifty. Cause of death, fractured skull due to blows to the head, inflicted with a hammer or similar implement. The assailant tried to remove the victim's right hand, unsuccessfully as he lacked the correct instrument. Doctor Waring reckons he used a knife and would have needed a saw or an axe to complete the job. Waring also found a deep cut to the top of the femur requiring a considerable amount of force. He thinks that it's possible our man was trying to remove the victim's penis." There was an audible intake of breath from the mostly male audience.

"I think if he's right that our man must have tried this while the victim was still alive, because he didn't manage it, and I don't see how he could have failed if the victim were dead. This is just conjecture, by the way." She walked away from the board and towards the group as she continued.

"It's now obvious that the body was transferred to the narrowboat after death. This implies that the murderer knew about it beforehand, and that they may be local. On the other hand, most narrowboat enthusiasts around here knew the wreck, so our man may be a narrowboat owner. DS Rankin has some information about the sunken boats original owner, Joe Ledbrooke. David, it's all yours."

"Thank you, ma'am. Unfortunately, the gent in question is now deceased. If he'd been alive he'd have been seventy-nine. I spoke to his daughter, who fortunately for us lives at the same address as he did, and she was very helpful.

"He registered the *Pied Piper* in 1950. He was a freelancer for several firms in the Midlands and used the boat to transport goods around the area for them. His daughter reckons he made a good living for the first few years, but as the motorway system grew business became harder and harder. He moored the boat in the disused arm, hoping he'd find another use for it. Trouble was, since it was one of the Joey boats it only had the small day cabin, so he couldn't rent it out for trips and the like. He just left it there, and got a job at the Rover. Our guess is that, unattended, it eventually sank. Anyhow, it's impossible for him to have anything to do with the murder, as he died ten years ago and the body's been in the sunken boat for no more than five years. Bit of a dead end, I'm afraid. We've more or less eliminated him and his family from the enquiry."

"Of course, there's always the fact that his family *did* know the boat was there!" DC Freeman stated.

"Yes, them, and anyone who was passing, knew the area or worked in the nearby factory. In fact you can better argue they're the least likely, as any discovery was bound to lead back to them, as the boat's owners," DS Rankin replied.

Josephine intervened.

"We need to talk to the winos and tramps around the area to see if they can recall anyone who corresponds to our description disappearing around that time. Though it's a long time ago in the life of a down and out. A lot of bottles of Diamond White under the bridge since then. Anyone got a better idea?"

"I can't see them talking to us, ma'am," Rankin began, "I mean let's face it, they really only talk to each other. It's like the Mafia, only smellier." A wave of laughter ran around the room.

Josephine glared at him.

"I can tell you one thing—if we go in with that attitude no-one *will* speak to us. We may have to try a bit of bribery, but we'll have to try."

"I still think it's a waste of time," Rankin continued.

"Well, sergeant, what brilliant scheme do you have? Or if we're asked about how the investigation is going, are you suggesting we inform the media that we decided not to pursue the only avenue open to us in this investigation because it would be 'too smelly'?" Rankin didn't answer.

"Well?" she asked again, sharply.

"No ma'am, we'll do our best," he replied, after a pause.

As they left the incident room Rankin followed Josephine down the corridor to the lift, much to her annoyance, as she really didn't feel the need to talk to him further. It was obvious that he knew he'd antagonised her and wished to make amends.

"What's on the agenda now, ma'am?" he asked.

"I'm going to fill the chief in on our progress, such as it is, and them I'm going home to have a long soak in a hot bath. I've got a family party tonight." After she'd spoken, she wondered why she'd bothered telling him her plans.

"Lucky you," he replied.

"And you?" she asked.

"I picked up a nice blonde the other night, so we're off for a meal and a few drinks, and who knows? he said, winking at her.

You arrogant and egotistical man, she thought, despite harbouring the feeling that his evening would be far more exciting than her own.

She couldn't know how wrong she would be!

Chapter 12

JOSEPHINE ARRIVED HOME to chaos. Auntie Win was running around the house like a demented chicken.

"I'm not sure we've got enough bread rolls Arthur. I told you to buy more, we could always have frozen the ones we didn't use."

"For God's sake woman! There's enough food there to feed an army," he replied, as he looked over the long dining table that was covered with an array of food of every conceivable variety.

"I've forgotten the pickles!" she exclaimed, as if it were a matter of great urgency. "You know how George loves his pickles. You'll have to go to the corner shop," she told her husband.

"I'll go," Josephine volunteered.

"I wouldn't hear of it. I could do with a breath of fresh air," Arthur said, grabbing his jacket. "I'll take Max." He was only too grateful of the opportunity to escape from the bedlam. At the sight of his lead, Max leapt from his comfortable chair and started jumping up Arthur's legs.

"Calm down boy, we'll be off in a minute, thank God!"

"Right, listen carefully," Win began "Only you always forget something. I want a jar of pickled onions, beetroot, and pickled cabbage, and if you think of anything else we might need, just buy it."

As Arthur slammed the front door behind him, Josephine turned to Auntie Win who looked flushed

117

and irritated.

"This is far too much for you, you shouldn't have gone to all this trouble."

"Nonsense, I'll be fine, now it's all finished. He moans there's too much food and yet you want to see the amount of drink he's brought. I've already caught him having a tipple. At this rate he'll be drunk before they arrive."

"Sit down," Josephine said sternly as she pointed to a nearby chair. Josephine pulled the footstool over.

"Now put your feet up, I'm going to make you a cup of tea, and if you dare get up—" Auntie Win was so taken aback, she obeyed her immediately. She wasn't used to people telling her what to do; it was usually the other way round. After seeing Win's shocked expression, Josephine could barely stop herself from laughing as she made her way to the kitchen. Some minutes later, she returned with two cups of tea and a plate of biscuits.

When they had finished, Win said,

"I won't be cooking a meal this evening, if that's okay."

"I shouldn't think you would, we'll probably be eating this for days," Josephine said as she looked at the food on the table. "Anyway, I'm going for a shower now, what time are they arriving?"

"About eight o'clock," she replied.

"I might even have time for a nap," Josephine said as she went upstairs.

After she had showered and rested on the bed

for a while, Josephine glanced at her watch; it was 7:15. She walked over to the wardrobe and looked through the few clothes she had brought. There wasn't much of a choice, as she'd only packed a few outfits; her really good gear, she'd left back home in Devon. She regretted not bringing at least one or two stylish dresses or suits. Her mind flashed back to last summer, when she had worn a lovely cornflower blue dress on her first date with Andrew.

He had often jokingly remarked that it was the sexy tight dress that had caused him to fall for her. She lay back down on the bed and closed her eyes for a few moments; she'd missed him more than she thought possible.

Suddenly, for no explicable reason, the image of the bloodstained, slashed tracksuit that she was wearing when she was relentlessly attacked came to mind. Josephine felt sick and frightened, she had re-lived the nightmare many times, and thought she had overcome the terrifying incident that had brought her so close to death. Although the psychologist had warned her, she would get flashbacks for no apparent reason. She started to feel sweaty, so she opened her bedroom window and lay her head back on the pillow, breathing deeply in an attempt to calm herself.

After a time she felt better and looked at her watch, it was ten minutes to eight. She quickly splashed her face with cold water in the bedroom wash basin, and dabbed on some moisturiser. After applying her make-up, she decided on a plain black dress. She had always suited black in the past with her blonde hair, although lately, she'd looked pale, as the tan she acquired on holiday had faded. She added some extra bronze blusher to her cheeks and used a slightly brighter shade of lipstick, in an attempt to add more colour and light to her face.

She stood back and looked in the mirror, there was something missing, the dress looked too plain. She suddenly remembered a lovely gold and turquoise pendant necklace that Andrew had bought her in a small street market in Spain. She removed it from her jewellery box and put it on, it was just what the dress needed. Now she was ready to meet the family she hadn't seen in a long time.

At around nine o'clock, the party was in full swing; she had spoken to several uncles, aunts, and cousins and reminisced about the good old days. She told them about Jessica's degree, her divorce from Tom, and her house that overlooked the sea. Although she tried to change the subject when they asked her about her recent ordeal and the injuries she received. Josephine never went into detail when asked about the 'new man in her life' but just said she had met someone she cared for. Her relatives remarked how Birmingham had changed over the years in some ways for the better, and others for the worse. Her one uncle said in his opinion she hadn't changed since her twenties, which she didn't believe for one minute. He then went on to say that perhaps it was living by the sea that kept her looking so vibrant and well. She was tempted to admit her beauty secret was Elizabeth Arden blusher and lipstick, but said nothing.

She was later introduced to a distant cousin, who had divorced his wife two years previously. When he introduced Josephine to his current partner, she recognised her at once. It was Emily Morgan an old school friend of hers, so they had a good chat as they discussed old boyfriends, and the antics they got up to in their youth. Josephine ate, drank, and reminisced; it was the first time she had really enjoyed herself since she had arrived in the Midlands.

Suddenly she looked up and saw a friendly and familiar face smiling down at her. It was her cousin Mark. Before she had chance to say anything he put his arms around her and gave her a hug. She felt emotional and her eyes filled.

"Mark, it's so good to see you."

"I just can't believe it took a brush with death, to finally get you up to Birmingham to see us all." He took hold of both hands and held her away from him at arm's length. "Let's have a look at you, you haven't changed much, even though you're a famous Detective Inspector."

"Don't lie, I've lost my slim waist and gained a few lines and wrinkles since we last met."

"That may be true, but you've still got those lovely blue eyes." Mark observed.

"Anyway, what's this 'famous', no-one knows me here."

"Don't you believe it, I remember you made the

national newspapers with that Ripper case."

"Don't remind me," she winced "It was bad enough in all the Devon newspapers, and the Torbay Tourist Board complained it was bad for the holiday trade."

Dear Mark, she thought. *He hasn't changed.*

They had been so close as children and during their teenage years. He had always teased her when she'd worn hot pants and mini-skirts, and criticised her choice in boyfriends. Though Josephine always retaliated, making fun of his kipper ties, afghan coats and girlfriends. But despite the teasing and banter that went on between them, they would always be protective and supportive of one another. They both felt justified when criticising each other, until an outsider did the same and then they would quickly jump to each other's defence. They'd had a special bond between them in youth, which they had lost over the years.

"You know Mark, it's rather sad that it takes a tragedy in peoples lives to bring them closer together," she remarked.

"Anyway, enough of this emotional rubbish. How are you settling in, I bet you've noticed a few changes?" he began.

"The place is so crowded, and the traffic! And I must admit the ethnic population has increased. The team I'm working with seems to be under the impression that there's hardly any crime in Devon. Still, I've put them right on *that* score."

"I'm sure you have," Mark replied smiling. "I was

sorry to hear about you and Tom."

"Well, these things happen. I'll always feel a certain fondness towards him. Living with a person for twenty years forms a bond that's hard to break, but he's found someone else and I think he's happy."

"And you?" he enquired.

"I do have a good man in my life, he's a forensic psychologist. He didn't want me to leave, but still, it's only for six months. Anyway, enough of me, what's your news, are you and Rita still together?" she asked.

"No, we divorced five years ago. Our son Roy is at University, but I try to stay in contact."

"I'm sorry to hear that, I always liked Rita," Josephine told him.

"At first I blamed the pressures of my work for the break up, but I suppose there were several factors."

"What line of work are you in at the moment?" Josephine asked.

"I'm a private investigator," he announced.

"I don't believe it! You were always anti the police."

"I still am, I'm afraid. There is a difference between a private investigator and the force, quite a few in fact."

"I've got to hear about this," Josephine began. "Get us some drinks and we'll sit out there," she said pointing to an vacant sofa in the conservatory.

A few minutes later, they were in deep

conversation about his profession.

"I know the police don't approve of, or give the credit that's always due to, private investigators," Mark began "And yet the most conventional route into the job is from the police. The vast majority have previously been in some branch of law enforcement."

"Was it something you just decided upon, or had you always yearned for such a profession?" Josephine asked.

"Do you remember me having a paper round when I was younger?"

"I can remember you hardly ever putting them in the letterbox. You would always throw them on the front step!" Josephine said laughing.

"Well once, our local bobby was chasing a man that had just mugged an old lady. Although they didn't call it mugging in those days. Anyway he was running towards me, and I took my shoulder bag, full of papers, and hit him in the stomach. As he collapsed on the ground, I put my bike on top of him and sat on it. I got such satisfaction that I'd caught him I thought these guys in the police have great jobs."

"Yet you never joined the force," Josephine remarked.

"No, it didn't appeal to me at the time, but come on, admit it Jo, the police don't like private investigators."

"Alright, I agree, that's the general feeling in the force, though I've worked with a couple of private detectives during my years as a police officer, and they've given me some good information on certain cases. I've always tried to see both points of view," Josephine announced.

"We don't have the powers of the police. There's no official system or warrant card to back us up, and because of that we have to learn to communicate better," Mark told her.

Josephine sipped her wine and was thoughtful for a moment or two. "Yes, I can see that to a certain extent, although I class myself as a very communicative copper."

"I know I'm getting a bit heavy here Jo, but I feel that private investigators should be recognised. I mean, the Legal Aid Board is reluctant to fund an investigator's fee to assist in defence, and yet, you still get your pay cheque at the end of each month, no matter how the case you're working on is progressing. If I don't get a result, I don't get paid."

"You'll be crying on my shoulder in a minute," she joked. "But seriously, you do have a point. I'm seeing the life of a private investigator from a different angle. Tell me, do you work alone or have an assistant?"

"I did have a female assistant, but it didn't work out," Mark informed her.

"I suppose you're going to tell me she was no good."

"On the contrary, she *was* good. Women operate intuitively—they listen more. She could always negotiate better than I could, and would be able to calm hostile situations."

"I agree," Josephine began. "My DS Bill, back in Torquay, used to criticise me for being too pleasant. It never pays to lose your rag no matter how aggravated they make you feel. Persuasion goes a lot further than aggression," she declared.

"Bit of the feminist rearing its ugly head," Mark said.

"Not at all," she corrected him. "I don't regard myself as a feminist. I love men, and although I may not be as strong in the physical sense, I believe I'm as capable as any man, I'm an equal and should be treated as such."

"Err… isn't that a pretty good working definition of feminism?"

"If that's feminism, then I suppose I'm for it."

"Carol, my assistant, was very good at her job. I once sent her to an unoccupied house. She profiled the type of person who had lived there just by the furnishings and personal touches. I could send her to check on things, No-one pays much attention to a woman, especially if she's walking her dog or pushing a pram, and a woman's appearance can so easily be changed with a wig. It was a pity, but we took on extra work and the hours got longer. Her husband and family were suffering, so she left and I've never found anyone to replace her."

"Were you physically attracted to her?" Josephine asked.

"Nothing like that. We just worked well together."

"I believe you, thousands wouldn't," she teased. "Seriously though, have you ever got into any bad situations?"

"You're not kidding. And of course, I can't call for backup on a radio. I've had death threats, but over the years, I've learnt how to deal with them. Normally when people threaten you, they rarely carry it out. It's just mental terrorism. It's the quiet buggers who come back at you."

"Since my brush with death I've often thought of fate as having a bloody strange sense of humour… oh dear, I'm getting maudlin again. Are you working on anything at the moment?"

"I get lots of divorce cases. One partner wants the other followed, that sort of stuff. I can't pretend it's elevating, but it pays the bills. A few months ago I was working for a businessman, who'd been swindled out of thousands of pounds, not by a business colleague but by an ex-lover, would you believe? It was tricky, but I got a result. At the moment, I'm trying to find someone's daughter. It's quite sad really. She left home four years ago, when she was only eighteen. Her father's terminally ill and wants to see her to make certain that she's okay. He wants to make amends for the last time."

"That is sad. I've had various trials and tribulations with Jessica over the past few years, but I always knew she was safe and well. The turmoil and anxiety that the parents of missing children must go through, wondering if they are alive, and if they are, what state their health is in, are they on drugs or sleeping rough? I hope you find her, as much for her father's sake as for her own," Josephine added.

"Well, she's been sighted in the city, but with all the homeless it's like looking for a needle in a haystack. Anyway, enough about me. How are you settling in with the local force? Are your officers okay?"

"I haven't seen much of my chief, the others are alright, although I didn't hit it off with my sergeant when I arrived, but things are improving. He's young, blond, handsome and arrogant. Definitely a man about town, and if he's to be believed, he has a string of glamorous girlfriends."

"The lucky sod! He hasn't made a play for you yet?"

"Don't be ridiculous. I'm far too old for him, he's into dolly birds."

"Oh, I don't know... a mature woman... like a good wine," Mark teased her. "Any good cases to solve?"

"We've discovered a body in a sunken narrowboat in a disused arm of the canal system. According to forensics, he was murdered. The problem is that the body's been there for five years, and we're having a problem identifying him. He seems to have been a tramp or down and out... anyway, I shouldn't be discussing this with you."

"I don't see why not—we're almost in the same profession," he replied.

"Mmm... perhaps I should take early retirement and open my own private detective agency," she remarked.

"You'd never manage," he told her, with a grin on his face.

"What a bloody cheek! Of course I could," Josephine replied.

"How long have you been in the force?" he enquired.

"Almost eighteen years."

"Precisely. After that length of time police procedure is a way of life. It's harder in the private sector, and difficult to adjust."

"I won't argue with you Mark, as I always win," she said smiling.

"You haven't changed since you were a teenager, Jo... I..."

Auntie Win came out into the conservatory.

"So this is where you've been hiding yourselves. Come on Jo, your Auntie Edna wants a chat with you, she's considering buying a mobile home in Brixham... and as for you, Mark, let's get some food. I was just saying to Arthur, that lad looks as if he hasn't had a square meal in weeks."

Mark jumped up and put his arm round Win.

"Well, I'll say this, dear Cousin," he said to Josephine. "We may be able to deal with knife wielding maniacs, drug dealers and mass murderers, but when it comes to Auntie Win we don't stand a chance.

Chapter 13

IT WAS A WARM sunny Sunday afternoon and the temperature was above average considering it was still only mid March. Brindleyplace was bustling. There were people sitting outside the cafés and pubs along the canal. The Sealife Centre was packed with visitors and people were milling in and out of the Convention Centre foyer. Tom Peters was having one of his busiest days for a long time as people queued to board his brightly painted boat 'Rebecca' for the hour-long trip down the canal.

As he stood on board, he shouted,

"Come along now just three seats left for the two o'clock trip, only five pound for adults and three pound for children." He looked at his watch; it was 1:55 and the passengers who were already on board seemed to be getting a little impatient. *I'll just give it another couple of minutes and then I'll start the engine*, he thought.

Due to the severe winter, business had been bad, and at one stage he thought he might have to sell his beloved 'Rebecca', but things were picking up slowly and he thought he would probably just about scrape through.

It doesn't look like there's any more takers for this trip, he thought. He was loath to start a journey unless the boat was full, as the price of fuel had soared. As he was trying to decide whether to cast off a woman and a young boy of about ten years of age approached the boat.

"Oh Mum, can we please—you did promise—"

"Okay, but just make sure you behave," she looked up at Tom and asked the price.

"It'll be just eight pound for the two of you," he told her. She handed Tom a ten-pound note rather begrudgingly, and after he'd given her the change, he helped them both onboard.

"Right ladies and gentlemen, we're just about to leave," he spoke into the crackly microphone that was in his small cabin at the end of the boat. "I shall point out various places of interest along the way." And the boat began its journey along the canal.

Jack was bored, he now wished he'd asked his mother if they could have gone into the Sealife Centre instead. *There's nothing here along this dull and boring canal bank,* he thought to himself. After another ten minutes or so had passed, the journey for Jack was becoming more tedious and tiresome, especially since his mother was now talking to the lady sitting next to her. He decided to go to the far end of the boat to see if he could reach into the water. As the boat moved slowly along the canal, the water rippled over his fingers. He was still fed up, but at least it was better than having to sit and listen to his mother prattle to the old lady. Suddenly he saw something floating in the water just a few yards ahead of him. *I'll catch hold of that as we go past* he thought, as he leant forward to stretch his hand further in the hope of grasping the floating object. As he got closer, he realised to his horror it was a human head. A girl or woman might have screamed, but Jack was made of sterner stuff. He turned and ran down the boat shouting to the driver.

"Hey Mister. Stop the engine! There's a body in the water!"

Tom at first ignored the boy's request, thinking it was just a childish prank or that perhaps all the boy had seen was an old coat, that someone had thrown in the water. It wasn't until the narrowboat pulled up alongside the body floating face down in the water he realised it was no joke!

An hour or so later, Josephine and her team had assembled on the side of the towpath. The body bobbed gently up and down in the water two or three yards or so from where they stood. About ten minutes after their arrival, Doctor Mortimer the forensic pathologist appeared at the scene with an assistant.

He walked towards Josephine.

"I felt the body needed to be examined in the water before it was removed, and since I'm not the best of swimmers, and a touch arthritic these days, I've brought an assistant." He introduced the young man as Robert Walker.

"Getting him to do your dirty work, eh, Doc?" DS Rankin joked.

"Not at all, he offered, didn't you dear boy?" he said as he turned to the young man standing next to him.

"I'm quite looking forward to it," Walker said excitedly.

"The scene of death will be gone the moment the body is moved. So we need to take as many photos as we can from different angles," Doctor Mortimer informed the SOCO team.

One of the police divers walked over to explain the situation to him.

"Although you may not need to be underwater it's possible you may have to submerge your head in order to see the underside of the corpse. So if you come over by the fence, I'll get your gear," he told Robert Walker.

When he had struggled into the wetsuit, and put on the required equipment, he carefully got into the water with the police divers. The police kept a prudent distance, as requested by Doctor Mortimer so that Walker could see the body without distraction or interference. As he went underwater he could look up and see the dead man face to face. The canal water was murky so a light had to be used. After a while, when his task was completed, he told the divers they could lift the body out of the water. As they did so, water poured everywhere. The corpse that was placed on the black body bag had straggly long wet hair. Mortimer examined it for a short while and then said,

"At a guess I'd say he's been in the water forty eight hours and probably dead the same length of time."

"Did he drown?" Josephine asked.

"I'm not sure at this point, I need to examine him thoroughly."

By this time quite a crowd had gathered, despite the fact the body in the canal was some distance away from the main busy social part of Brindleyplace. But news travels fast, and people had started to walk the half mile or so down the towpath to the spot where the body was found.

"Right, get rid of this lot," Josephine told two officers, "While I go and speak to the owner of the boat and the young boy who spotted the body."

Jack was so excited, he told her he'd never found a dead body before and went on to say how a really boring day had turned out to be a great adventure.

"Just you wait till I tell all my mates at school. They'll never believe it; they'll be dead jealous. I'm glad I didn't go into the Sealife Centre, because if I had I'd never have seen the body, would I?" he told Josephine excitedly.

The boy was of no real help; Josephine hadn't thought for a moment he would be. To him, it was just a humdrum day that turned out to be thrilling. The novelty and euphoria would probably last a day or so, and then be replaced by a new game on the Playstation.

The owner of the boat, however, proved more helpful. He'd worked on the canals for many years before buying his narrowboat and organising day trips. The multi-million pound facelift and development of that stretch of the canal had brought him lots of business. The Convention Centre, National Indoor Arena and Sealife Centre, along with all the shops, bars and cafés situated on the canal, had attracted thousands of visitors not just from Birmingham but all over the country. Due to the weather the winter months had been difficult, but generally trade was good and his boat would be sometimes booked for office parties and day trips from schools and other communities.

"I'd like you to view the corpse, to see if you recognise him," Josephine suggested to Tom Peters, although she wasn't very optimistic. She was pleasantly surprised when he said,

"It's old Bob Melchett I think," he looked at the face for a few moments longer "Yes, it's definitely Bob. He's one of the winos who spends time up and down the canal. He's pretty harmless and I sometimes give him money for food. It's strange though he never usually comes down this end, it's a bit too posh for him now, he prefers the other end of the canal."

"I suppose he could have fallen in the water further down and floated to this spot," Josephine suggested "But there's no doubt about his identity, you're certain?"

"Yes, it's definitely Bob," Tom Peters assured her.

"Do you know if there's any next of kin?" Rankin asked.

"Not as far as I know, always been a bit of a loner, though he's friends with the other dropouts."

"We'll probably need you to come to the morgue and identify him again officially," Josephine told him.

"That's not a problem, I'll give you my mobile number—poor sod. He was always half cut, I suppose he just missed his footing and fell in," Tom Peters said dismally.

"Two bodies, in as many weeks and both in the canals; is that usual?" Josephine asked Rankin when they had returned to Police Headquarters.

"Not really, in the two years I've been at the Major Investigation Unit, it's the first time it's occurred. I don't suppose it's connected in any way to the body we found in the boat, do you?" he asked.

"It's doubtful there's nothing to suggest the two are linked, still, something might turn up in the forensic pathology report."

Josephine and DS Rankin donned the usual protective clothing and made their way to the autopsy suite. Doctor Mortimer was there along with Robert Walker, the young man who had examined the body whilst it was still in the water.

"You've both met my assistant," Mortimer said to them, "Since he was present at the scene of crime I thought he'd like to hear the post-mortem results."

"It's the first time I've seen a drowned corpse,

although Doctor Mortimer is not sure if that was the cause of death," Walker added.

"Are we looking at a murder case then?" DS Rankin enquired.

"It's difficult to say, as it's rather more complicated than that. I'd like to go through each stage of the report with you. We've also got the written reports and photos that were taken at the scene. They're here at the morgue, in my office ready for you to take away," Mortimer told them.

"Now, I don't want to blind you with science, but here goes. Despite the fact thousands of deaths by drowning occur in the UK each year, our knowledge of the events is by no means complete. Usually the victim will hold their breath for a variable length of time until carbon dioxide accumulates in the blood and tissues. When this gets to a certain level the stimulation of the respiratory centre in the brain leads to inhalation of large volumes of water. What follows is swallowing of water, coughing, vomiting and loss of consciousness. The next phase is the escape of remaining air in the lungs and replacement with water, unconsciousness and convulsions are followed by heart failure, and death occurs in a very short time."

"God, it sounds an awful way to die," Josephine observed.

"I'd have thought you'd have experience of several cases of drowning, living on the coast," Rankin remarked.

"A few, but they've never been described to me in such specific detail before," she replied.

"I believe in giving all the details to the police," Mortimer began, "And the point I must stress is that drowning in fresh or brackish water in a canal is different from sea water. Because of the low salt content in these waters there is an abrupt violent increase in blood volume. This causes the heart to be over burdened, which can lead to death in about three to five minutes. Disposal of a murder victim to simulate drowning is possible, and yet I'm afraid there are no completely reliable tests that show that a victim definitely drowned."

"So what we really need to know in this case," Josephine intervened, "Concerning the body that was recovered from the water, is was that person alive at the time he entered the water."

"I suppose, we can only go on the scene and circumstances surrounding the incident," Rankin added.

"We once found an alcoholic floating, some fifty feet below a cliff at Babbacombe, and his zipper was open. The conclusion we came to was that he had been urinating before he fell, and foul play was dismissed," Josephine informed them.

"I did discover a drug addict dead in a water filled bath, but usually they've been put in there in an attempt to resuscitate them," Rankin enlightened them.

"Abundant foam is usually noted exuding from the mouth and nostrils of a drowning victim, hence the presence of foam in an airway does indicate beyond doubt, that the victim was alive before submersion. But since he'd been in the canal for a matter of days, this cannot be determined," Doctor Mortimer informed them.

"So do you believe death had occurred longer ago than your original estimate of forty eight hours?" Josephine enquired.

"A body in water will sink, unless air trapped between the clothes keeps it afloat. The body will then re-surface when gas is formed as a result of putrefaction. This is slower in seawater compared to fresh canal water. The time of re-appearance of the body depends on the temperature of the water. It may be two to three days in summer and longer in winter. Despite the time of year, the past couple of days have been unusually warm, which would cause the body to re-surface. So I'd hazard a guess that the body had been in the water about four days."

"Okay, I understand that, but you still haven't told us if he was alive or dead when he entered the water, and if there's any indications he was murdered," Josephine said.

"I'm coming to that my dear," Mortimer replied smiling. "Bodies found at sea are usually subject to injuries from rocks or the propeller blades of ships or boats. Despite the fact this is unlikely to occur in the canal, a passing barge may have caused the body to be thrown against the sides. After careful examination of the skull, I've discovered two types of injuries, one possibly caused by a hammer, but I can't be certain. The indentations are not as clear as those found on the corpse in the boat, as there are also surrounding cuts and abrasions. The other injuries occurred after death, it looks like these injuries were caused by a passing boat," he said pointing to a deep cut and round indentation on the victim's head.

"But I've kept the strangest thing till last," he lifted the bottom half of the sheet to reveal the mans genitals.

"See this cut along his penis?" They all looked and nodded. "I can confirm this injury was inflicted before death, and I'd go so far as to say before he entered the water."

"You've given us all the medical and scientific facts, but can you draw a picture of what might have happened from past experience?" Josephine asked.

"I'd say the most likely explanation is that he was attacked with some sort of weapon, although I cannot determine which at this point, and his assailant attempted to cut off his penis, but was unsuccessful," he replied.

"So it's possible there was a struggle and then the victim fell into the canal," Josephine suggested.

"Yes. Due to his head injuries and blood loss, even if the victim *was* conscious on entering the canal he'd be dazed and weak, so couldn't save himself and drowned."

"As far as I'm concerned, it's still a murder

enquiry," Josephine began. "He'd probably have finished the job, so whether the victim was pushed or fell into the canal is irrelevant."

"One thing that occurs to me, ma'am," Rankin said, "Is that it must have happened at night, because surely someone would have noticed something during the daytime."

"We don't know how far from the point the body was found when it entered the water. Although there's very little current in the canal, so I doubt it could have travelled far," Josephine observed. "The police divers are still dragging the canal for a weapon and another team of officers are searching the surrounding areas, so we'll just have to wait and see what turns up."

"Are there any similarities to the first death?" Rankin asked.

"His penis, or what was left of it, showed no signs of injury, so it's impossible to say if the surface flesh had been cut. There's also the deep mark on the top of the left femur. It's a knife wound, so it's possible the deaths may be connected. I'll carry out further tests to see if there's any relation between the two."

They thanked Doctor Mortimer for a very interesting, and somewhat educational, morning as they left his department.

At Josephine's request DS Rankin and DC's Lloyd and Freeman were assembled on the towpath next to Vincent Street Bridge where the body was found. At this point there were two separate bridges across the canal marked with black and white ornate nameplates. Although the narrowboat was travelling under the right hand bridge, the body was found floating under the adjacent bridge that was only a matter of feet away. As they walked up the towpath some four hundred yards or so they came to The Fiddle and Bone pub on the left-hand side. Rankin told Josephine it was a popular venue for all ages, due to the fact the pub had some very talented jazz bands performing there throughout the week. Next to the pub was an old round Victorian building known as the Roundhouse. It had originally been used for industrial purposes but was now converted into rather quaint small shop units. A long dark cobbled pathway went down the side of the pub and under the Roundhouse.

"This would be an ideal place to attack anyone," DC Freeman remarked.

"Mm—I'm not so sure, although this spot is deserted, an assailant could possibly be seen by customers leaving the pub. Anyway we've seen enough here but I'd like you and DC Lloyd to make enquiries in the pub and shop units to see if anyone noticed anything," she told Freeman.

When they returned to the towpath they were by Sheepcote Bridge where the murder weapon, a hammer had been found. The water taxi stop was situated on the towpath outside the pub.

"How far does this travel along the canal?" Josephine enquired.

"All the way to Wharf Street Market," DC Katie Lloyd informed her.

"Speak to whoever's responsible for operating the water taxi, it's possible they may have noticed something. And I've just noticed there's a cycle path along here, surely someone on a bike may have seen something."

As they continued their walk along the canal side, Josephine remarked how clean and smart the area looked. There were several decorative lamp posts and several shrubs and bushes had been planted along the canal borders. A few yards further up on the opposite side stood a complex of luxury flats with rather impressive bay windows.

"I bet you need a bob or two to buy one of those," DC Lloyd observed.

"Yes a friend of mine brought one, and he didn't get much change from £150, 000, and according to the estate agent he got a bargain," Rankin told them.

"Sounds like he paid over the odds to me," Josephine remarked.

"Not at all, this is a prime location, where the property is sought after."

"Well, let's hope we catch this murderer, before the prices start to fall," she joked.

As they walked past the opulent looking buildings Josephine turned round and looked back down the canal towards the bridge.

"The people on those two top floors would have a good view of the canal, especially those corner ones," she said as she pointed up to the building. "We'll get one of our officers to interview the residents there; it may be a long shot, but who knows."

As they continued to walk, the NIA multi-storey carpark was on the left and a little further down they came to a spot where the canal widened to almost a circular shape, there was a man-made island situated in the centre, where several ducks were nestling. In the middle of the island stood a signpost showing the distances in miles to various towns along the canal. On the left hand side stood the Malt House pub, a rather traditional looking building with circular wrought iron balconies along the front.

"That's where Bill Clinton was photographed drinking a pint," Rankin said proudly.

Directly opposite stood the Sealife Centre and as they passed they could hear strange sounds of water music coming from the entrance. Josephine didn't like the architecture it looked modern and space age, almost like a NASA building. She felt the same about the Convention Centre with its large smoked blue glass windows, and yet opposite that was another traditional looking building.

Josephine felt as if she had landed in a confused time warp where modern monstrosities surrounded traditional Victorian style buildings and pubs. She had always felt she didn't belong in this century, as she preferred the remoteness of Dartmoor, which some people found depressing. She had always perceived cities as concrete jungles, and for a moment wondered why on earth she had asked for a transfer. She expressed her views to those around her.

"You sound very nostalgic, ma'am, maybe it's your age. Remember, we're only months away from the Millennium," Rankin told her. Morgan and Lloyd winced at the sergeant's remark, thinking that their Inspector might take offence but she replied,

"You could be right there sergeant, but to me the Millennium is just a date. I can't see what all the fuss is about."

They walked further along towards a busy area where lots of bars, shops and restaurants were situated. They were now surrounded by crowds of people.

"I think if the chief agrees, we could get a couple of officers to patrol the canal," Josephine suggested. She stopped walking and looked around her and was thoughtful for a few moments then she said,

"We've been assuming the victim was attacked on the towpath and was either thrown or fell into the canal. But looking at those signposts, it's possible he was murdered elsewhere and transported to this spot on a boat and then thrown in the canal."

"That's feasible, in fact a car could have parked

on the bridge at Vincent Street and the body could have been thrown into the water from there, though the killer would have taken a gamble on not being noticed."

"Let's get the flats on the road side checked and go through the register of narrowboat owners. I know it's a chore, but it's all we've got to go on."

"The worst chore will be asking the chief for extra manpower," Rankin added.

"At the far end of the canal there are tramps and homeless people. We'll speak to them and see what they can tell us about the victim Bob Melchett. According to Tom Peters, the boat owner, they all knew him."

"I can't see them being very co-operative, that's if any of them are sober," Rankin said.

"Well if we offer them some incentive, they might talk."

"If you mean money for food, I can't see the chief agreeing to give us any more funds."

"There's no time like the present, let's ask him," Josephine said, and they headed back to the station.

Chapter 14

THE TWO MEN sat on the sloping grass verge by the canalside, passing the bottle partly concealed in a brown paper bag between them. They looked considerably older than their years, due to their weather beaten complexions. One man's hair was long and straggly, and so badly matted it looked like the comb had never been invented. The few teeth that were left in his mouth were black with decay, and his breath smelt foul. He wore an old dirty brown bedraggled coat, that he held up to his neck in an attempt to keep out the biting wind. His companion wore a knitted black hat and a string vest under what appeared to be an old dinner jacket with a black satin collar. It was covered in food stains and drink, yet despite his attire he didn't seem to feel the cold like his friend.

As he swatted a fly that had landed on his leg, he looked up and said

"Pigs, filth, that's what you are, I'm telling you nothing."

The young smart clean shaven DC turned to his colleague.

"I'll accept pigs, but filth, looking at the state of him is beyond a joke." The PC laughed.

"What's it worth?" The other one said as he tucked the bottle under his overcoat. The officer took some coins from his pocket.

"At least you can get yourself a hot mug of tea and some breakfast to keep out the cold," he said pointing to a sign outside a nearby café that read, FULL ENGLISH BREAKFAST + TEA + TOAST ONLY £1.99, knowing full well if he accepted the money it would be spent on booze.

He was just about to speak when the other one said,

"Keep your mouth shut Frank, just piss off you two!"

"If there is someone going along the canal killing your sort, you should tell us anything you know, I mean, you might be the next one," the DC told him.

An old woman walked up behind them. She smelt of stale urine, and when she smiled, she looked like an old witch. She had obviously overheard them talking.

"These two are okay, nothing will happen to them or me," she told them.

"How can you be so sure?" DC Freeman asked.

"Because they're too old," she replied.

"What do you mean?"

"It'll cost you," she said, wiping her runny nose on her sleeve. He reached into his side pocket and removed a crumpled five-pound note. "Bob was always after the young blokes for sex, someone said they'd slashed his cock, should've cut the bloody thing off!" she told them.

"Are you sure about this?" The PC asked.

"Of course I am, I caught him once—up some poor young thing's arse. The dirty swine!"

"No matter how hungry I was, I'd never do that,

148

even if I was offered money," the man in the hat uttered.

No, but I bet you'd do almost anything else, DC Freeman thought.

"The body was found just a few hundred yards down there," he said as he pointed down the canal path. "Did you see him hanging about with anyone last week?"

"When was that?" she asked.

"Last Thursday."

"I don't know, I never know the day or date, all the days are the same to me. Now give us that money, I've told you what you want to know," she said as she lurched forward in an attempt to grab it from his hand.

"Not so fast—here, you can have it," Freeman said giving her the money "But you'll need to come to the station with me. My DI will want to talk to you."

"That wasn't the deal, now clear off!" she turned and went to walk away.

"What's your name?" he said as he grabbed her arm.

"Flossie."

"Look Flossie, you can either come with us now quietly, we only need to talk to you for a short time. It's nice and warm in the station, and I'll make sure you get a hot meal. Otherwise, we can arrest you and keep you in a cold cell for hours," DC Freeman told her.

"You can't, I've done nothing wrong!"

"I can always think of something," he said.

"Pigs!" she shouted. "Okay, but one hour, no more."

As they walked away with Flossie to the police car that was parked on the nearby road, Frank said to his companion,

"You see, she's got money off them and now she's getting a meal. We could have told them that, I'm bloody starving," Frank said.

"Shut up, and give me the bottle," the other man said as he snatched it from his hand. "We'll get the money off Flossie when she comes back."

"She'll have spent it on booze or meths by then," Frank replied.

Flossie Trafford sat in front of Josephine and DC Freeman and sipped tea from a mug.

"Have you got a cigarette, dearie?" she asked Josephine.

"I don't smoke anymore, I'm afraid," she replied.

"It's Detective Inspector Blake you're talking to Flossie—show some respect," DC Freeman intervened.

"It's okay," Josephine assured him. "Now, Flossie, from what my DC here tells me, you knew the deceased."

"Yeah, him that was knocked off. Old Bob Melchett. Good riddance to bad rubbish, that's what I say. He was a bad lot. Always had a fancy for young lads he had. Not that any of them'd go near him. But I seen him looking over kiddies—there's more of 'em around since they poshed the canals up."

"Rent boys?"

"Nah. Where'd he get the money for rent boys? He preyed on them as had been thrown out by their own. They can't go to the police, you see—vulnerable they are. I heard those he couldn't jolly along with some drink he took by force."

"Rape, you mean?"

"Unless you've got a posher word for it."

"Tom Peters, who owns the pleasure boat, said he'd known Melchett and he didn't tell us anything about this."

"He kept it a secret from anyone who could have caused him trouble. Tom would give him money every so long, and pay him to clean his boat. Bob wouldn't have wanted him to know. Ask any of the others who hang around, they'll tell you the same. We couldn't do him any harm."

"Do you sleep rough, Flossie?" Josephine asked.

"I've got a nice cardboard box all of my own, dearie. You don't need to worry about Flossie."

"Is there no chance of you getting into a hostel? I'm sure if you cleaned yourself up you might find some sort of employment. You must be suffering terribly in the cold weather."

The old woman rocked back and forth in a bout of laughter. Wiping the tears from her eyes she said "Oh dear, that's a good one. Get real lady! You can sit there in your nice suit, talking la-di-da to me. Do you know what it's like to be so cold you cry? Or that hungry you'd do anything to get some food inside you? To have finally got to sleep under some plastic in the cold when some bloody copper moves you on? Suffering! You don't know the meaning of the word!"

"Well, not in the sense you mean, Flossie, I don't suppose I do."

Josephine could have told Flossie of the terrible pain and the horrific nightmares she'd endured after her injuries, but knew she'd be wasting her breath.

"Have you any idea who killed Melchett?"

"So it *was* murder!"

"He was badly injured when he entered the canal. Someone had beaten his head to a pulp. Whether his actual death was caused by drowning, we don't know. But yes, it was murder. Do you know anyone who'd have a reason to murder him?"

"Nah. Not really. Of course there was loads as would have *liked* to. But I don't think any of 'em 'ud have the bottle."

Josephine picked up a picture. It was an artist's impression of the face of the unidentified man found in the sunken boat.

"Do you recognise this man?" she asked.

Flossie looked at the picture for a moment or two.

"Nah, can't say I do."

"It might have been some years ago!"

"Nah, not that I can think of."

"Right. Look Flossie, I want you to keep your eyes and ears open. If you get to know anything, I want you to report it back to me."

"Why should *I* help *you*? What's in it for me?"

"I'll pay for any information you give me. As long as it's genuine. Don't try and fool me—even posh birds in smart suits can spot bullshit, would you believe! I'll try and get you a place at a hostel for a few weeks."

"Gawd, if you could do that old Flossie'd be grateful. It's so long since I last slept in a real bed."

"Right then, it's a deal. DC Freeman here will take you to the canteen and make sure you get a meal before you go."

"Thank'y ma'am, you're a real lady… a real lady…" She kept repeating the phrase as she went out of the door.

"My God, she's changed her tune a bit since she arrived," Freeman observed.

Josephine left the interview room and returned to her office. As she entered DC Katie Lloyd was waiting to see her.

"I don't know how you do it, ma'am!"

"What's that?" Josephine asked, a little confused.

"Get all these men after you. Not that I'm jealous, you understand. Now if it were the opposite sex…" The DC lifted a piece of paper and started to read, "A Doctor Blythe called. He's left his number in Devon. DS Bill Hughes phoned and started chatting me up, would you believe?"

"Yes, that sounds like Bill," Josephine agreed.

"Oh, and your cousin Mark Hitchen. I've written all the numbers down."

"Thanks Katie. I could do with a cuppa if one's going."

"No problem, ma'am. I'll get you one from the canteen."

As soon as she left Josephine picked up the phone and dialled Andrew's number. She managed to get straight through.

"Hi… how are you?" he asked.

"Not bad," she replied.

"Missing me?"

"Well… yes."

"You don't sound too sure, Jo."

"Of course I am. It's just that we've found another body in the canal," she told him.

"Has it been there some years, like the first?"

"No… only a matter of days, in fact. He was attacked and thrown in."

"So the two cases aren't linked?"

"No, it seems not. This latest victim is a known paedophile. I suppose the only link at the moment is the canals."

"And you thought you'd miss the sea!" Andrew joked.

"There's a difference between Birmingham's canal network and the sea you know! Mind you, they've spent millions developing Brindleyplace, and it attracts loads of tourists. I'll take you there for lunch when you come up to Birmingham."

"I don't know when that will be," he told her. "I've got so much work on at the moment it's untrue. I took extra leave while you were in hospital and afterwards and I've never really got caught up."

Josephine's mind was in turmoil. She desperately

wanted to see him, and was a little annoyed with him. She knew his excuse was valid—she remembered how guilty she'd felt when he'd put his cases on hold to look after her.

"No problem, I'll take Bill instead. I'm sure *he'll* enjoy himself," she said, sharply.

"Please yourself," Andrew said and hung up.

Usually when they'd argued over the phone she'd brood and feel sorry for herself, but she wasn't to have the chance. DS Rankin entered the office.

"I'd like a quick word with you on the progress report on the identification of the corpse in the boat, ma'am."

"Oh good, have a seat."

"We put what details we had through the HOLMES computer after we'd checked through the missing persons reports, and we put a press release out. Although the Photo-fit wasn't that good we boiled it down to a list of seven men reported missing at the time who fitted the build, height and description. I want to run a check of their dental records against the victim's, to see if we can come up with a match. It's a long shot I know…"

"No, go ahead, get it checked," she said vaguely.

"You don't seem very enthusiastic, ma'am—I know it's not brilliant, but it's something to go on."

"The reason I'm not too optimistic is that if he *was* a loner or a tramp, he'd wouldn't have had a base to go missing from—if he did leave home it would have been years earlier. Can you see my train of thought?"

"Yes, I can. If a youngster or teenager goes missing the family and police automatically assume the worst. That they've been abducted, killed or enticed by drugs and so on. But when a middle aged man goes missing, they assume he's left his wife, gone off with another woman or just got fed up with his life and done a Stonehouse. There doesn't seem so much concern or importance attached to the case."

Rankin placed the list of missing persons on Josephine's desk. "We've got the names and addresses and the times of disappearance. I think there are three possibles. Those are the ones I've marked with a cross. The first four are John Burns, Nigel Holmes, Alfred Caldicott and Michael Downs. All left homes and families behind them. Burns and Holmes took clothes and possessions with them and cleared out their bank accounts. Pretty obviously they intended leaving, even though their wives reported them as missing. Caldicott and Downs were both suffering from depression according to their doctors. I'd guess we could assume there was no foul play involved there."

"Now we come to the three who look hopeful. Alec Morton went to work one morning and never returned. It was as if he'd disappeared off the face of the earth."

"Abducted by aliens?" Josephine said wryly.

"You've been watching too many episodes of the X-Files," Rankin countered. "Then we come to Charlie Reid. What a star! According to his wife they had been happily married, with two kids, then she came home and found him having sex…"

"Well, infidelity is common enough," Josephine remarked.

"With the next door neighbour's son!" Rankin added. "She threw him out and hasn't seen him since."

"So why did she report him as missing? Surely it was a breakdown in the marriage due to his perverted sexual tendencies?"

"She thought that something had happened to him. He didn't get in touch with her or the children."

"Well, perhaps he was too ashamed to face them?"

"Yes, but their joint bank account had a healthy balance, and she thought he'd have contacted her just to get his share of the money," Rankin said.

"Mmm, sounds promising… The recent victim, Melchett was a paedophile. Still, there's nothing to suggest the body found on the boat is connected with the latest victim, especially given the time difference. It's a pity we haven't a more accurate date."

"The last one is William Fryer, married, no children. According to his missing persons report he just left one Sunday morning to get a paper and never came back. In all the cases no bodies were ever found—in fact they're real enigmas."

"What dates do they cover?"

"The earliest is 1993, the latest is 1996."

"So they're in the range. The body could have been in the cabin from two to five years. So we're looking at dates between 1994 to 1997, but of course the missing person could have been killed *after* they went missing.

Still, it's a bit of a pot-pourri. We'll just have to wait and see if we get a match."

"I've got all the dentist's names and addresses from the families."

"Right. Well, let's see what turns up. We're still waiting for the list of all owners of narrowboats in the area, although not all are registered. From what I've been told one or two slip through the net."

"Oh, by the way, ma'am, can you see the press officer? The Evening Mail and Central News have been on to him about an update on the murder, and he wants to check with you before releasing any information. Apparently Radio WM have asked if someone from the department could comment on the case."

"Well, there's not really much to comment *on*," Josephine replied.

"They're a good station ma'am, and they did help out when we were trying to identify the body on the barge."

"Okay—would you like to talk to them?"

"Yes I would, ma'am," Rankin said enthusiastically

"Okay, but let's check it out with the duty solicitor first to ascertain what information we can give out."

"Will do, ma'am," he said smiling, as he left the room.

Chapter 15

ANNIE JENKINS was tucked up in bed in her narrowboat, which was moored at Gas Street basin, near the James Brindley public house. Sipping the steaming hot mug of cocoa that her husband had made for her, and ready to start an Agatha Christie paperback, she was in seventh heaven. As far as Annie was concerned there was nothing in the world better than to be in a warm comfortable bed, with a good book, her cocoa and a packet of milk chocolate digestives.

As she finished reading the first chapter, she put the book face down on the covers of the bed and reached over for a biscuit. She was about to dunk it into her cocoa when she suddenly heard a huge splash that rocked the boat so fiercely she split her drink all over her nightie.

"Ohhh… damn and blast! Not again! And just as I was getting comfortable. I'll have to change now," she muttered to herself as she got out of bed and began to walk the length of the still rocking boat to where her clothes were kept.

"I suppose some bugger's dropped another old bike in the canal. It's disgusting the way some people use the canals as rubbish tips. I tell you Annie, I've had enough, I'm reporting it in the morning," her husband Bert said angrily.

"Never mind about tomorrow, just help me out of this nightie, I'm drenched," she moaned.

Some twenty minutes or so later she was back in

bed, wearing a clean nightie and a fresh mug of cocoa.

"Now don't spill this one!" her husband said, as he handed her the mug.

"Right, let's get back to this murder mystery. D'you know, Bert, even Agatha's red herrings haven't fooled me this time. I reckon I've worked out who did it!" Little did she know that a real body lay floating just feet from where she lay engrossed in the book!

Josephine dialled the number of the Torbay Police Department in Devon. She didn't recognise the voice of the girl on the switchboard, so she asked to be put through to DS Hughes.

"About time too!" Bill moaned.

"What do you mean?" she asked.

"I've been trying to get hold of you for days."

"Well, I've only received one message."

"How's it going, anyway?"

"We've found a body in the canal," Josephine told him.

"Yes, you told me, the one on the boat."

"No, there's another one. A fresh killing."

"So you're busy then?"

"Well, to be honest we've come to a bit of a dead end. How are you coping?"

"Fine. You DI's have an easy job of it," he joked.

"Just don't make yourself too comfortable in my office."

"No. Joking apart, there's not much happening. Just the usual burglaries and street crime. No murders since you've left. You're jinxed—they've followed you to Brum!"

"Well thanks. We had a party here and I saw all the family. I met a cousin I hadn't seen for years, Mark. He's a private investigator now."

"Why's that, couldn't he make it into the force?" Bill asked.

"No, it just appealed to him. Being his own boss and everything. He's got his own agency now and seems to be making it work."

"I've got no time for private investigators. But you know that—most of us coppers don't like them."

"I suppose I've been as biased as you in the past, Bill, but I didn't really understand what they're up against. Talking to Mark certainly makes me think of it in a more favourable light."

"Well, he's your cousin. On to business." It was obvious to Josephine that Bill didn't want to debate the relative merits of private versus public detectives. "I've got a few days leave and I was wondering when I could come up to Birmingham."

"I could spend the weekend with you. I'm moving into single quarters next week."

"That'll do me. Now, will Auntie Win put me up or will I bunk down with you?"

"Bill! I'll get you a bed and breakfast."

"Well... er... I'm a bit short at the moment, got my solicitor's bill—it was ridiculous!"

"Okay, I'll see what I can arrange," she said.

"So if I arrive Friday evening and leave on Sunday night?"

"Yes, that sounds okay to me."

DC Katie Lloyd burst into the office.

"Sorry to interrupt, ma'am, only they've found another body!"

Bill had overheard on the other end of the phone.

"I told you, you're jinxed! I'll see you Friday."

It was a foggy, damp morning when they arrived at Gas Street basin. It was a small basin with about twenty boats moored alongside one another in the water, looking rather cramped. There was only a foot or so between each boat, and one or two had smoke coming out of the small tin chimneys. It was all rather quaint, like a small village on the water. Josephine and DS Rankin made their way to the far end where a boat was moored on the corner, situated a short distance from the others in a more private position.

The scene of crime team were cordoning off the area with fluorescent rope as they waited for the forensic pathologist to arrive. The body was clearly visible, floating face down in the water, a foot entangled in the ropes that were used to moor the boat. From what they could see in the dark murky water, the corpse had black curly hair and was wearing what looked like an old grey overcoat.

"Who found the body?" Josephine asked a nearby PC.

"The owner of the boat, Mr Jenkins. He heard something fall into the canal last night. He says it was about midnight. He thought at the time that someone had dumped a bicycle in the water. Apparently the kids throw all sorts of things in here."

Doctor Mortimer walked along the narrow path to where they stood.

"We'll have to stop meeting like this, my dear," he said, smiling.

"I know. I'm beginning to dread seeing you— not in the personal sense, you understand..." Josephine replied.

"Well, I've come prepared this time. I've bought my waders, and I see the body's on the surface. That's good."

"I'll go and have a word with the boat's owner while you examine the body, and I'll see you shortly," Josephine walked a yard or so and descended the wooden steps that led into the boat's interior.

Despite the boat's narrow interior being bright and well-lit, Josephine felt at little claustrophobic as she walked down the narrow passageway that led past the bathroom and cooking area to the living area at the front. *I don't know how people can live like this* she thought, as she ducked her head passing though into the front of the boat.

Mr Jenkins turned out to be a white-haired man in his late sixties. His wife looked slightly younger, with grey curly hair and wore a bright pink flowered blouse over slacks. Her lipstick was a vivid shade of cerise that matched her top.

Her husband looked pale and tired, but she looked the opposite with flushed cheeks and bright eyes. Before Josephine could speak she said,

"Isn't this exciting? I mean, I've read lots of whodunits, but to have a murder happen next door to our boat. It *is* murder isn't it? Not just some drunk who fell in." She rattled on without pausing for breath. "I've been following the case in the newspapers, I bet he's the latest victim!"

As she listened to the woman prattle on, Josephine looked round the boat, noticing as she did the shelf crammed with Agatha Christie paperbacks. The woman's weird fascination with the murder became clear. Josephine was also a Christie fan, but had experienced death at first hand, and realised the distance there was between the fiction and the actuality. She wondered whether, if this woman ever had to encounter the real horror and grief of it, she would ever pick up another murder mystery again.

"If I'd known when me and Bert heard that splash! A real body, lying only feet away from where I was sleeping…"

Josephine decided it was time to interrupt.

"Right, thank you Mrs Jenkins."

"Call me Annie,"

"*Thank* you Mrs Jenkins," Josephine repeated in a louder and sharper tone. "Now, Mr Jenkins, if you could tell me what happened?"

"Not a lot I can say, really. We heard a loud splash and the boat rocked summat fierce. Annie here spilt her cocoa on her nightie... she was soaked."

"Yes... I," the woman began, but Josephine was determined she wouldn't interrupt again.

"Didn't you go outside to check?" she asked Mr Jenkins.

"Well, no. I thought someone had probably just dropped a bike or something into the canal. Tell the truth I didn't want to run into anyone who'd have done that. Getting on a bit now, y'see—some of these young lads haven't got any respect for age. Mind you, I regret it now—I might have saved the poor bugger."

"Why do you say *him*? We haven't removed the body yet, how do you know it's a man?"

"Well, they've all been men, haven't they? All those that have been murdered. I just assumed..."

"Are you moored here permanently?" Josephine asked. "There's a lot of boats for such a small area."

"Aye, most of them are permanent moorings. There are a few hire boats at the end of the basin, which are let for holidays, and a few business boats."

"I noticed smoke from a few chimneys," Rankin told him.

"Aye, even though most of us run on butane gas cylinders, some boats still burn coal or wood. We've got everything you'd have in your house, even a microwave."

"So are some boats connected to the mains?"

165

"Some are. Some use gas, coal or wood and run their power from batteries. Of course, you have to run your engine a bit to keep them charged up. Not a problem if you're travelling, moreso if you're moored."

"Going back to last night, the body seems to have become tangled in your mooring ropes."

"He never ties them tight enough—he's always doing that!" Anne said.

"They were tight enough. It's the damp that slackens them off. You can't have them too tight, anyway. Maybe the force of him going in loosened them a bit more."

"Now, going back to last night, did you hear anything unusual at all?" Josephine asked.

Mr Jenkins looked a little vague.

"I mean, anyone arguing or rowdy or the sounds of someone fighting," Josephine continued.

"No, nothing. Sometimes we hear people leaving the Tap and Spile, and they can be a bit rowdy especially those that are drunk, but thinking about it, it was quiet last night," Mr Jenkins told her.

"Well, please contact me if you remember anything at all that may help," Josephine said, handing him her card.

DC Lloyd came to the door of the boat.

"Doctor Mortimer has asked me to inform you that the body has been recovered from the water, ma'am."

"Right, thank you, we'll be there shortly," Rankin replied.

The body was lying in the black body bag, but it hadn't been zipped up. Doctor Mortimer stood over the corpse wearing his white protective clothing and gloves; he stood out like a ghost against the dull misty background. The face was a mass of congealed blood and slightly disfigured, unlike the previous victims who had received mainly head injuries.

"What can you tell us?" Josephine said looking down at the mutilated corpse.

"Not a lot at present," he said looking at his watch "I'd say he died approximately eight to ten hours ago."

"According to the owners of this boat they heard a loud thud and splash at around midnight," DS Rankin informed him.

"Mm, that ties in; I'd say he was possibly dead before he entered the water."

"So you'd rule out drowning in this case?" Josephine asked.

"I can't confirm officially until I've carried out further examinations, but yes, if I had to commit myself, I'd say he died approximately fifteen to thirty minutes beforehand, was dragged to the edge of the towpath, and then rolled in the water. Although the Forensic boys will be able to confirm that, depending on where they find his blood along the pathway. Even though the face is a mess, he also received several blows to the back of his head, which was probably cause of death."

"Any wounds or lacerations inflicted on his

penis?" Josephine asked.

"I haven't examined that part of his anatomy yet," Mortimer replied. "Let's look, shall we?" He carefully unzipped the victim's trousers and examined the genital area. "No, it looks fine to me."

"Perhaps the killer didn't have the time," Rankin suggested.

"Well, he certainly inflicted enough injury to his head and face," Josephine remarked.

"Even these terrible injuries could have been inflicted in less than thirty seconds in a frenzied attack with the right sort of weapon," Mortimer informed them.

"I suppose he may have been disturbed, or heard someone coming, so decided to dump the body and make a quick getaway," Josephine added.

"To me, this man has little or no fear of being caught; look, this isn't exactly what you'd call a remote spot," Rankin remarked as he looked round at the surrounding pubs, boats and cafés. "In fact, it's one of the busiest areas along the canal. He took a real chance that no-one was passing by, even at that time of night."

"What's worrying me is, with the state of his face, we're going to have another problem with identification," Josephine announced.

They stood back as the SOCO team continued to take photos of the corpse and surrounding areas. Just then a man slipped through the cordoned-off area and was making his way towards them. An officer caught up with him and grabbed him by the arm.

"I'm sorry sir, you can't go any further, this is a crime scene, I'm afraid."

"It's just the coat—I think I recognise—" he said, leaning to one side in an attempt to look at the body.

The man's face looked familiar to Josephine.

"Let him through," she ordered the PC. As he came closer to them he said,

"Tom Peters, do you remember, I own the cruise boat."

"Oh yes, of course, we've spoken to you before."

"It's just that, the coat—"

"Did you know this man?"

"Yes, it's Terry Ryan," he replied.

"Are you certain?"

"Of course, I've known him for ages."

"But his face—how can you be so positive?" Josephine asked doubtfully.

"Despite the way he looks—my God—I mean, how could anyone—?" He was quiet for a few moments as he looked down at the body slightly dazed.

"His arm—look at his right arm. Terry has a small cherub tattooed at the top with the name 'Nathan'."

Doctor Mortimer carefully removed the victim's arm from his coat, and there it was, a rather artistic design, in blue and red, of a small cherub about three and a half inches long.

"I suppose it was one of his boyfriends," Rankin suggested.

"What the hell do you mean?" Tom snapped.

"All my sergeant meant, was that the previous victim had a preference for young boys."

"Well I don't give a damn about that, Terry was as straight as a die!"

"How can you be certain of that?" Rankin asked him.

"Well for one thing, he lived with his girlfriend."

"That's not absolutely conclusive, some homosexuals appear to be happily married men on the surface," Rankin added.

"He had a part-time job at the pub over there, and from time to time, he'd clean my boat and help me with odd jobs. We've often chatted about his life with Karen, and I'm telling you, the bloke's straight!" His voice was becoming loud and slightly aggressive.

"Okay Mr Peters, let's assume what you say is true. How can you account for his tattoo?" Josephine asked.

"Nathan was his son, he was killed in a hit and run road accident when he was nine years old. Terry's ex-wife blamed him; he was supposed to be looking after the kid when he ran over the road to see one of his mates. Terry and his wife eventually split up, and he was lonely and depressed for some time until he met Karen. The tattoo was done a few years ago, as Terry's sort of token of love to his son. It's sick to imply it means anything more perverted," he said indignantly.

"I can understand your anger, now you've

explained, but you must realise this is a murder enquiry, and up to now the assailant seems to have been targeting homosexuals. So obviously we would assume this victim to be similar to the previous one, unless facts came to our notice to prove different," Josephine retorted.

His anger subsided.

"Yes—I do see that now—it was the shock of seeing him with his face battered."

"We want to find out who's responsible for these deaths, so please work with us rather than against, and contact me if there's anything else you remember," Josephine said, as she handed him her card.

"Oh by the way, do you have Terry Ryan's address?" Rankin asked.

"No, but the pub will give it to you, as he worked there part time."

After he'd left, Josephine instructed the team to interview the residents of the adjacent narrowboats, and make enquiries at the surrounding pubs and cafés. She looked up at a skyscraper office block "I don't suppose they could see anything from there; still, check it out," she told Rankin.

"You never know, there might be someone who has a pair of binoculars, who can see in the dark," he joked. "Anyway, when we get his address, I'll go and speak to his girlfriend and break the news to her, and I'll take DC Lloyd with me."

Two days later, they all assembled for a briefing in the incident room, after certain information had been obtained. The photos of the two recent victims, and shots taken of the surrounding areas of the canal were pinned on the board. Photos of the remains of the corpse discovered in the sunken narrowboat were also pinned up.

A further five officers had now been assigned to the case which was classed as a category A crime. Chief Inspector Robert Lyle was present, and he didn't seem pleased at the way the investigation into the three murders was progressing. Since Josephine had been quite high profile in Devon, and solved several major crimes, she felt he expected the same performance with these cases, but they had so very little to go on, and every avenue they explored seemed to lead to a dead end. They had, however, made some progress.

As the briefing began, DS Rankin stood up.

"We now have a positive ID on the remains found in the boat," he told them.

"Right, that's a good start, go ahead sergeant," Josephine said.

"About time too," the chief muttered.

"After going through the names of local people reported missing in the rough time span we had, we short listed seven possibles, and I'm pleased to announce we now have a positive ID, thanks to the dental records. The body in the boat was that of Charlie Reid, and what's even more interesting," the sergeant's voice became slightly louder due to his excitement, "Despite the fact his wife reported him as a missing person, she actually threw him out of their home, when to her horror and disgust she found him having sex with a young boy. When I went to tell Mrs Reid we'd identified the remains as those of her late husband, she did say someone had told her a year or so ago they'd seen a vagrant along the canals who resembled her husband."

"So now, at least we have some sort of connection," Josephine began. "Charlie Reid, the first victim discovered in the sunken boat was homosexual or bisexual, and he was murdered. Cause of death was due to severe blows to the head, although Doctor Mortimer could not ascertain if any damage had been inflicted to the genital area, due to the state of the body. Then we move on to victim number two, Bob Melchett, found in the canal with head injuries and his penis cut, although not amputated. Again he had a preference for boys. Then finally we come to the latest victim, Terry Ryan, who again sustained head injuries and was disposed of in the canal."

"Yes, but in this instance," the chief began, "There was no injury to the penis, and nothing to suggest the man was gay, so where's the link?"

"Yes, that's correct sir," Josephine agreed. "But after interviewing Karen Bridges, his girlfriend with whom he shared a flat, she was adamant he was totally straight, and that they had a normal and fulfilled sex life."

"More than most of us can say," DC Freeman

joked as one or two people sniggered.

The chief gave him a stern piercing look, and the room went suddenly quiet.

"Sorry about that interruption, please continue, DI Blake."

"Karen Bridges also confirmed that the tattoo on his arm was in memory of his young son."

"Quite so, Inspector, but if this man wasn't gay, you have just reinforced my opinion, that there is no link to the previous murders."

"I disagree sir. Terry Ryan worked in the Tap and Spile pub and helped out on the boats. Karen told me he was well known along the canals. He would often talk to young boys who were fishing or cycling along the canal, but she said this was because he'd lost his own son. So let's say he wasn't a paedophile, but the murderer might have mistakenly assumed he was, if he saw him talking to young lads. As far as the fact that no injuries were inflicted to his penis, it's possible the assailant was disturbed, or heard someone coming and decided not to risk inflicting further injuries on his victim, so he just dumped the body and ran."

"Mm, that's feasible," the chief replied, although he still sounded doubtful.

"What seems odd to me, is that he picks relatively busy locations. I'm amazed he wasn't spotted by anyone. It's obvious he has a good knowledge of the canal network, but he always seems to run a high risk of getting caught," Rankin stated.

"Have we had any luck interviewing the people

174

on the surrounding boats and buildings?" Josephine asked.

DC Mike Freeman stood up,

"I know it sounds incredible, ma'am, but they all say they didn't see anything. I know that the pubs and cafés were closed at the time, but you'd think someone living on the boats or passing by may have heard or seen something."

DC Katie Lloyd intervened.

"I know this sounds odd, and it may have no significance, but one woman I spoke to said around about midnight she heard someone whistling the rhyme 'Rock A Bye Baby', but apart from that as DC Freeman said, no-one heard any shouting or arguing."

"I doubt it's of any consequence, but we'll make a note of it on the file," Josephine replied. "So let's re-cap; concerning the three victims so far, all male, all found in the vicinity of the canal even though the corpse in the sunken boat was found in a disused arm in the Aston area, and the other two were less than a mile apart in Brindleyplace. The one victim was found by Vincent Street Bridge, only yards from the Fiddle and Bone pub, although it could have been dumped in a different location. Since the victim's head had lacerations from the propellers of a passing boat it's possible he could have been killed some yards further down the canal. But the fact the weapon was located under the bridge, near the Fiddle and Bone pub, does suggest the murder was committed somewhere along that stretch of water."

"I think it's safe to assume the person we're looking for is local, with a good knowledge of the canal. The murderer obviously didn't want his first victim to be discovered and that's why he hid the body in the sunken boat. Whereas in the last two cases, the body was just dumped in a location where it could be easily found in a matter of hours," Rankin told the team.

"If all three cases are connected," Josephine began, "It's seems odd that the murders would start up again, just weeks after the newspaper report about the body recovered from the boat. If it's the same man, us unearthing his original victim may have started him killing again for some psychological reason that we don't understand. Or is it possible the person responsible for the last two deaths, is some sort of nut who has read the newspaper report about the body in the canal and has just decided to follow suit, and copy the killer? As far as we can tell, the victims didn't know one another, but I suppose it's possible Terry Ryan might have known Bob Melchett, as they both hung around the canal."

Rankin turned to the team and said "If Terry Ryan was straight and loved kids, I should think he'd be appalled at Bob Melchett having sex with young boys. I doubt if he'd associate with him, other than to give him a punch on the nose."

"That's a valid point," Josephine agreed.

"What about the notion that the killer owns a

176

narrowboat? Have we checked the register?" The chief asked.

"We're working our way through the list sir. There is one thing that's come to our attention, a John Conway who has a boat moored locally is a convicted paedophile; he's served his time in prison, which most people thought wasn't long enough."

"Is it ever long enough?" the chief commented.

"Well, when he returned to his mother's house, the neighbours revolted. Threw bricks through his windows, said he should be locked up for life, and they didn't want him living in the same street as their children, you know the sort of thing. He moved a couple of times but was still hounded, so he decided the only way to escape it was to live on a narrowboat. Although I, personally, don't think an animal like that should ever be allowed any peace," Rankin declared.

"Everyone in this room probably shares your view, but we're not here to air our grievances," the chief reprimanded him.

"Look into it further, but when you interview him, don't use any unnecessary force or abusive behaviour. We don't want any complaints of police harassment. Do I make myself clear?"

"Yes sir," Rankin replied.

"It's quite obvious our murderer has some sort of an aversion to the gay community. So we need to make enquiries at all the gay clubs in the area and see if any of them have noticed anyone strange hanging about, stalking or being abusive, so could you arrange that area to be investigated?" Josephine said to Rankin. She then turned to the chief.

"What I'd like to do, sir, is stake out the canal area; I think we need some officers on the spot in case he strikes again."

"I see your point Inspector, but I can only give you two of your investigation team," he told her.

"That should be sufficient sir. I suggest they disguise themselves as tramps, and if we can get another two officers to take their place when they change shift, we can get the area covered both night and day.

"That's a valid point, you can have four officers, but only for a short time and they change over for the night shift," the chief agreed.

Josephine chose DCs Lloyd and Purvis and two others. Rankin was relieved she didn't ask him, as he was such a snappy dresser, especially when he socialised with his string of girlfriends. The thought of getting togged out in old decrepit clothes was just not his scene.

When the briefing had finished, Josephine instructed the four officers on their assignment.

"Talk to as many people as you can, especially the vagrants and homeless, they may open up to you if they think you're the same as them, whereas there's a lot they wouldn't tell the police. I'll see if I can arrange for you to have a supply of cigarettes and the odd miniature bottle of spirits, that you can share with them in the hope of getting them to divulge any information. Right, that's all for now. If you've got no old clothes that will suffice, go to your local charity shop, as long as you get a receipt we'll reimburse you, just make sure the clothes look old and tatty."

"I don't like the idea of wearing someone's cast-offs, you don't know where they've been," DC Freeman said.

"I wouldn't worry about that, God knows what diseases the people you'll be associating with will be carrying," Josephine replied teasingly.

Chapter 16

THE INVESTIGATION into the murders was becoming complex. They had a lot of facts, but didn't seem to be making any headway. Even though they'd had a breakthrough of sorts, Josephine was frustrated and tired, and also had the additional pressure of not living up to her so-called reputation. Although he hadn't said as much, it was obvious that Detective Chief Inspector Lyle expected far greater things from her. She was disappointed, and knew that it was both unrealistic and impractical for the chief to expect an arrest, but if only they had a list of suspects to work with, they could at least have eliminated them one by one. Perhaps she needed to consult a forensic psychologist. She could, of course, always run through what they'd got so far with Andrew, but dismissed that idea. She thought if she phoned him just to discuss the case and ask for his professional opinion, he would be hurt and annoyed. He'd done so much for her already and she felt she would never be able to repay him. She still cared for Andrew, but decided if she was going to stand any chance of getting to the crux of this case she would have to put their relationship on hold for a short time, as she didn't need the added pressures of an emotional involvement. She suddenly remembered Bill was coming to see her at the weekend and was in two minds whether to ring him and cancel but thought *Oh, what the heck. I'd love to see him, and he always manages to cheer me up. I'll discuss the case with him;*

he might have some fresh ideas.

She picked up the phone and dialled her home number at Babbacombe.

"Jessica here."

"Don't you say the number when you answer?" Josephine asked.

"Oh, hi Mum, no. I only did that when you were here. I know if anyone rings it won't be important. When you were at home, there were always lawyers, doctors, and magistrates ringing. Now it's just my mates."

"How's the house?"

"It's still here!"

"Jessica, I hope you're keeping it tidy."

"Well, I think it's okay. I don't know if you would, you're so fussy."

Josephine decided not to pursue the state of the house further. She'd rather not know what sort of mess it was in so she changed the subject.

"How's the job hunting going?"

"Nothing as yet."

"Are you trying, Jessica?"

"Of course I am. They either say I'm over qualified or have no experience. I tell you Mum, I can't win."

"How's the garden looking?"

"Fine, me and Sally have been doing it."

"What do you mean? Where's Ben the gardener? I left you the money to pay him every fortnight. I'd arranged to have the trees pruned and the hedge cut back."

181

"I err—had to dip into it, I'm afraid. Only I ran short, so I told him to leave it for a few weeks."

"Jessica! This is too much! I left you plenty before I went, I'll phone Ben and send him a cheque and ask him to start coming again from Monday. Do you know how hard it is to get a good gardener nowadays? I don't want you and Sally to touch another thing—I just hope Ben agrees to come back. You've let me down Jessica. I feel really disappointed."

"I'm sorry Mum. I tell you what, I'm going to tidy the whole house from top to bottom, I'll even clean the windows," Jessica told her.

Josephine took no notice of this rash promise and continued,

"Now look, I want you to sort me out some more clothes, put them in that small red suitcase and I'll ring Bill and ask him to collect them. He's coming up to Birmingham this weekend. Have you got a pen handy?"

The phone went quiet for a short time and then Jessica said, "Okay, I'm ready."

"Pack my brown trouser suit, and that creamy coloured camisole. Oh, and I'll have that red mandarin dress—my black trousers and that little blue dress."

"Er, there's a problem with that—" Jessica sounded nervous.

"A problem!"

"Yes, one of my mates borrowed it to go on a date, I knew you wouldn't mind, the thing is, she

182

hasn't returned it yet."

"That's the last straw! I'm going now before I say something I'll regret. Just make sure it's all ready for Bill to collect," Josephine put down the receiver.

Later that day, Josephine rang the number of the Private Investigation Agency run by her cousin Mark Hitchen and left a message on his answerphone leaving her mobile number.

He returned her call an hour or so later.

"It's Mark here, I got your message, is everything okay?"

"Well, as good as it can be with three murders to solve and no suspects."

"I read about the last one in the Evening Mail; I was tempted to ring you, but I knew you'd be tied up with the investigation."

"How's your work, busy?" she asked.

"I'm up to my eyes in it at the moment, with three cases on the go. I've been managing to grab about four hours sleep a night maximum," he told her.

"It's just that my DS, Bill is coming up from Devon this weekend, and I was going to ask you if you wanted to join us one night. Mind, I warn you he's anti private investigators."

"What copper isn't?" he replied. "No, seriously Jo, I'd love to come but I'm so tied up at the moment."

"No problem, I realise you've got to take the work

when it's there. Anyway, you probably need to catch up on your sleep, and knowing Bill he'll keep us up till the early hours."

"Perhaps we can arrange something for next week," Mark suggested.

"Well ring me, and I'll see how the case is going. It should be okay," Josephine replied.

"How's Auntie Win?" he asked.

"The same as ever, God bless her! In fact I'm moving into the singles quarters in a day or so and I don't think she's too pleased," Josephine told him.

"No, I don't suppose she is, she won't be able to keep an eye on you and make sure you're eating properly. Don't be surprised if she turns up with a home-made pie one day."

"Oh don't! I've got enough on my plate as it is—Oh God, I'm even cracking jokes now, I'm off, I'll be in touch," Josephine said and put down the receiver.

DS David Rankin considered himself an authority on all the best clubs and restaurants in Birmingham, so he insisted on tagging along with Josephine and Bill. Josephine tried to explain to Rankin that her old DS Bill would be quite satisfied with a good Balti curry and a few pints. But Rankin wouldn't hear of them going round the City unchaperoned.

Bill turned up at Josephine's at six thirty in the evening, carrying a holdall with a few things he needed for the weekend and the suitcase from

up and added a quick squirt of her perfume as a finishing touch.

"Will I do?" she asked Bill.

"Not a babe you understand, but not bad for an old un," he laughed.

About half an hour or so later they were heading towards the City Centre in Rankin's car. At his suggestion they went into two fashionable pubs in Broad Street. Bill wasn't impressed with either of them, as they were both packed and the prices of the drinks in his words were 'bloody extortionate'. Rankin then took them to Ronnie Scott's, where a jazz band was performing. Bill liked Ronnie Scott's; the seating was comfortable, and the band was excellent. While Rankin was at the bar, Bill turned to Josephine and said,

"It's okay in here, a bit pricey though. I thought we were going to some local pubs and then for a curry. It's nice of the bloke to give us a tour, but I bet if he picks a restaurant, it'll be that Nouvelle Cuisine stuff. It looks pretty and all that, but there's never enough and it costs a bomb."

"Don't worry, I'll sort it. I've already told him you want to go for a Balti," Josephine replied, wondering how she and Bill could make an exit without offending her sergeant.

There was no need for her to have worried. Five minutes or so later Rankin returned to their table, with a tall, well-endowed young blonde woman. She wore an exquisite, yet low cut tailored dress and jacket. He introduced Annabel to Josephine and

Bill. She seemed a very pleasant young woman and chatted to them for a few minutes, before making her excuses, to visit the ladies.

David Rankin leant over to them and said "Look, I hope you don't mind, but I'm going leave you to it now. Only I've been after her for months."

"I thought you were going out with someone," Josephine began.

"I am, but you know what they say Variety is the Spice of Life," he reached into his pocket "Here's the card for that Balti house, it's excellent if you like that sort of thing, not my scene you understand."

Bill took the card and read it "Five courses for six ninety-nine—sounds like my type of place," he said.

When Annabel returned, they said their goodbyes and left. Bill couldn't keep his eyes off her breasts and as soon as they'd walked away, he said,

"Did you see the tits on that?"

"Bill!"

"Oh, err—sorry, but you must admit, they were huge. Do you think they were real or silicone?" he asked Josephine.

"I've no idea."

"Well, ask Rankin, when you get back to work."

"I shall do no such thing! I don't know, Bill. You men!"

"Look we're only human. I bet even your loverboy Andrew would have noticed them."

188

"I'm sure he would, but the difference is he wouldn't be asking if they were real or not."

"That's because he'd probably know, being a doctor."

"I think it's time we went for that curry," Josephine suggested.

They went outside and jumped in a black cab. Josephine told the driver the address on the card, and they arrived some ten minutes later.

They ordered poppadoms and dips. Bill had Lamb Tikka and Josephine had Tandoori Fish to start, and afterwards the waiter bought their Baltis. He placed large black metal dishes with a handle on each side in front of them. The contents were sizzling hot, as the various spices, meats and tomatoes created a wonderful aroma. They shared a large Peshwari Naan and Pilau Rice, and it all tasted delicious. Bill mopped up the last bit of his curry with a piece of Naan Bread and as he picked up his glass of lager said,

"I'm stuffed, I couldn't eat another thing, marvellous meal."

They stayed in the restaurant for another hour or so, drinking and talking. Josephine told him about the murders and her frustration at not progressing as far with the investigation as she would have liked. She mentioned how Birmingham had changed since the sixties, told him about Auntie Win, Uncle Arthur and her cousin Mark and finally admitted just how much she was missing Andrew. Bill didn't have much news; nothing exciting was happening it Torquay, just the normal run of the mill crimes. His love life was boring, as he'd split from Joyce who he'd been dating for over a year, and there was no-one else on the scene.

As they were leaving the restaurant, Josephine felt a little tipsy. Bill had drunk far too much and was slurring his words, despite constant denials that he wasn't drunk. They arrived back at Josephine's and Bill lay on her sofa: within minutes he was dead to the world. Josephine only had one duvet so she tucked him in with a pillow and her coat. Bill snored so loudly that he kept Josephine awake, even though she was in the next room. He awoke the next morning, declaring that it was the most marvellous night's sleep he'd had in months.

"I'm glad for you. I didn't sleep a wink," Josephine said, "Thanks to your snoring. Did Joyce complain about it?"

"The couple of nights a week I stayed at her house, she said I sounded like a foghorn."

"No wonder she finished with you," she teased him.

"It was mutual, actually. She didn't finish with me," he corrected her.

"Well, if you ever do get back together I suggest you find some sort of remedy. There's a device you can get from chemists to stop it. I'm making coffee, which in my case will be black and strong to keep me awake after last night!"

"Great! Stick some bacon and eggs on for me while you're in the kitchen," Bill shouted as she walked from the room.

"No can do, I'm afraid. You were supposed to be staying at a B&B, remember. I've got nothing in the fridge."

Bill had to make do with two rounds of toast for his breakfast. Luckily Auntie Win's invitation to lunch, which consisted of roast beef, Yorkshire pudding and all the trimmings, set him up for his journey home.

As he was leaving he hugged Auntie Win and planted a big kiss on each cheek.

"I've never had such a marvellous meal, thank you," he turned to Josephine. "You must be mad leaving a lovely place like this to live in that rabbit hutch."

As he drove away Auntie Win said,

"What a lovely young man. If I had him for a few weeks, I'd soon feed him up, poor mite."

Josephine looked at her in bewilderment. Bill was in his late forties, although Win regarded anyone under the age of sixty as young. As far as feeding him up went, he weighed fifteen stone, and was the last person anyone would consider to be undernourished.

"You amaze me Auntie Win! Josephine said.

"Really, dear!" Win replied, under the illusion that Josephine had paid her a compliment.

Chapter 17

DC KATIE LLOYD strolled down the canal past Vincent Street bridge. She was pleased her DI had chosen her for this assignment, and it didn't bother her in the least dressing in old tattered clothes. In fact she felt quite comfortable in her overcoat and trousers. About a year earlier she had gone undercover with two WPCs as a prostitute, and had loathed every minute of it. In fact she didn't know whether she hated the tarty clothes and high heels or the lewd remarks from the punters (and her colleagues) most.

She only wished she had the same confidence in the assignment that she had in her disguise. The past six days they had patrolled the canals undercover, working different shifts during the day and night. She'd spoken to vagrants, fishermen, and cyclists—in fact, anyone who might have seen anything. At the present time both she and Purvis had struck out. It was about seven o'clock in the evening, and she had been on duty since one o'clock, and was looking forward to eight-thirty when she would finish her shift. It had been quite warm when she started, but now it was becoming cold and the light was fading.

Katie knew Purvis was somewhere at the other end of the canal, down towards Gas Street Basin. She had radio contact with him. She'd seen so many suspicious characters over the last few days, all of whom had come to nothing, that she paid no attention to the young man in the long dark raincoat, who was walking down the slope leading to the tow path on the opposite bank. He stopped and lit a cigarette, looking around as if he were waiting for someone. He was smartly dressed and Katie thought he was probably on a date. She put her hand in her pockets as a sudden breeze gave her a chill, deciding she'd treat herself to a brandy when she came off duty. She walked further ahead of the man on the other side and was about forty yards before him when another middle-aged man came up beside her and crossed the bridge to the other side. She decided to carry on walking back towards the Pit Stop Café, where she'd arranged to meet DC Purvis. Suddenly the sounds of a commotion drifted towards her. She paid little attention at first—in the last few days she'd come across mothers shouting at their kids not to get too close to the water, tramps arguing over a bottle of cider and an assortment of bickering young couples. As the voices became louder she turned to look and saw that the young man in the raincoat was arguing with the older man who'd just crossed the water.

"It might be nothing," she thought "but I'd better check it out."

As she crossed, keeping the two men in view, the younger man violently struck the older man. She broke into a run, deciding against shouting at them. The older man reeled from the blow but came back with a left hook that sent the younger man flying, back into the canal.

"Fucking bastard!" the man left on the towpath snarled.

Katie ran towards him shouting, "Police! Stay where you are!"

He looked towards her, seeing only her rags and shouted, "Piss off you old cow and mind your own business!"

Katie pulled out her radio and radioed to Purvis, "Quick, I need help—Vincent Street bridge—Hurry!"

At that moment the man realised it wasn't a joke and Katie really was a copper. He grabbed hold of her and they struggled on the path. Katie was strong, but her big overcoat hampered her. She could hear the man in the water shouting for help. She looked around and at that moment her assailant punched her in the face. She fell away from him, her face throbbing with pain. He started to run and she launched herself at his legs. He fell heavily, turned and kicked back at her arms and face.

"Fucking bitch!" he kept screaming.

Where the hell are you Purvis? she thought, as the man gave one last kick. Her hands were forced apart and he scrambled to his feet. She rolled over and noticed Purvis, twenty yards away and closing on the man. "Get after him," she shouted as the man made off. She got to her knees, threw off her coat and jumped into the water. She was a strong swimmer and the canal was only shallow, but she knew that the layer of silt on the bottom was what she had to avoid. If she got mired in it she could easily drown. The water was still and ice cold. The man's head had surfaced once or twice as he gasped for air. Katie pushed herself under the dark and murky water, to catch a glimpse of white—his T-shirt! She tried to grab him and pull him up, but he wouldn't budge—his feet had become stuck in the silt. She tried to hold her breath and keep the pressure up, but started to swallow water. She surfaced and took deep gulps of air, feeling as if her lungs were on fire. *Here we go again* she thought, as she submerged again, determined to save him. This time she timed the kick of her legs as she grabbed his clothing and he came free. She pulled him to the surface, but in his panic he thrashed out and hit her and they went under again. She felt her strength waning, but had one last attempt. As she dragged him up this time she aimed for the bank, and pulled him with her. Luckily he'd passed out by now. She remembered her lifesaver training and got behind him with her arm locked around his neck. Keeping his head above the water, she shouted for help to the crowd of passers by who had now collected. Two men came forward, and as she kept him afloat, manhandled him out of the water, and then pulled her to safety. Katie knelt on the towpath coughing up water. After a few moments she stood up and walked over to the man. One of the crowd was giving him mouth to mouth ventilation. After a while he started to cough, and began to vomit up the canal water he'd swallowed.

Katie had saved his life.

DC Purvis was still pursuing the other man who had run up the slope and on to Vincent Street. As Purvis chased him, he radioed for help.

As they reached the far end of the canal where all the bars and cafés were situated, crowds of people were walking about. Purvis, dressed in tramp's clothes, had no badge or uniform to excuse his roughness, so he just pushed and shoved his way through the crowds avoiding eye contact. Some people didn't mind being jostled, while others swore at him. Purvis thought he'd lost the man when he suddenly spotted him some yards ahead in the crowd.

One young man in a baseball cap grabbed hold of Purvis and said,

"Hey mate, who the fuck are you shoving?" He grabbed hold of the DC and pushed him into a young woman who was passing. She started to scream and the crowd around him separated slightly. Purvis sat up and got out his police radio.

"He's getting away. If he's still on the canal path he'll be heading towards the James Brindley pub. He's wearing a long black raincoat."

"We're at the bridge now, by the Brindley, I can see him running towards us," a voice answered.

DC Purvis's aggressor suddenly realised he'd assaulted a policeman.

"Right, you're nicked!" Purvis shouted, but the man just turned and ran. Purvis got painfully to his feet, his head was pounding and his cheek was scraped and bleeding. He decided not to pursue the thug that had just knocked him to the ground. His first priority was the man he was chasing.

He got to his feet, and a message came over his radio.

"Purvis, you can relax, we've got him," a voice said.

"Thank God for that!" He uttered. "DC Lloyd needs assistance, she's by Vincent street bridge. If you can send back up, I'll make my way to her."

Two days later they were all assembled in the incident room. DCs Lloyd and Purvis were present, although they looked like the walking wounded.

"Before we begin, I would like to commend Lloyd and Purvis. In my opinion they both acted with courage and determination; and I feel the young man who fell in the canal, Paul Ramsey, would most certainly have drowned if it hadn't have been for Katie. And although, Purvis didn't actually apprehend the other man, Ron Arkett, he chased him for some time and radioed ahead giving his fellow officers the assailant's position," Josephine then turned to them and continued, "Since you haven't been on duty for past 36 hours, neither of you'll be aware of our findings. Unfortunately, the man who attacked and pushed his victim into the canal, isn't the serial killer we've been looking for." The team groaned in disappointment.

"But all wasn't lost," Rankin began "Both Ramsey

and Arkett were drug dealers and we found a considerable amount of crack on both of them, although Ramsey's was somewhat wet! It appears Ramsey had muscled in on Arkett's patch, which was the local school, and that's what the row was about."

"I wish now I'd let the bastard drown. To think I nearly died saving that scum!" DC Lloyd exclaimed.

"The one who was attacked has given us quite a lot of information. They'll both be charged with possession and dealing, but the drug squad will make a deal with Arkett if he gives them the information they need," Josephine told the team.

"So we've got some of the scum off the streets, for a time, anyway," Rankin declared.

"Yes, but there's always someone waiting to step into their shoes. Still, we've done the drug squad a favour but we're no closer to catching our man," Josephine announced despondently. "I think we'll keep surveillance on the canals for another week at least, if I can clear it with the chief, but I think you two should have a break," she told Lloyd and Purvis. "DC Wright and Freeman can take your place, and once again well done both of you, it's just a pity it wasn't our man."

Later that day, she telephoned Andrew and told him about the other murder.

"And did Bill enjoy his weekend?" he enquired.

"I think so, you'll have to ask him, but I warn

you he may be seeking your professional opinion on breast implants."

"Why, you're not thinking of having yours done, are you?"

"Don't ridiculous, at my age."

"Some women do it to keep their man," Andrew joked.

"God, you've seen me in a hospital bed with no make-up on for weeks. I'd have thought that would be enough to put anyone off," she replied.

He didn't answer for a moment and then said, "I miss you Jo."

"Oh God, me too Andrew. In fact I'm beginning to wonder what I'm doing here. This case is getting me down. We've identified the victims and the rough profile I've done on the man we're looking for is that he definitely has an aversion to homosexuals. His last victim was straight, though. I think the murderer took him to be gay. All the murders have been committed in or by the canal. Does that suggest anything to you, other than the fact he has a good knowledge of the area?"

"Assuming it's a man, he may have some sort of obsession about the water, or had a bad experience as a child near a canal, or some other deep rooted trauma," he replied.

"One thing that strikes me as odd, is that the locations where the last two bodies were found are quite busy. The killer seems to be taking a chance and the murders don't appear to be planned or calculated."

"Maybe he wants to get caught," Andrew suggested.

"I don't get it," Josephine said slightly confused.

"What I mean is, his need to kill is greater than his need to protect himself and delude you, it could be revenge killings," Andrew explained.

"But none of the victims knew one another, I can't see any link, other than their sexual preferences."

"It's only guess work on my part, but I think the assailant is male, since he has a revulsion for homosexuals. It's interesting that he's pushing the bodies in the water after he's killed them," Andrew remarked.

"I know, in some cases he had to drag the bodies to a certain spot in order to get them into the canal. It would have taken considerable time and effort—whereas most murderers like to get away from the scene of crime as quickly as possible," she added.

"The fact that he's inflicted injury to the penis, shows he has a particular abhorrence of that part of the body. It's possible he had a bad experience as a child or might even be gay himself and has been rejected or hurt by a lover. Talking of which, I'm feeling a little rejected at the moment," Andrew told her.

"I'll make it up to you when I get back, I promise," Josephine replied. "Can't manage the huge bosom, I'm afraid, but there's always that sexy black basque…"

"Enough of this, I'm getting horny!" he

announced.

"Do you know Andrew, I think I'm losing it, this case is really baffling me."

"Don't worry, something will turn up, it always does; you've just got to keep looking into every angle."

"I wish I had your confidence," Josephine answered. "Anyway, I won't be solving anything while I'm talking to you I'd better go. I love you," Josephine told him, before she put down the receiver.

Chapter 18

BETH HAD HAD A LONG DAY, she'd walked about for hours trying to keep herself warm, and now she was tired, cold and hungry. Don had given her half a can of lager, which was flat, although she was so thirsty she drank it, but the alcohol had only increased her appetite. Her stomach rumbled and she felt weak, as the pangs of hunger increased. Then she suddenly remembered her mate had got a part-time job in the chip shop. *Maybe if she's there, I might be able to get something to eat,* she thought.

As she reached the door of the shop, the man behind the counter said,

"Get out of here. You'll put my customers off with that smell."

"Is Mo here?" she asked.

"She's cleaning up, round the back. You'll have to wait for her outside."

"I'll have a cone of chips then—" Beth told him.

"Let's see your money first then."

"Can't I pay you later?"

"Look, clear off. I won't tell you again." His wife, who stood next to him in a white cap and pale blue overall, glanced at Beth and thought how pale and ill she looked.

"Surely we can spare a few chips, there's some pieces of batter as well that we'd only throw away." She put a portion of chips and batter into a bag and gave them to the girl.

"Thanks," Beth said "Tell Mo, I'll catch her later."

And she went out of the shop.

The man turned to his wife and said, "What do you think we are, a bloody charity. She'll be sending all her mates in now for free chips."

His wife lifted a huge basket of cut potatoes and pushed then into the boiling fat.

"You mean sod. You could be hungry one of these days. Mind you, I reckon you could live off that fat for a month," she said looking at her husband's huge stomach.

Beth made her way down to the canal, and sat on a wall eating her chips. It was the first food she'd had in over forty-eight hours. One or two pigeons landed at her feet, but today, they were unlucky, she wasn't even going to give them the bits left over in the bottom of the bag, as she picked at the last few and licked her fingers clean. Beth felt better after she'd eaten and decided to head back to her hostel. She pulled the old black knitted hat further down over her ears to keep out the wind and made her way down the towpath in her old boots. When she reached the bridge, and started to walk beneath it she could hear the sound of her footsteps echoing, and some distance behind her someone whistling a familiar tune, that she couldn't put a name to. The noise got louder and louder as they got closer, but it never occurred to Beth to turn round and look; she was a big tall girl who'd lived on the streets for a long time, if anyone could look after themselves, it was Beth. The whistling began to resound as the person walked under the bridge, it became louder and louder as they got closer. Beth was just about to turn round and ask the name of the tune, when a hand whipped across her head jerking he back; and a hard palm covered her mouth. In the darkness of the tunnel, from the corner of her eye, Beth suddenly saw a glint of metal.

She struggled and twisted her body, but his grip was like a vice, she could hardly breathe as her assailant crushed her larynx.

"Your sort are scum of the Earth! You just spread disease and innocent people die!" A voice said.

Her heartbeat rocketed. *What the hell's he talking about*, she thought.

For a split second something ran past their feet, Beth wasn't sure if it was a rat, but whatever it was, it startled him for a few seconds. So she took her chance and shot her leg out, bringing it up between his legs with as much force as she could muster. He was stunned for a few moments, but as Beth tried to escape he recovered.

He lurched at her through the dark tunnel, breathing like a desperate animal.

"You won't get away," he shouted. Beth fought with all her strength, but suddenly felt something tightening around her neck. *I don't want to die like this!* she thought, gasping for breath. Everything started to spin as her strength waned; suddenly a black cloud rolled over her consciousness. She had lost her fight for life.

As the scene of crime team put the fluorescent tape around the opening of the tunnel that led under the bridge, where the body was found, Josephine knelt next to Doctor Mortimer.

"I can't believe a woman's been killed, all the past victims have been male," she told him.

"It looks like she put up a fight, as there's blood and skin under her nails, and see these marks around her neck. She may have been strangled, even though there are still head injuries. After I've had a better look at her back at the morgue, I can give you a more definite cause of death."

"None of the other victims had any marks or abrasions on their neck," Rankin observed. "Still it must be the same person, I'd have thought."

"What's this?" Josephine said as she reached for what appeared to be a photograph, at first glance. She carefully picked it up by the corners in her gloved hand. It was a black and white blurred image and at first it looked like a half moon with a face on.

"It's a picture taken when a baby is scanned in its mother's womb," Doctor Mortimer enlightened her. "There's a date on here, 3/5/98 and it says in the top right hand corner, Queen Elizabeth Hospital."

"I suppose it must belong to her, I wonder where the baby is now?" Josephine queried.

"We'll soon know if she's given birth when I examine her," Mortimer replied.

She looked down at the long thin body with its cropped black hair.

"I bet she couldn't be much more than her early twenties."

"She looks older to me," Rankin observed.

"That's probably due to the life she's led," the doctor said.

"Any ID on her?" Josephine asked the one officer.

"No, nothing, although there's this tattoo," he said pointing to her shoulder, where there was an engraving of two serpents entwined around a flower.

"I wonder if this was done locally," Josephine began. "We'll have to make enquiries. This is the fourth body in as many weeks, and we're no closer to finding the murderer. How soon can you give me the autopsy results?" she asked Mortimer.

"If we get her back now," he said looking at his watch, the time was 10:05 am. "And if I work on her straight away, I might possibly have something by about late afternoon," he told her.

"Right, let's get photos of her and also a close-up shot of the tattoo. We need to get them developed as soon as possible; we've got to find who she was, and soon.

They were successful in identifying the victim, as a local tattooist recognised his work and the victim straight away.

"Yes, that's Beth. I can remember doing that tattoo for her about six months ago. Here's the pattern I worked from," he said as he showed them the exact design, on a sheet of paper, that was engraved on the victim's shoulder.

"Do you know her surname?" Josephine asked him.

"I'm afraid not."

"Well, wouldn't you need it for the receipt? Surely you keep records."

"We don't usually give receipts, and Beth didn't have much money, so I told her just to buy me a drink some time. But I've just remembered, she sold the Big Issue, so she should be registered at their offices. I think they all have to give their name and address. If they've got one, that is—most of them are homeless," he told them.

Josephine and Rankin made their way to the Big Issue offices on the Bristol Road in Birmingham. When they arrived they were taken upstairs to the manager's office.

After they had shown their ID cards, Josephine got out a photo of the victim.

"Do you recognise this girl?" she asked.

"Well, I personally don't, but I'll get my assistant, she has all the vendor's photos on file."

He buzzed through on his intercom.

"Joan, can you bring me a list of the Issue vendors and their photos in the Birmingham City Centre area?"

"Okay," she replied, "It'll only take me a few minutes."

"All our vendors have a badge with their name

and number on, and the location at which they are allowed to sell the magazine," he told them.

"Where would that be?" Rankin asked.

"Well, for instance, let's take New Street in the City Centre. We have five vendors registered, the first one's pitch is at the top by the Central Library and they stand about three hundred to four hundred yards apart, the last location being at the far end of New Street."

"We didn't find a badge on the victim," Josephine informed him.

"They are supposed to wear them at all times when selling the magazine, but some don't stick to the rules and regulations."

A few minutes later, his assistant entered the room with a list of names and a photo at the side of each one. The manager handed the list to Josephine and she studied it for a minute or so.

"Here she is," she said pointing to a picture half way down the page. "Elizabeth Gunter, it says here her location was at the corner of Newhall Street and New Street. We'll go down and speak to the others," she told DS Rankin. "Can you tell us what sort of people sell the magazine?" she asked.

"To start with, they have to prove they are homeless or living in hostels. As I've explained, they are all given a badge with their details on. They buy the Big Issue from us for 40p a copy and sell it for a pound, or what ever they can get."

"Can they return any they don't sell?" Rankin asked.

"No, I'm afraid not," he replied.

"So what if they can't sell of them all, surely they'd be out of pocket?" Rankin suggested.

"I don't think that's ever been the case. They can buy as little as six at a time from us and the locations where they sell are very busy areas, they normally dispose of what they've got and come back for more. It's a popular magazine with some good articles. Here, take a copy," the man said as he handed them two of the magazines.

"Would any of your staff here know Elizabeth Gunter personally?" she asked.

"I'm really not sure, you'd need to talk to them. Some of the vendors often stop and chat to the girls in the office when they come in to buy the magazines, so I'm sure someone would know her."

"Right, thanks a lot. DS Rankin here can stay and speak to the staff and I'll go and chat to the Big Issue vendors in the New Street area; it's more than likely they'd know her, working in the same vicinity."

"There's no need for you to do that, ma'am, we can arrange for the officers to make enquiries," Rankin told her.

"They can cover the other areas and I'll concentrate on the ones in New Street, I'll enjoy it. It's years since I've spoken to people on the streets during a murder enquiry; it'll be quite nostalgic. Thinking back, the last time I did house to house enquiries was when I was a detective constable."

"Things have changed since then, some of these people on the streets can get really nasty," Rankin warned her. "Would you like a PC to accompany you?"

"No way, that will put them off, seeing someone in uniform; I'll go alone, I'll be fine," Josephine said and she left the offices.

She started at the far end of New Street. The first vendor she spoke to was a man in his early twenties. He wasn't very helpful, and didn't seem to understand what Josephine was asking him. So she came to the conclusion he was taking something, whether it was drink or drugs, she wasn't sure. All she knew was that it was hopeless talking to him, so she left and started to walk down towards the next vendor who stood on the corner of Newhall Street and New Street, which was normally Elizabeth Gunter's pitch. In her place stood a young woman with purple hair. She had her nose, chin, and ears pierced with silver studs.

As Josephine approached her she said, "Buy a copy of the Big Issue miss?"

"I already have one, but here take this," Josephine said as she handed her a five-pound note.

"Thanks," the girl said slightly taken aback.

"I'm DI Blake," Josephine said showing her ID card.

"I knew there was some catch, here, take your money back! I've done nothing wrong. You gave it to me," she said raising her voice.

The people passing by began to slow down and stare at them, but Josephine wasn't going to be put off. She looked at the girl's badge, it read AMY VINE.

"Look Amy, I'm not trying to catch you out. Do you know Elizabeth Gunter?"

"No, I've never heard of her."

"How long have you worked this pitch?"

"It's none of your business," the girl replied sharply.

Josephine was becoming impatient.

"Look, this was Elizabeth Gunter's pitch," she told her.

"Oh, you mean Beth."

"Tall girl with short black hair?" Josephine added.

"Yeah, that sounds like Beth, she's not in any trouble is she 'cause I ain't twitting on a mate!" She started shouting again, and a very vicious looking man with a shaved head and tattooed arms came up to her.

"You alright Amy? Any trouble?" He came right up to Josephine and stared menacingly into her eyes. Her heart started to pound, but she was determined, she would not let her fear show.

"She's a copper," Amy told him.

He stood back and eyed Josephine up and down in her grey suit.

"Well, you could have fooled me. She looks like one of them posh secretary tarts from the offices. Look, Doll, we have enough police harassment.

211

Now what's your problem?"

"I don't have one, but you will, if you don't leave me alone," she turned to the girl. "Listen, Amy, Beth's been killed and we're trying to find out who's responsible. Now if she was your friend, I suggest you forget your prejudices and talk to me."

"Killed! But I only spoke to her a couple of days ago!" Even though the girl's face looked pallid, due to her make-up and purple hair, what little colour she did have started to drain away.

"Let's go and have a coffee, I only want a chat, I'm not here to hassle you or anybody else, I just want to find out who murdered Beth."

"Okay," the girl agreed. "Vinnie, will you carry on selling these for me, I won't be long," she said to the man as she handed him the magazines. "And look after Rusty."

Josephine looked down at a rather old mangy looking dog.

"We'll bring him something back to eat, poor little thing," she said as she reached down to stroke the dog.

"You wanna watch it," Vinnie said, "He'll have your hand off!"

"I don't think so, dogs have a special instinct, they know when someone is kind to them, and if I have any more mouth off you I'll book you for insolent behaviour. You might be a big brute of a man, but I've met a lot worse than you in my time." She looked over at Amy, "Come on we'll go there," she said pointing to the café opposite, "I'll buy you breakfast."

As Josephine sipped her cappuccino Amy tucked into scrambled eggs and muffins. *God she must have been starving*, Josephine thought, as she watched Amy consume the food like a vulture.

"Most people find Vinnie quite intimidating, he's a bit of a bully."

"I'm sure they do," Josephine agreed.

"You didn't mean what you said about knowing a lot worse than him—" she said.

"I certainly did. I've dealt with mass murderers and serial killers that make Jack the Ripper look like a pussy cat," Josephine announced.

"Well, I've never seen anyone stand up to Vinnie before. Weren't you nervous?"

"Not in the least," Josephine lied.

"I can hardly believe what you've told me about Beth," the young girl said.

"Her body was found on the canal path and she was badly beaten about the head and strangled," Josephine told her.

"Oh God, by the canal. So I suppose it's this killer that's been in all the papers lately, but I thought he only killed men?"

"We believe it's possible it was the same man, but do you know anyone who would want to hurt Beth or who had some sort of grudge against her?"

"No, she was well liked, she had hard times like the rest of us, trying to get a roof over her head and food in her stomach."

"Did she make any money on the Big Issue?" Josephine asked.

"Just enough to scrape by."

"I don't suppose you know if she was ever pregnant or had a child?"

"Not as far as I know, but Beth was a bit of a loner, she didn't talk much about her past life. I suppose it's possible she could have had a kid somewhere."

"And what about you?" Josephine began.

"Me?"

"Yes, how come you're doing this?"

"I left home a couple of years ago. Oh, I had big ideas of getting a job and a nice flat, but it all went sour. The streets weren't paved with gold. It's just a vicious circle, you can't get a job unless you've got a permanent address or experience, and no-one will give you a chance. We all try to help one another when we can, but it's hopeless. It's so demoralising doing this, but what else is there?"

Josephine noticed some small puncture marks on Amy's arm.

"I see you're a user," she remarked.

"Yeah, well, what else is there? Although I am trying to kick the habit."

"The money you get from this, you should spend on food not drugs. You're slowly killing yourself."

"Look, cut the lecture, you ain't my Mum you know."

"I've seen first hand the damage drugs can do to bodies, minds and families, they destroy lives," Josephine warned her.

"That may be true, but they're all I've got to keep

214

me going," Amy replied.

"Yes, going to an early grave."

"Who cares? Life's not worth living anyway," Amy stated.

Josephine felt very sad and depressed as she looked at the girl's face, old before its time.

"Look, take my card if you can think of anything else about Beth, phone me, and if you really want to kick the habit, I could get you in a rehab unit."

Amy took her card.

"I'll think about it. I don't suppose you can spare any more money."

"No, you'll only spend it on drugs, but since you've polished that food off so quickly, I'll get you another coffee and a doughnut." She paid the bill as Amy was eating her second course.

"You're not too bad for a copper," Amy told her as Josephine left.

Chapter 19

JOSEPHINE ENTERED the morgue with Rankin and put on the required protective clothing. She hated the thought of going through the detailed injuries of yet another victim.

Doctor Mortimer began,

"Female, in her early twenties, reasonably well nourished considering she lived rough. She has abrasions and bruises on various parts of her body, but some of these are old and they were probably just due to sleeping rough and her way of life. Cause of death, now this is a little tricky. She had pressure marks on her throat as you can see here," he said pointing to marks on her neck. "There were also injuries to the top of her head, but there were more pronounced indentations on the back of her skull, which suggests to me she could have been attacked from behind. She obviously fought for her life as there was blood and skin under her nails which came from the assailant, I sent these to the lab for examination."

"The one thing I really need to know is,, was she ever pregnant?" Josephine enquired.

"In my medical opinion, no. I've examined the uterus in detail and I'm quite confident that this woman had never given birth," he stated.

"Could she have miscarried at any stage?" Josephine asked."

"I'd say that was highly unlikely."

"I was thinking that the photo of the scan of the

baby found close by belonged to her," Josephine began.

"She may have had the photo on her person, but it definitely wasn't a picture of *her* unborn baby; it's possible that it belonged to one of her friends or a member of her family, if she had any that is," Mortimer suggested.

"There is one other plausible explanation," Josephine said, "The photo could belong to her killer."

In the incident room, all the photos of the previous victims including Elizabeth Gunter's picture were pinned on the board.

Josephine opened the meeting "This is the first female victim, since all the previous victims were men and homosexuals apart from Terry Ryan, who we believe the killer mistakenly thought was gay. As you know, the profile of the man we're looking for, assuming the killer's male, definitely has an aversion to homosexuals. Equally obvious, the canals have some sort of significance. He may have morbid fascination with the area for some reason. And his revulsion to gays could be because he had a bad experience with one in the past. He may even have been raped. It's also possible the killer himself is gay and is out to get revenge on his own kind, because a previous lover spurned him. The other aspect of this case is that his victims are vagrants and down and outs, or if not exactly destitute, most seem to be relatively poor. What has thrown us completely off track, is that his latest victim is female. Having said that, as you can see from this picture," she said as she turned and pointed to the board, "Elizabeth Gunter, known locally as Beth, was quite a tall if somewhat thin woman. Her hair was very short and she wore trousers and a long coat and finally, her face was devoid of any make-up. In a nutshell, Elizabeth Gunter wasn't feminine in any way."

"So what you're suggesting is that the killer may have mistaken her for a man," Rankin remarked.

"Precisely. With the past two victims, the killer had inflicted wounds on their penises, but no damage was caused to her vagina or surrounding areas," Josephine added.

"So let's assume for a moment," the chief began "This serial killer we're dealing with only attacks men. I wonder if he realised he had made a mistake in this case or whether he still believes his victim was a man."

"Well, when he reads the newspaper, which I'm sure he will, as most killers get a kick from seeing themselves and their crimes in print, he'll realise he's made a mistake, assuming of course all his intended victims are meant to be male. Then again, he may not have made a mistake at all and realised his victim was a woman and yet still went ahead and killed her," Rankin replied.

"Now moving on to Doctor Mortimer's report," Josephine began "Elizabeth Gunter was never pregnant, so the photo of the scan found at the scene wasn't her baby. It's possible it could have belonged to someone she knew, or Elizabeth could have found it in a purse or wallet that she'd either found or stolen. The other alternative is that the picture was dropped by the murderer."

An A4 enlargement of the scan was pinned on the board. Josephine pointed to it and said,

"It says here the scan was taken on the third of May, nineteen ninety-eight and as you can see, it was done at the Queen Elizabeth Maternity Hospital. So we need to speak to whoever's responsible for that department in order to get a list of all the expectant mothers who had scans taken on that particular day. If it does belong to the murderer, we may have our first real lead, although I hate to be too optimistic." She then turned to the one DC standing close by and asked, "Any luck on enquiries at the gay clubs?"

"We've spoken to the owners and members of all those in the area, but unfortunately no-one's noticed anyone suspicious hanging about," he replied.

"As you all know, Elizabeth Gunter sold the Big Issue. I've spoken to a girl who is now selling on Elizabeth's pitch, who knew her reasonably well, and she tells me she didn't think Beth had any enemies, although she was a bit of a loner," Josephine told the team.

"Perhaps she was just in the wrong place at the wrong time, and there was no personal vendetta,"

Rankin suggested.

"Yes, you could be right. The killer saw her walking along the canal probably thought she was a man, saw his chance and struck. Obviously he's unhinged and perhaps he's not targeting any particular individual now, but killing at random."

"The only definite link is the canal, for some reason he needs to kill them in that vicinity, and since Birmingham's got more canals that Venice, he's got plenty of locations to choose from," the chief added.

"The crime was committed at least a mile further down the canal than the previous two murders, that's why our surveillance team were of no help," Josephine told them. "And it's possible he was about when the two drug dealers were arrested. He might have guessed we'd put police on the canals disguised as vagrants, so decided his next location would be slightly off the beaten track."

Chapter 20

HE THOUGHT OF HIS OPTIONS long and hard, but always came to the same conclusion; she had to be killed by the canal.

It would have been easy to follow her when she came out of the hostel one night and beat her to a pulp. He could even have mowed her down in his car or pushed her off a high bridge, or some high-rise flats, but no, there was no other alternative. It had to be the canal, but how would he get her down to the spot where he intended to end her life, and more importantly get her to come alone?

Money. Would she come for money? Could he say he had a message from him? No, too risky, she might contact him and then she would know it was a lie.

He would have to just say he needed to speak to her urgently, as it was vital she keep the appointment.

What if she refused? Oh well, he'd cross that bridge when he came to it. But he felt confident she wouldn't.

She'd always been curious, even as a child, to the point of being down right nosy. No, she couldn't resist; it would be like a lamb to the slaughter!

He picked up his mobile and dialled the number.

Josephine was taken to Doctor McGuire at the Chief Administrator's office at the Queen Elizabeth

Hospital. After showing her warrant card and introducing herself, she showed him the picture of the scan that had been found by Beth's body.

"We thought at first it belonged to the victim, but after a thorough examination by our forensic pathologist, we discovered she hadn't given birth," she told him.

"Well, as you can see, it clearly shows the date and time it was taken, in the top right hand corner. So we can go through the records of the scans taken on that day and give you a list of the names and addresses of all the then expectant mothers," Doctor McGuire replied.

"Do you think it's possible the radiographer might remember the woman in question?" Josephine asked.

"That's doubtful, they do hundreds of scans each week on different women. There's always the chance if there was a rare complication or abnormality of the foetus; they may remember a particular woman. But looking at this scan, the baby appears perfectly normal to me. Having said that, until we get the mother's name and are able to check her records, I couldn't positively say."

"Do all pregnant mums get a picture?" Josephine asked.

"Only if they ask for one, and it costs one pound," the doctor informed her.

"When I was pregnant with my daughter, there was nothing like this then, and you couldn't know the sex of your child until it was born. In my opinion, it was far more exciting to find out at the birth. Mind you, I'm going back over twenty years."

"We've advanced considerably in medical research, and can detect abnormalities much earlier than we could in the past. Though I do agree with you, about telling the parents the sex of the child. It's far better not to know until the moment of birth. Anyway, I'll go and get that list compiled for you. It may take an hour or so, do you want to wait?"

"Yes, I think I will. I'd like to look around the hospital if I may, not in a professional capacity you understand, I'm just curious to see how things have changed over the years."

Doctor McGuire looked a little puzzled.

"I used to live in Birmingham," Josephine began to explain "But I moved to Devon, about twenty-five years ago."

"While my secretary is checking the records on the computer, I can give you a short conducted tour," Doctor McGuire offered.

"That's very kind, if you're not too busy," Josephine said.

They went to the Radiography Department where the scans were taken and then to the Special Baby Care Unit. Josephine looked through the large glass panel at the small infants in their incubators.

"They look so frail and tiny to have all those tubes and equipment connected to them," Josephine remarked.

"They are tougher than you think, and it's that equipment that's saving their lives," he informed her.

"I'm sure you do a wonderful job. It's quite odd

223

really; we seem to be at different ends of the scale. You help bring new life into the world, and I deal with dead bodies, in the hope of getting justice for the victims and their families."

"Death is a certainty. It's the only thing we can all be sure of," Doctor McGuire stated, "Whereas, even with today's advanced technology, even birth isn't inevitable. Things still go wrong from time to time and we do lose babies, both at birth and in the womb. Only thankfully, we can save more lives than our ancestors."

"Some months ago, I had a close shave with death, and it's made me somewhat philosophical. Sometimes, with the way the world and society are today, with the crime rate and drugs increasing, I often wonder, what sort of future these poor little mites will have," Josephine pondered.

"All we can do is give them the best start in life that we can, and all their parents can do is love and care for them. They then have to face the big bad world, with all its drudgery."

"It must be fulfilling, helping to bring new life into the world," Josephine observed.

"No more than your career," the Doctor replied "At least you rid the streets of some of the evil people that take lives. That in itself must give you some satisfaction. Anyway, I think that list of names may be ready for you now." And they made their way back to his office.

Josephine sat at her desk and showed the list to DS Rankin. Eighteen women in all had scans on that day, and they had the names and addresses of them all.

"We need to go through them and contact everyone on the list as soon as possible," Josephine told him.

"It seems an odd thing for anyone to carry on their person. I know people keep small snaps in their wallet or purse, but a scan of a baby—it just doesn't make sense," Rankin remarked.

"I was shown the card they normally put the scans in and it states that if the picture is kept under plastic in a photo album, they tend to fade. So that's probably why someone was carrying it about," she enlightened him.

"Don't you think it's possible that one of these women might have lost their purse, or had it stolen, say by the killer?" Rankin suggested.

"Then why keep a scan? They'd just take the money and throw the rest of the contents away. I think the picture belonged to the killer and it's a scan of their own child. Still, it's no point speculating, we'll have to wait and see. All I know is we must catch this maniac, before he or she kills again."

It was as if Josephine had tempted fate by her last statement, as the following day another body was discovered.

Chapter 21

A FISHERMAN discovered the body, about two miles further down the canal on the route out of Birmingham to Wolverhampton.

The victim was another woman, which put paid to their theory, that all the serial killers victims were men, and that he had mistaken his last female victim for a man, due to her appearance.

As they fished the body out of the water, it was obvious, the murderer had made no mistake in this particular case. Despite the fact the victim wore jeans and a sweatshirt she was very feminine. She had long red hair and small delicate features, and it was obvious she once had been a very pretty girl. As Doctor Mortimer examined her at the scene, she was found to be clutching a cufflink, with the initial I on it. Apart from that there was nothing on the body to identify her; no jewellery, personal effects or credit cards. Her photo was taken and a team of officers showed it to all the shops, pubs and clubs in the area, but no-one recognised her. Even Tom Peters, who ran the cruise boat, and seemed to know everyone who lived and worked around the area, didn't recollect ever having seen her.

They went through the list of persons reported missing in the last forty-eight hours. There were only two, a young lad of fifteen, had been reported missing by his parents, and a woman of forty-eight years old had not returned home from work according to her live-in boyfriend, but there was no-one that fitted the description of the young woman.

"She's such a pretty little thing," Josephine said to Doctor Mortimer, looking down at the pale freckled face and body. "I'm amazed some boyfriend or lover hasn't come forward and reported her missing. Surely, someone somewhere must have loved and cared for this girl."

"Sadly, in today's society, there are lots of lonely, desolate people out there, who literally have no-one. The family unit will become a thing of the past, with the soaring divorce rate," Doctor Mortimer observed.

Josephine pondered for a few moments and then added,

"We're approaching the millennium, and have supposedly come far in modern technology and medical research, but I often wonder, if the quality of life is really any better than our forefathers'."

"My God, you two have got very philosophical, all of a sudden," DS Rankin observed.

"You may feel the same, when you reach our age," Josephine replied.

She turned her attention back to the body.

"So what can you tell me about her?" she asked the Doctor.

"She weighed seven stone, ten pounds which is underweight for her height; five feet, four inches, I'd say she was under nourished. Cause of death was due to severe blows to the head. I can't eliminate drowning completely but all the points suggest she died of her head injuries. She was a drug user, can you see these pin marks?" he said, pointing to the victim's arms. "Probably used what money she had on drugs, instead of feeding herself. I can't tell you the exact drug she was using, until I get the results back from the Toxicologist. But I'll say this, even if she hadn't been murdered if she carried on abusing her body the way she had, I doubt she'd have lived much more than a year or two at the most. I can't find any traces of blood or skin beneath her nails, and no marks on her body to suggest a struggle or fight for her life. I doubt she'd have had the strength to defend herself to any extent."

For the first time since these murders began, Josephine became very emotional and her eyes filled tears.

"What a wicked waste. To think what this girl might have achieved, if only she'd chosen a different lifestyle."

Even though Josephine was of the opinion that no-one deserved to have their life taken away by another individual, she didn't feel the upset or distress about the other victims that she did with this one. Possibly because one victim had a reputation for abusing and having sex with young boys. Being a professional, she would always devote the same time and effort to each particular case, whether the victim was a young innocent child or a drug dealer. It was just that some cases affected her far more than others.

"One thing that does appear different," Mortimer continued, "Is that the previous victims were struck with a hammer, or similar type of weapon, hence the crescent shaped indentations. Whereas the marks and depressions on her skull are a different shape."

"So you believe a different weapon was used this time?" Rankin asked.

"Yes, these hollows measure about three to four centimetres across and are so severe, that the skull has almost concaved."

"So what are we looking for in the way of a weapon?" Rankin asked.

"Mm, difficult to say—possibly something with a rounded head—"

"A club?" Rankin suggested.

"No, rounder still. Perhaps a paper weight—or a ball."

"Like a billiard ball," Josephine proposed.

"No, heavier, you know the ball shot putters use, or it could be something the murderer made himself," Mortimer told them.

"Surely a paperweight or ball would be difficult for the killer to hold?" Josephine remarked.

"Yes, but it would be easier to conceal on their person. Whereas a hammer would be difficult to carry, unless the murderer wore a long overcoat with big pockets," Rankin added.

"But if he's always used a hammer in the past,

why change his weapon?" Josephine queried.

"Who knows how the sick bastard's mind works!" he replied.

"I've sent a sample of her blood away to be tested, as I suspect she may have been HIV positive. In fact, the disease could have progressed further into full blown AIDS, but I can't be certain until we get the results."

"What makes you say that?" she asked Mortimer.

"She has lots of scabs and abrasions on her body, and her chest was congested with mucus. Since there are no nicotine stains on her fingers, or yellowing of her teeth, I don't think she was a smoker. Her immune system had started to break down."

Josephine looked again at the poor girl and felt very melancholy. She desperately wished she was back home, where she could walk along the beach and cliffs and watch the waves crash against the rocks as she gazed at the sunset over the water. The beauty and enchantment of the sea would always renew her faith in human nature, and the belief that something so wonderful must have been created by a far greater force than anything on Earth.

She left the morgue and went out into the streets, which looked grey and lifeless, staring up at the gigantic buildings that surrounded her. For the first time since she'd arrived, she hated the city.

The victim's photo was circulated to different departments of the police force, and was also put in the Birmingham Evening Mail and other local newspapers, in the hope that someone would recognise her. Regarding the photo of the ultrasound scan found beside Elizabeth Gunter's body, the investigating team were working through the list of names they had been given by the hospital. The women they had interviewed to date still had the photos of their scans, and none of them had been in the vicinity of the canal where both the body and picture had been found. But they still had about another ten women left to speak to. The ones they'd interviewed so far had all given birth to lovely bouncy babies, except one unfortunate woman whose baby had died at birth, so she was understandably very distressed when the officers questioned her about the scan she'd had taken of her unborn child.

The forensic department had carried out a detailed examination of the cufflink found on the latest victim's body. It was 22 carat gold, and obviously one of an expensive pair. Apart from that, no other information could be gleaned from the cufflink. Josephine and Rankin could only come to the conclusion that it belonged to the unidentified victim's assailant.

Two days later, Josephine received a call from her cousin Mark Hitchen.

231

"How lovely to hear from you, how's work?" she asked.

"Very busy as usual, and you—?"

"Don't ask, things couldn't be worse, five victims, and we still don't have any suspects."

"Well, I have some good news for you."

"What's that?"

"I recognise the photo in the Mail," he informed her.

Two hours later, Josephine was sitting in a café in Broad Street drinking coffee.

"So you say, she's the missing person you had to find for the family?"

"Yes, it's Annette O'Connor," Mark told her.

"And you're not mistaken?"

He looked a little put out.

"I wouldn't be in this business if I couldn't recognise a face," he said a little brusquely.

"Of course, I'm sorry, It's just that this is the best bit of information we've had."

"I told you the police don't give us private detectives the recognition we deserve."

"Alright, let's not get into that argument again," Josephine said, smiling.

"It wasn't just her photo, which I spotted in the paper, but the whole description; long red hair, freckled skin, pretty features, it's Annette alright."

"I'll need you to identify her formally at the morgue, and then we can contact her family."

"That's no problem, we can go now if you like," he agreed.

They finished their coffee and left.

As they drove back towards the city, Josephine said "So, fill me in on the whole story."

"Her father Raymond O'Connor asked me to find her. I've only been to his home once, and he's very ill, I don't think he has long to live. Apparently she'd left home four years previously and never been in contact. But a friend of the family had sighted her in Birmingham. He never told me why she'd left. I suppose it was some sort of family row, and he just wanted to make amends before it was too late. The photo he gave me was a few years old, but she hadn't changed that much. I searched for her for weeks, and then finally found her in a hostel."

"Did you speak to her?" Josephine asked him.

"No, he just wanted to know where she was, he said if I approached Annette, it might frighten her off. When I telephoned Mr O'Connor to tell him the good news, his son answered and said he was too ill to speak on the phone or have visitors. So I wrote to him stating I'd located his daughter, and gave him the address of the hostel where she was staying. A few days later I received a letter from him, thanking me, and with a cheque enclosed, which covered the amount of the bill plus an extra fifty pounds on top, which was a nice little bonus. The cheque was made out very neatly and precise, even though his signature was a little shaky. I suppose he didn't trust himself to fill the cheque in correctly, so he may have got his son or someone else to write it for him."

"How long ago was this?" Josephine asked.

"Oh, about two or three weeks."

"I'd have thought he would have contacted his daughter in that time," Josephine said.

"Maybe he did, and she wouldn't come back home," Mark suggested.

"Well, all I can say is, if she preferred her futile existence, to a warm bed, and decent food in her stomach, it must have been something pretty awful that caused her to leave, and not even return to see her dying father," Josephine remarked.

Several minutes later they pulled up outside the morgue and Josephine asked reception to let the staff know the body was to be viewed. They had moved Annette O'Connor from the clinical looking examination department to another room that was far more restful and appropriate.

There was soft lighting and dark blue curtains in the room, and she had been put into a white dress that covered the large incision made on her body by the pathologist. Her long red hair cascaded over her shoulders and she looked like 'Sleeping Beauty'.

"Yes, that's her," Mark said, a small tremor in his voice. "If only I'd found her sooner, maybe this wouldn't have happened."

"You can't blame yourself, the family had been informed of the hostel where she was staying, they could have gone the following day, if they were that desperate to see her," Josephine tried to reassure him. "This maniac serial killer, seems to strike anyone at any time. The only uniform thing about his murders is the location of the canals. This poor girl was at the wrong place at the wrong time. No-one else is to blame."

They left the morgue and went outside.

"If you can give me the family's address, we'll notify them at once," Josephine told him.

"Of course, give me your fax number and I'll fax it to you the minute I get back to the office."

Chapter 22

The two officers knocked at number forty-nine Sherham Crescent, a terraced house in the middle of twelve. When, after a minute or so, there was no reply, one of the PCs looked through a window. There was no sign of life. Prompted by curiosity, the next door neighbours, a man and his wife in their sixties, ventured out.

"You're wasting your time there, son," the man said, "That house has been empty for months now."

The officer looked at his list.

"Did Mrs McCallum live here?"

"She did, but she died months ago," the man replied,

His wife pushed forward.

"Look, come on in, it's starting to rain. I'll tell you what happened."

The PCs removed their caps and entered the house.

"Go and make these two young men a cup of tea," she ordered her husband. They were both grateful of some refreshment, as they had called at several houses so far that morning, without a break.

"It was a great shame... so sad..." the old lady began.

"What do you mean?" the officer asked.

"She died, and the baby... so very tragic."

"Was she married?"

"Oh yes... to young Ian. He was devastated of course. Left the house, and no-one knows where he's gone."

"Did she die giving birth?" The PC asked

"Oh no, it was about nine months later."

"Do you know what the cause was?

"We could never really find out," the neighbour told him. "We asked Ian several times, but he never wanted to discuss it, which is understandable, I suppose."

"Would you happen to know who their doctor was, by any chance?"

"I do, as a matter of fact. They used the same medical centre as us. Although I don't know who their doctor was, as there's five at the practice."

"Is there any member of family we could contact?"

"I think her mother's still alive, and Ian had a brother, but I don't know his address."

Her husband returned with the tea and after they'd finished drinking the officer said,

"Can I take your names, just for the record."

"Betty and Joe Adams," she told them.

"Right, and the doctor's address?"

"Yes, I'll go and fetch it for you." She came back a minute or so later with an address and telephone number written on some paper. As he look it from her the officer said,

"Right, thanks for your help, I'll leave you the station's telephone number, in case you think of anything else. If Mr McCallum does happen to return to his home, I'd like you to ring us."

"He's not in any trouble is he?" she asked.

"We'd just like to speak to him," he replied, handing her a card with the station's address and telephone number.

When they returned to the station, he passed the information on to DS Rankin

"You did well to get the doctor's address, well done," he told the officers.

"The neighbour was a bit of a nosy parker," the PC told him.

"Don't knock it, lad. It's their sort that usually give us the information we need."

When Josephine returned he gave her the information.

"Definitely worth chasing, I suppose," she began.

"It may be nothing, but it's odd that both mother and child died," Rankin replied.

"Would you like to know what I've discovered today?" she began.

"Go on, surprise me," Rankin replied.

"We have the identity of the latest victim."

"I knew when we put her photo in the Evening Mail, someone would recognise her," Rankin stated.

"It was my cousin, the private investigator who identified her," she informed him.

"Really!" Rankin sounded surprised.

"Her father was his client, and he had been given the job of finding her. Apparently she'd left home four years previously. So at least we have the family's address, though it probably won't bring us any closer to finding the killer, and if the family haven't been in touch with her for some time, it's doubtful, they'll know any of her friends," she said despondently.

"There's no need to sound so pessimistic," Rankin told her, "at least now we have two lots of information, one may prove fruitful."

As they parked on the long paved drive leading to the detached house, Rankin observed,

"Fancy, leaving all this to live rough, she must have been mad."

"We don't know what caused her to leave home. Maybe she was desperately unhappy and needed to get away, despite the consequences," Josephine remarked as she rang the front door bell. A tall dark rather attractive looking man in his thirties answered the door. They showed their warrant cards and introduced themselves,

"We've come to see Mr Raymond O'Connor concerning his daughter," Rankin began.

"Oh, Annette! Is she in any trouble?" he asked.

"May I ask who you are?" Josephine said

"Oh, I'm sorry, I should have introduced myself. I'm James O'Connor, Annette's brother. I'm afraid my father passed away last week, he'd been ill for some time."

Josephine was already aware of this, as Mark had informed her, and she decided that it was probably for the best. The old man had hoped to be re-united with his daughter before he died. The news of her death would probably have killed him. At least he died thinking she was still alive. Now she had to break the news to the son, who in the space of two weeks had lost two members of his family.

"Perhaps we could go somewhere more comfortable?" Rankin suggested, a little candidly.

"Yes certainly," he said as he led them into a large lounge over looking the rear garden. It was tastefully decorated, and no expense had been spared. There was a large green tapestry suite in the centre of the room, which matched the drapes. On the highly polished parquet floor lay a large Chinese carpet. Around the room were paintings and sculptures and one or two rather nice antique clocks. As she sat on the plush sofa, Josephine began.

"I'm so sorry to have to tell you this, Mr O'Connor, but we have found the body of a young woman, who we believe to be your sister. We need you to identify her to confirm this.

The colour drained from his face.

"Er… are you sure… I mean, how do you know it's Annette?

"Were you aware that your father had employed a private investigator to try and trace Annette?" Rankin asked him.

"No I wasn't. He'd mentioned it, some time ago, although I didn't think he was serious."

"Surely, knowing he was ill, you'd understand that he would want to see his daughter?" Josephine suggested.

"Er… Yes… I suppose…" He sounded shocked and dazed. It was obvious he hadn't taken in the bad news.

"The private investigator working on the case recognised the photo in the newspaper. He found Annette living in a hostel in Birmingham, although on your father's instruction, he didn't approach her, he just gave your father the details and the address where he could contact her. Your father settled his bill in full, and said he'd make his own arrangements," Rankin informed him.

"I find it odd your father didn't tell you what he intended to do," Josephine said.

"When he mentioned it some time ago. I'm afraid I was very much against the idea, and I told him so. That's probably why he didn't tell me what he was doing, I had no idea he'd employed someone."

"Why were you against the idea? I mean she was your sister, and your father was dying," Josephine asked.

"There's a ten year age gap between Annette and myself. Being the younger child my parents always spoiled her. When my mother died, several years ago, my father was so stricken with grief, he hadn't really got that much time for us. It didn't really bother me, being older I suppose I understood; but Annette rebelled because she wasn't getting the attention she wanted. She was about seventeen at the time and she started drinking, smoking, taking drugs and smashing things up. Once she had the audacity to bring some of her so called friends back here. They stole money from my father's desk, obviously to buy drugs. He told her if she couldn't improve her ways, to get out. I don't think he meant it really, he just wanted her to see the pain and destruction she was bringing upon herself and everyone else. But she took what he said literally and left. She never got in contact, from that day to this."

"How did you father know she might be in the city?" Rankin asked.

"Someone had seem her there some time ago. You haven't told me how she died. Was it a drugs overdose?"

"What makes you think that?" Josephine asked.

"She started to get into the heavy drugs before she left. That was about four years ago. I thought she'd never be able kick the habit," he explained.

"Your sister was still a user, but I'm afraid she was murdered, and her body was dumped in the canal," Josephine informed him.

He put his head in his hands.

"Oh God, not the serial killer that's been in all the newspapers?" he uttered.

"We believe she may have been one of his victims," Josephine told him. "You'll have to accompany us back to the coroner's office in Birmingham to officially identify your sister. I do have a picture here if you feel..."

"Yes, I'm okay," he replied, looking at the photo Josephine held in her hands. "Yes, that's Annette," he confirmed, his eyes filling with tears.

"Did you live here at home with your father?" Josephine enquired, wondering why such an attraction man had never married.

"Yes..." he replied looking at Josephine. It was as if he'd read her thoughts. "I'm not gay, if that what you're thinking, I've had several women friends. In fact I almost got engaged once. It's just that mother died, and then there was the problem with Annette, and on top of it all father's illness. I just felt I couldn't desert him," he explained.

"Well, that's to be commended sir. At least now, you'll be free to do your own thing," Rankin told him.

"Yes, but I have no family left, I have this house," he said as he looked around the opulent lounge. "And I won't be short of money. But what's the use of all this when there's no-one to share it with?" He sounded despondent.

"I'm sure in time, you'll be able to put all this behind you, and make a new start. You have to look to the future," Josephine tried to re-assure him.

Some fifteen minutes or so later, they left the house with O'Connor, and took him to the coroner's office, where he made a positive identification.

"Yes, that's Annette," he confirmed and then he broke down and cried. After they'd arranged for a police car to take him back home. Josephine and Rankin went into the office.

243

"It's hard to believe such an angelic looking creature could create such distress and havoc," Rankin remarked.

"Yes, she was a pretty young thing, but you can't judge a book by its cover," Josephine replied

"Do you think he's telling the truth, about not knowing originally, that his father had hired the services of a private investigator to trace his sister?" Rankin asked.

"There's no real reason for him to lie. Raymond O'Connor was so ill, he probably didn't want the added stress of his son objecting."

"If James had looked after his father, he probably couldn't understand why he needed to contact her, as she'd never done anything for him, apart from bringing him upset and grief. I can see his point; the father must have been mad."

"Wait till you're a parent yourself and then you'll probably understand how Raymond O'Connor felt," Josephine began. "Sometimes it doesn't matter what your children do, or how badly they behave, you never stop caring. It's a special bond that's hard to break. Blood is definitely thicker than water."

"Since you're a parent and I'm not, I can't really argue with you on that point," he replied.

"That's right sergeant," Josephine said smiling. "Now, what's next on the agenda?

"A visit to the Yew Trees Medical Centre. We have an appointment with Doctor Newton at four o'clock."

As they sat opposite Doctor Newton, in his consulting room, he had Anna McCallum's medical record open on his desk.

"It was a very sad case, you know, very sad. Anna died and then her baby died about a month later. A tragedy."

Josephine was becoming impatient and tried to steer him back to the point.

"What was the cause of death?" she said firmly.

"Oh, I'm sorry, I thought you knew. They both died of AIDS."

"AIDS?" Josephine repeated in surprise.

"Yes, a terrible shame!"

"I'd like you to give me all the facts," she said.

"Anna had been my patient for many years, since before she married. She'd stayed in the area after she married, you see, so there was no need to change doctors."

Josephine came to the reluctant conclusion that there was no way she could rush Doctor Newton, and decided to let him continue at his own pace.

"After she married and became pregnant she discovered that she had contracted AIDS when a routine blood test was done at the maternity clinic. Understandably she couldn't come to terms with the fact—she kept insisting that they must have got her blood test mixed up with someone else's. She said Ian was the only man she'd ever slept with, and it just wasn't possible. I explained there was a high risk of the virus passing to her child, and urged her to consider an abortion. She wouldn't hear of

245

it. To her a termination was out of the question."

"How did her husband react to the news?"

"Worse than Anna. He kept saying she was the only woman he's ever slept with and it was impossible he could have infected her. Since Anna had never had a blood transfusion or taken drugs it would seem that the only way she *could* have been infected was through sexual contact. And Ian was the most likely source of the infection. To begin with he refused to take a blood test, but I persuaded him."

"And the result?"

"He was HIV positive."

"Surely he'd know? Wouldn't there have been symptoms?"

"Not necessarily. HIV slowly progresses into full-blown AIDS. In some people that process can take many years, in other cases, such as Anna's, it's swift. People can be HIV positive and not know. They can then sleep with other people, infecting them. Those contacts, like Anna, can develop AODS swiftly and they can die before the person who infected them, or they can develop slowly, and spread the disease in ignorance. It's like a game of roulette. Some are lucky, some are not. It's a chance you take with unprotected sex."

"So what happened after that?"

"How they dealt with the facts personally, I'll never know. The baby was born normally, and to an outsider the mother and baby were doing well. It was only short lived. Anna's illness seemed to accelerate, possibly due to her being in a low mental and physical state. She deteriorated rapidly, developed pneumonia and died. Ian had to cope for the baby's sake. She lasted a few more weeks and then lost her fight for life. Anna's mother called him a murderer. He was totally overcome with grief."

"He's left his house. Do you have any idea where he's gone to?"

"No, I'm afraid I don't. No-one does. Is he in any trouble?"

"We found this photo at the scene of a murder, and we believe it may have been dropped by the killer. We've been through a list of over twenty women, but all of the others still have their scan photos," Josephine handed the photo to Doctor Newton.

"Mmm. It says thirty-five to thirty-six weeks on here. Let me just check Anna's record." He studied the charts for a moment.

"According to this Anna's baby was born full term, approximately four weeks after the date on this scan. I'd say there's a very good chance this is hers."

"Do you have her mother's address?"

"She's still a patient with us. Her name is Jane Wright. I'll get the receptionist to give you the details."

They got up and both shook hands with the Doctor.

"Thank you for your help, Doctor Newton," DS Rankin said.

"Not at all. Please contact me if I can be of any further assistance."

As they drove back to the station Josephine turned to Rankin and said,

"I suppose there's little doubt that Ian McCallum is our man. I know this may sound strange, but if he is I almost feel sorry for him. I don't suppose you feel the same?"

"I think it's a terrible story. To have his wife and child die like that. From what the doctor said, he seemed genuinely shocked he was carrying the virus. I suppose he must have had an active sex life before marriage, whatever he told his wife," he replied.

"You talk to Anna's mother and see if she has a key to the house. Explain we just need to look around. I'll speak to the chief to arrange a search warrant. We still don't know where the connection to the canals comes into it, though I suppose he derives some morbid satisfaction from it. See if the mother has any contact with other members of his family—telephone numbers and the like. I hope you don't mind this—I've had as much grief as I can stand for the day."

"Not a problem. I'll get on to it as soon as we get back," Rankin told her.

They managed to contact John McCallum, Ian's brother, who apparently hadn't seen him since the baby's funeral.

"We've never been that close. I don't know if you understand me, but he was always young for his age. When he was in his teens, where the rest of us were off clubbing, chasing women and drinking, he was fishing and playing with model railways. It was a hell of a surprise when he fell for Anna. But even that wasn't like an adult relationship. It was like two kids playing house. It was lucky for them he was so skilled with his hands, and could make a good living doing something he liked, because he didn't live in the real world much.

"It was terrible—when they buried Anna he threw himself on the coffin and sobbed like a child. We had to drag him off. And then a few weeks later he had to go through the ordeal again when he buried the baby. To be honest, when you contacted me I thought it was to tell me he'd committed suicide. It's what we've all being expecting, he felt so guilty and responsible for their deaths."

"I'd imagine even the most stable person would find it difficult to accept and live with," Josephine replied. "If he's the man we're looking for, I think that they're revenge killings, in some way that we don't understand. What I can't fathom is the connection with the canals."

"He always loved them. When we were kids he'd spend hours fishing on the canals. Funnily enough in his late teens he just stopped going. He'd never tell me why, when I asked him. He always said he'd love to own a narrowboat. I think he'd have liked to live on one, and make the canals his home, if he hadn't met Anna and fallen in love."

"Did he ever show any violent tendencies?"

Rankin asked.

"No... never. We used to fight when we were kids, of course, but he was a bit of a softie really. He was too busy reading books and making things. He wouldn't have hurt a fly. And he adored Anna. He'd have been a good husband and a good dad—he just never got the chance."

"Have you any idea where he'd have gone?"

"No. I can understand him leaving the house. The memories must have been unbearable. I suppose sooner or later it'll be repossessed by the building society."

"Where did he work?"

"A small jewellery factory in Hockley, on the edge of the Jewellery Quarter. But he left his job when Anna died and went on the dole to look after the baby. And then there was no-one for him to care for."

"Thanks for your help, Mr McCallum. We'll be in touch. Here's our number if you need to contact me. If you remember anything else, or if Ian contacts you, let us know. It's in his best interests, you know," Josephine said, handing him her card.

"I realise that Inspector."

The chief was present at the next briefing and was pleased at the progress they'd made to date.

"So, there's little doubt," he began, "that the picture of the ultrasound scan found at the scene of the crime belongs to Ian McCallum?"

"I suppose it could possibly belong to someone else, sir, but there are a number of circumstances that make him the likely suspect," Josephine answered.

"It's an odd thing to carry on your person," he remarked.

"Due to the tragic circumstances surrounding their deaths I could imagine he'd carry whatever pictures of them he could. I think he's obsessed by their deaths, and in some way the pictures feed his need for revenge," Josephine replied.

"I can understand ordinary photos, but this one?"

"You can't put them in a normal frame or photo album, because the picture fades. He feels terrible guilt for infecting his family, and he may think it's significant that the child was infected in her mother's womb. This is a constant reminder to him," Josephine explained.

"Okay, it's obvious he hates paedophiles, especially those that prey on young boys. Possibly something similar had happened to him in the past, and that's how he'd become infected. That I can understand—but why kill women?"

"Look," said the chief, "we need a result on this quickly. The papers are all over it—you've only got to mention serial killers and the public panics—and the Chief Constable has let it be known he's keeping an eye on us. So we have to get moving pretty damn quickly."

"I've dealt with several serial killers over the years,

and they usually have a pattern to their crimes, a theme, if you like. Some of them are just monsters in human guise, but I don't believe our killer fits into that category. He's obviously unbalanced, but due to circumstances, not to his basic nature," Josephine said.

"He's killed five so far, if the one in the boat's one of his, so in the public's mind he's a monster, believe me," the chief said.

"Yes, but he's not the kind of serial killer who gets real joy from inflicting suffering. That's why he's been so difficult to profile and track down. The similarities are in the physical details of the crimes. All the victims have been in the vicinity of the canal, and have been attacked with a hammer-like implement. Although in Annette O'Connor's case Doctor Mortimer believes that a different weapon was used, something with a more rounded shape, like a paperweight. A forensic psychologist told me he once profiled a killer who'd use a different weapon at each crime. I asked about our suspect changing from killing men to women, and he said that if the killer really needed to express his anger, sex and appearance would be irrelevant."

"I wonder how he accosts his victims," the chief said, "Does he talk to them first, or just attack them?"

DS Rankin stood up.

"At least we have a possible ID on the killer now. We'll get a recent photograph and circulate it. Wherever he is, no matter how remote the location, he's still got to eat, to buy groceries. He's been killing these people in busy areas—someone must have seen him. We also need to talk to the neighbours in the road where he'd lived. Before the tragedy he may have given someone some information that we need. Even if he's a recluse now, we know he hasn't always been one."

"Anyway, you've got your warrant, so you can now search the house," the chief informed them.

"Right, there's no time like the present. We'll take two officers and go there now," Josephine told DS Rankin.

Chapter 23

AS THEY ENTERED the small terraced house it was dark and musty, due to the fact all the curtains had been drawn and the windows hadn't been opened for some time. Even though Anna's mother had a key, she said she couldn't go into the property as she found it too traumatic.

There were two small rooms downstairs, and on a table in the back room there were several photographs. Josephine examined each one carefully with gloved hands. There was a picture of Ian McCallum with Anna, holding hands in a disco, possibly taken when they were dating. Several other photos of Anna when she was pregnant also stood on the table and there were pictures of the baby. It was obvious; despite the fact she knew Ian had infected her, she still loved him, by the way she looked at him and the close contact they had with one another in each picture.

He looked a pleasant young man and nothing like a murderer, but Josephine knew from past experience that the most sadistic killers could be charming and amiable. In the one photo she studied for some time, Josephine noticed a strange look in his eyes. It wasn't an evil or malevolent guise that she'd seen many times, but a lost, confused almost cynical expression, as if he distrusted everything and everyone.

"Get all these tagged and put in plastic," Josephine told one DC.

"I'd have thought he would have taken these with him when he left," Rankin observed.

"Mm, I agree, still, he may have another set of pictures with him. I feel that no matter how mentally disturbed he may be, he must still be grieving for his wife and child."

Josephine entered Chief Inspector Lyle's office.

"Right, take a seat, I'll keep this brief. Can I assume you have no doubts that this Ian McCallum is our man?"

"Yes… Well, everything points to him being the killer. I can't get my head around the fact that this distressed and grieving man, who was once a good husband and father, has become a murderer."

"So are you saying you're *not* certain he's the killer, DI Blake?"

"No… well… I mean nothing's a hundred percent, is it sir? It's just that I can't see why he started. Even if they *are* revenge killings, I'd have thought his grief stricken state would have been stronger than his hatred. I just can't figure out how his mind works, it's baffling," she reflected.

"Why are you trying to analyse him? That's the psychologist's area when we find him, not yours, and we'd better get him quick. Have you read this?" He threw a copy of the Evening Mail down on the desk; it carried a large article on the killings. She read it for a few minutes and just before she finished the piece the chief said:

"They're saying the streets aren't safe and questioning why we haven't caught the killer. The proprietors and landlords of the pubs and cafés along the canal are saying they are losing trade because people are afraid to visit the area."

"I don't believe that for one minute. In my opinion, most people don't stop going to a particular area just because there have been crimes committed. In fact, some people are curious about these things and normally go to see the scene of the crime, to the point of revelling in the idea that they could be somewhere close to where the murder happened. I'd have thought trade would have increased. Okay, I'll accept the fact people shouldn't walk alone at night in the area, but most of the people that frequent Brindleyplace and the canals go in groups," she replied.

"The one paper's saying that President Clinton's visit increased trade and now because of this there's a slump," the chief added.

"Their aim is to sell papers; anyway trade is always bad in most places the first three months of the year, as people pay off the credit cards that they've overspent on at Christmas," Josephine remarked.

The chief became angry and red in the face, "For Heaven's sake Blake! This isn't a debate about whether what the papers say is true. Most people believe what they read. I frankly don't give a damn if businesses in the area have genuinely lost trade because of this or whether it's an excuse. The West

Midlands Police are under fire. We've had a lot of criticism, and I hate to have to admit this, but a lot of what the press are saying is true. We need to find this maniac and quick, so I'm putting another ten officers on the case. Their job will be to talk to everyone in the area, and show his photo around. We also need to put his picture in all the newspapers, and appeal for witnesses on all the local radio stations. We need a result. When you have gone back to Devon, I'll be the one who has to face the music!" he announced angrily.

"I've never shirked my responsibilities or obligations," Josephine declared. "And I wouldn't dream of going anywhere until this case is solved. We have encountered many obstacles, the problems with identification have been the worst, and I am personally prepared to work round the clock to get a result. As to your earlier point, about me trying to analyse the killer. I feel it's an advantage if you know their mind and their reasons for killing."

"How can you know his mind, unless you're as bloody deranged and insane as he is? He's a maniac!"

"I disagree. He's unbalanced, but circumstances have changed his temperament and personality dramatically," she retorted.

"DI Blake, I'm not in the least bit interested in your assessment of this man. Just make sure we catch him before he kills again."

Over the next three days there were sightings of the man in question, and a few people contacted their local station, saying they recognised the man in the photo. When it was all checked out all the information proved fruitless.

Josephine knew it would just be a matter of time, and that eventually they would receive something from someone that would be productive. The problem was that time was running out. Josephine felt that if he killed again she might have to consider resigning from the case, as a last resort. She thought back to when they had first discovered the body in the sunken boat. At the time it hadn't seemed that significant, but that was the start. For some reason unknown to them it was the point of origin of the murders that were to follow. It was almost as if, by finding Charlie Reid's bady in the cabin, they had disturbed some sacred burial chamber. It was like a curse had been released and others would die; Bob Melchett, Terry Ryan, Elizabeth Gunter and finally Annette O'Connor.

Oh God, I hope there won't be a number six added to the list of the dead...

The next day it seemed her prayers had been answered.

They received a telephone call from John McCallum, the suspect's brother and made an appointment to visit him.

"It may be of no importance, but I was going

through some photos the other day and I came across this one," he handed them a picture of a young boy, about fifteen years of age, sitting on the end of a brightly coloured narrowboat.

Josephine looked at the photo for a few moments but couldn't see the significance. Then John McCallum said, "That was Ian when he was fifteen."

"I'd never had guessed, he looks so different on the more recent photos we've seen of him with his wife." She studied the photo more closely.

Yes. Now she could see the resemblance and yet... His expression in this photo, he looked so happy, carefree and innocent. Almost angelic. Yet on the more recent photos he looked haunted and tormented. The loss of his wife and child was tragic and yet... there was something else. Some other menacing force.

DS Rankin suddenly interrupted her thoughts,

"Why do you think this photo could be of use to us Mr McCallum?" he asked.

"I'm sorry, I'm not making myself clear," he began. "It's not the photo, it's the boat Tigerlily. It may be a long shot, but the owner, Robert Downes, was a family friend. When he was young, Ian loved the canals; he'd fish on them, and cycle down the towpaths. Most of his weekends and school holidays were spent on Robert's boat. He loved it."

"Tell me, this Robert Downes, was he gay?" Josephine enquired.

"Good Lord no! Robert was married, that's not the point I'm getting at."

"Then what exactly do you mean?" Josephine said a little impatiently.

"Well you see, Ian loved that boat, it was his second home, and in later years whenever Robert and his wife Jill went on holiday, or to visit their son who lived in Dorset, Ian would look after the boat for them."

"Does Robert Downes still own the boat?"

"Well yes, but he's been away in Australia for the last nine months, and although I haven't seen him for some years, I know Ian still kept in touch with him. I think he may be living on Robert's boat," he told them.

"Yes, that's quite possible, since it held fond memories of his youth he could regard it as his haven, a safe place where he could retreat," Josephine agreed.

"Do you know where it's moored?" Rankin asked.

"It's on a stretch of the canal just outside Kings Norton, that's if it hasn't been moved. I can show you where it's situated," he offered.

"Well, there's no time like the present, we'll go now," Josephine said.

"I wish you'd have given us this information earlier," Rankin told him.

"I'm sorry, but with all that's happened over the last few months, I'd forgotten about Robert, it was only when I found the photo, it all came back to me," he explained.

"I think we'll need back-up, ma'am, just in case

he's there. He could be dangerous," Rankin said.

"It's hard to believe you're talking about my brother," John McCallum added.

"If he is our man, he's already killed five people," Josephine told him. "We can't take any chances, we'll radio for back-up on the way."

"I think we need to let the chief know what we're doing, as we may need armed officers," Rankin proposed.

"Yes, you're right, sergeant, we'll go back to the unit first."

Two hours later, they were heading out of the city with two armed officers in their car, and DCs Lloyd and Freeman followed in the vehicle behind. Josephine made it clear she wanted no police sirens and that they should park out of sight. She didn't want to alert McCallum, as she thought the best approach was quiet and unobtrusive.

They parked on the road by a bridge and walked down to the canal. She instructed the armed officers to stay some way behind. There were three boats moored on the canal at about fifty or so yards apart.

Josephine turned to DC Katie Lloyd and said "See if there are any residents on the other boats, because if there are we need to get them away from the area."

The first boat was unoccupied, but there was a family living on the next one. Josephine spoke to the father.

"Do you know if there's a man living alone on there?" she said as she pointed to the narrowboat Tigerlily.

"Yes, he's looking after it for the owner," the man replied.

"Do you know his name?" she continued.

"Yes, Ian, why, he hasn't done anything wrong has he?" he asked.

"We just need to speak to him. I don't suppose you know if he's on board?"

"I don't think so, he normally has a fire, and there's no smoke coming from his chimney."

Just then the man's wife said,

"He went out earlier on his bike."

"Do you know when he might return?" Rankin enquired.

"It's a fine day," she said looking upwards to the clear blue sky, "He may not be back till five or six this evening."

"Then we'll wait, but you'll have to leave your boat for a few hours," she told them.

"Whatever for?" the man asked.

"Things could get nasty, and you and your children may be in danger if you stay," Josephine told him.

"In danger from who?" he asked a little confused.

"Ian McCallum," Rankin replied.

"Don't be ridiculous. He wouldn't hurt a fly; I'm not leaving."

"I'm afraid I'll have to insist, it's only for a few hours, isn't there anywhere you can go?" Josephine asked.

"No, we've no other family or friends and we don't have any transport," the man told her.

Josephine was beginning to lose her patience with the man.

"One of my officers will take you anywhere you need to go in their car. Sergeant, give them some money," Rankin looked a little hesitant. "I'll reimburse you later," Josephine told him.

He got out a ten-pound note.

"There are four of them for heaven's sake, give me twenty-five pounds," Josephine ordered. He handed her the money and she said

"Right Mr—er—?"

"O'Brien," he informed her.

"Right, Mr O'Brien, take this money, and my officer will drive you wherever you want to go. Do as you like, treat yourselves to a meal, but don't come back until late, understand?"

"Yes," he said, "No problem," he took the money out of her hand. "Come on kids, we're going to have a ride in a police car," he told them and off they went.

"Right, if he's gone on his bike, he'll be coming back along the towpath. Even if he went by road it's about six hundred yards ahead at that bridge," she said as she pointed up the canal. "Let's get officers positioned at either end of this stretch. We will wait in the boat, and you can radio through to

263

us as he passes you," Josephine told them.

"We need to look around the boat, but we'll probably need to break this small door open," Rankin said as he tugged at the locked door.

When they had gained entry they went inside the boat. The cabin area was very neat and tidy. As they opened the small cupboards in the kitchen, one housed various pots and pans and the other contained tea, coffee and some tinned food. They opened the small fridge door where they found a container of fresh milk; the sell by date was two days away.

"Well it's obvious he's been living here," Josephine observed.

"Take a look here," Rankin shouted, and Josephine dipped her head and made her way to the far end of the boat. There was a small table covered in framed photos of Ian's wife and baby.

"Do you know, this doesn't look like a killer's lair, but just the home of a very sad young man who's lost everything and wants to live alone, like an injured dog who wants to go in his basket and lick his wounds—I wonder?" she pondered.

Rankin carried on searching the drawers and cupboards. He came across a diary, which he opened and started to look through, on one particular page and date. It read:

TODAY I HAVE RID THE WORLD OF SOME VERMIN. AT LEAST NOW THERE IS ONE LESS ON THIS EARTH TO SPREAD THE TERRIBLE DISEASE.

I THOUGHT I WOULD FEEL BETTER AS I WATCHED THE ANIMAL TAKE HIS LAST BREATHS, BEFORE GOING UNDER THE WATER, BUT THE PAIN IS STILL THERE.

OH MY DEAR ANNA AND SOPHIE, THE KILLING DOESN'T MAKE MY LOSS ANY EASIER TO BEAR.

He showed the page to Josephine, and after she'd read it she noticed he'd written other pieces on different days. These dates coincided with the dates of the murders.

"This is a vital piece of evidence, get it bagged and give it to one of the officers," she told Rankin.

Josephine and DS Rankin had been on the boat for about four hours. It was almost five o'clock in the afternoon, and they were both feeling somewhat tense and yet at the same time bored and restless. There was no radio or television on the narrow boat, which they could watch to while away the time. Josephine came across some old newspapers, and she read those for a while.

They had never spent such a long time in each other's company. Although their working relationship was now on a better footing than at the beginning, they still didn't have that much in common to talk about to pass the time.

Josephine put the newspaper down, looked at her watch and sighed,

"I don't know about you, but I'm absolutely

famished. I haven't eaten since seven o'clock this morning."

"I must admit I'm starting to feel hungry too," Rankin replied.

"Why don't you go and get us both some food?" she suggested.

"I don't know about that, ma'am, I shouldn't really leave you here alone," he replied.

"I don't see why not. It could be hours before he returns and we do have officers posted at either end of the canal. So whichever way he returns along the towpath on his bike, they can let me know in plenty of time, that he's approaching. In fact, they'll most probably stop him before he gets anywhere near the boat."

"I suppose you're right... And to tell you the truth, I could do with getting off the boat for some fresh air. I don't know how people can live on these things, they are so confined and cramped," he remarked.

"Yes, I know what you mean, I felt a bit claustrophobic when we first came on board, but I'm okay now. I suppose it's like anything, you get used to it in time. Though I must admit to needing quite a bit of room myself," she replied thinking of her large spacious house back in Devon.

"I'm wondering where to go for the food. I think I saw a fish and chip shop along the road, just before we turned on to the canal."

"I didn't see one, but then I was rather preoccupied. I suppose you could always send one of the officers," she suggested.

"No, I'll go myself, I could do with stretching my legs. What do you fancy?"

"Oh anything, fish, chicken, as long as it's with chips and a pickled onion," Josephine said, the thought of the food was making her more ravenous.

"At least at this time they'll be nice and fresh," Rankin replied.

He left the boat and walked five hundred yards to his left, where DCs Lloyd and Freeman were positioned on the towpath.

"Nothing doing, then?" he asked them.

"No, bloody boring in fact. Purvis and Jones are fed up waiting down the other end, the only life they've seen is some kids throwing stuff in the canal, so they chased them off."

"I know. Me and the DI are fed up with waiting about," Rankin told them.

"It's alright for you, Sarge, at least you're in the boat where it's nice and warm, it's bloody freezing hanging about here," DC Lloyd moaned.

"I'm just off to that chip shop we passed earlier, to get us something to eat," he said.

"Do you want me to go for you sir?" DC Freeman offered, desperate for a change of scenery.

"No it's okay, I could do with the exercise. It looks like we could be here for some time," he said as he walked away.

The towpath was deserted, the officers positioned at each end had a good view down the canal, and could see anyone approaching from some distance away, but there was no sign of their suspect.

Some half a mile or so down the canal, another boat was travelling towards the spot where Tigerlily was moored. On the boat were two men.

"It's good of you to you to give me a lift, Jack," the younger man said.

"No problem, I couldn't see you walking all the way back with your bike. Mind you, the speed these boats go you could have walked home faster, I doubt I've saved you any time."

"It's been a change to chat to someone," the younger man told him. "I normally carry a puncture kit with me, I must have left it on the boat."

"Any idea when Robert is coming back from Australia?" the other man asked.

"No, I haven't heard anything from him, I suppose he's having a whale of a time and there's nothing to come back for except his boat."

"Well, I wouldn't change my life on the canals," Jack told him.

"I used to feel like that, but things change," the young man sounded bitter.

"There she is, just ahead, I'll pull up alongside, are you sure you can get your bike off okay?"

"Yes, thanks Jack."

"No problem, see you Ian," the old man replied.

Josephine heard the noise of the approaching boat, but didn't think anything of it. Several boats had passed by in the few hours they had been there. She suddenly felt the boat rock and heard voices followed by a banging and clattering noise. She thought for a moment that Rankin had returned, until she heard an unfamiliar voice. After a moment or two Ian McCallum came aboard the boat. Despite the fact the light was poor in the cabin area, she recognised him instantly from his photograph. Her heart started to pound, but she knew she wouldn't be able to radio for help, and yet for some strange reason, she didn't feel as afraid as she thought she would. This young man didn't look vicious or dangerous, though Josephine knew different.

Should she tell him outright that she was a policewoman, and had come to question him about the murders? Having found his diary, there was now little doubt he was the man they had been looking for. It was obvious he had not seen the police waiting at the one end of the towpath. Perhaps he had been inside the boat that had brought him along the canal and had not noticed them. Should she make some other excuse for being there; but what could she say? Her mind was in turmoil, as she tried to think of something to say, to convince him her presence on his boat was perfectly innocent.

He studied her for a few moments and didn't speak, which unnerved her even more. As he looked around the boat he noticed one of the drawers wasn't closed properly. He quickly opened it, noticing at once his diary was missing. Suddenly realising he had locked the door to his boat before he was leaving and that the lock would have to be broken in order to gain entry, he quickly weighed up the situation.

Just as Josephine was about to speak he said,

"So you've got my diary, I suppose you've read it."

"A page or two, yes," she replied. "I'm so sorry about your wife and child Mr McCallum," she began.

"My God, you know bloody everything, even my name," he suddenly became quite aggressive.

"I'm Detective Inspector Blake and I've come to question you about several murders that have occurred over the last few weeks in the vicinity of the canal," she told him.

For God's sake Rankin, where the bloody hell are you? It's just like history repeating itself, she thought as she remembered her encounter with the copycat Ripper murderer some months previously.

How the hell shall I handle it? Come straight to the point and accuse him, or take the sympathetic approach, for all I know he might attack me at any moment, but surely he would realise I wouldn't come alone without backup.

It was if he had read her thoughts.

"How come you're here alone?" He asked her.

"The other's will be here shortly," she replied.

"So I suppose you think what I've done is wrong?"

"Of course I do. That's my job; to reinforce law and order," she told him.

"Yeah… well… some of us have good reasons to kill."

"No reason is good enough to take a human life," she stated.

"Well, they took my wife and child," McCallum told her.

"Who are 'they'? Surely your family died of an illness."

"Why don't you say it, AIDS, spread by the vermin I've got rid of. They infected me and murdered my wife and child. The filthy gay bastards! I've done everyone a favour ridding the world of them!"

"You haven't done their families a favour though have you?" Josephine remarked. "And Terry Ryan wasn't gay."

"Of course he was, I'd often see him talking to young boys. He even had a tattoo on his arm of one of the poor little kids he had buggered."

"That was his son who was killed in a car accident. Terry Ryan was straight; he lived with his girlfriend. The boys he befriended just reminded him of the son he had lost," she told him.

For a moment he seemed to believe her and a sudden expression of regret passed over his face, but in a second it was gone.

"Rubbish! Don't lie to me!" he said as he came closer, staring into her eyes.

"What about the woman? Did you know you had killed a woman, Elizabeth Gunter?"

"Yeah, well that was a mistake. She was so butch I thought she was a man. Still, she was probably gay anyway."

"But she didn't have AIDS," she told him.

"How do you know?"

"We tested her in the morgue. And what about Annette O'Connor?"

He looked a little confused.

"The pretty girl with long red hair," continued Josephine, "She was such a frail, delicate little thing, I suppose she was a pushover."

He looked puzzled.

"I... er don't..."

"I suppose you're going to tell me, you thought she was a man," Josephine said.

"I never killed any girl with long red hair!" he declared.

"How would you know? You probably attacked her in such a frenzy; it's just another life to you. We found a cufflink on her body with the initial 'I' engraved on it!"

He came up to Josephine and grabbed her viciously as he pulled her towards him.

"I didn't kill her I tell you!"

Josephine felt frightened and tense.

"We've got both ends of the canal covered, you won't escape."

"Huh, it doesn't bother me. I've lost everything I ever cared for, and I'll develop the disease sooner or later, my days are numbered."

"There was no need to go on a killing spree. In time they will find a cure for AIDS, and you're only HIV positive, you haven't developed the full-blown disease yet."

"I don't want to be cured. Without Anna and Sophie... my dear baby Sophie... I don't want to live. I've killed them anyway, so I was already a murderer before I started killing," he said sadly, his anger subsiding.

"It was unfortunate you infected them, but not intentional, I'm sure."

"That dirty bastard who raped me when I was a boy, fishing by the canal, he was the one who infected me. I was only seventeen. I fought him off, God did I fight him, but he was just too strong for me. Still, I went back and killed him a few days later."

"Did you put him in the boat?" Josephine asked.

"Yes I knew it had been underwater for some time, so I thought it would be a good place to hide his body. I thought I could make a new start with him out of the way, and put it all behind me. I didn't know when he shoved his penis up my arse, as he beat me senseless, he'd given me that terrible disease that I would pass on to the only two people I ever really loved." He put his head in his hands and his eyes filled with tears.

Josephine suddenly felt very sorry for this young man, a murderer he might be... but still...

Suddenly his sadness turned to anger.

"Fucking filthy vermin! They should all be poisoned like rats and wiped off the face of the earth... oh Anna... Sophie... Oh God, what have I done?"

Josephine looked into his eyes and he stared at

her in a strange manner. He felt she understood. No, how could she, she was a copper, and yet… that look in her eyes he had seen that before, when Anna was dying, too weak to speak and yet she seemed to be saying "Don't blame yourself Ian" she had forgiven him but he couldn't forgive himself.

"You'll need to come back to the station and we can talk about it."

God he's a bloody murderer, and I'm talking as if I'm some sort of counsellor and yet…

She knew in her heart it was the only way to handle this confused, bitter, violent and yet pathetic man.

"Okay," he agreed. "There's nothing left for me now, I'll make a full confession."

She was quite taken aback that he had surrendered so readily, and she was just about to radio to the other officers when he said,

"No," as he grabbed her walkie talkie. "I don't want them all around me. I'll go quietly, but my way."

"Okay," she agreed.

"I need to take some photos with me." He took four or five photos of Anna and Sophie out of their frames, and put them into his pocket.

As they got off the boat, she looked down the towpath and could hardly see her fellow officers, as they were some way away, so she doubted they would see her with McCallum until they had walked a little further towards them. She desperately hoped they wouldn't come running, causing him to panic and try to escape.

Just at that moment, a child on a pair of roller skates came whizzing towards them. In a matter of seconds, the child had careered into her, causing Josephine to lose her balance, and she fell into the canal. She wasn't unduly worried, as she could swim a little. Her main concern was that McCallum would get away. The water was dark and murky and though the depth was only just over four feet in places, her feet were being pulled down by the silt on the bottom, like quicksand. She managed to free herself and get back to the surface, when suddenly he was in the water, pulling her down.

Oh, God, he's trying to drown me, she thought as she struggled against him.

She managed to get her head above the water, as she gulped the fresh air.

Oh no she thought. It's happening all over again!

She recalled the horrific details about fresh water drowning that Doctor Mortimer had explained to her. Now she was experiencing them first hand.

She was a child again, walking along the beach holding her fathers hand. Then in hospital giving birth to Jessica, and the church… the white gown… Andrew… no, Tom, waiting at the altar.

As she submerged again, she started to panic. *"When energy reserves are exhausted, the struggle subsides, and drowning begins,"* Mortimer's words rang in her ears.

She was making love to Andrew. Dear Andrew… and now the Ripper, slashing her to pieces. She surfaced again; coughing and spluttering. *"Coughing vomiting and progressive loss of consciousness, follow in rapid succession,"* the doctor had said.

Her heart was pounding and she was getting weaker. She was at Jessica's school play; now Tom was leaving with his suitcase. Her lungs were on fire. Her body ached, and she was desperate to breathe, but she couldn't.

Suddenly a hand grabbed her fiercely. *No... No he's pushing me back down.* But she didn't have the strength to fight. He started to pull her towards the surface, and she could see daylight again through the dark abyss. When they reached the surface, he held her head above the water pulling her to the side of the canal. It seemed like an eternity before Josephine was finally pulled up onto the towpath. As she lay on the ground he tried to resuscitate her, first giving her mouth to mouth ventilation, and then pressing on her chest to restart her heart. He carried on like this even when he could hear people running towards him, shouting at him to leave her alone. He continued the procedure, until foam exuded from her mouth and nostrils. Josephine started to cough, splutter and vomit water as she gained consciousness.

Ian McCallum had saved her life!

After fifteen minutes Josephine had recovered to the extent she could explain to Rankin and the team that McCallum had saved her. Although she was insistent that she didn't need to go to hospital, Rankin ignored her pleas and called the paramedics. When they arrived they checked her over and said she'd have to go to hospital for a thorough examination. Eventually she agreed, but insisted on walking to the ambulance instead of going in the chair they'd provided.

The ambulance was parked next to the police car where Ian McCallum sat handcuffed in the back seat with an officer to each side. She opened the door and looked at him. "Thank you for saving me from the water. I may have drowned if you hadn't acted so quickly."

"I told you, I don't kill women! And it was..." he began, and then stopped as his eyes filled.

"What? What was it Ian?" Josephine urged him to continue.

"The look in your eyes as you were going down. The fear and dismay. I'd seen it before when Anna was dying. There was nothing I could do to help her, except hold her hand and watch her die."

Two days later after she had rested on the doctor's advice, Josephine was ready to interview Ian McCallum.

As he had told her earlier, Charlie Reid had brutally raped him when he was just seventeen. He had been fishing by the canal when Reid had befriended him. He'd shared his flask of tea and sandwiches with Reid, but when he had the chance

Reid had attacked the boy, viciously beating him before he'd raped him. Several days later, when Ian had recovered he'd gone looking for Reid to get his revenge. McCallum claimed that his initial intention had been to just injure Reid, but when he started to hit him with the hammer he couldn't stop, When McCallum realised he'd killed Reid, he'd panicked, but then he'd recalled the sunken boat in the disused arm. It wasn't far away, so that's where he'd hidden Reid's body.

McCallum had tried to put it all behind him and start a new life. When he'd met Anna he thought his life was complete. They'd fallen in love, married and she'd become pregnant. And then the horrifying revelation that he'd infected the two people he loved most in the world with AIDS. When they'd died his world was shattered. It was then that he'd decided to avenge their deaths by killing "the sort of people who'd infected me." Due to his obsession he'd killed two people he'd mistakenly thought to be gay. His murders took place on the canals because of his morbid fascination with the place his own rape had taken place. He considered that he had nothing to lose—he'd lost his family and was HIV positive. In effect he already had a death sentence looming over him. He showed remorse for the killing of Elizabeth Gunter, who he'd really thought was a man. He confessed to all the murders except for that of Annette O'Connor. He continually claimed to know nothing about her killing. After a thorough search of his boat the hammer that had been used to kill Elizabeth Gunter was found; forensics matched blood and skin from it to her.

"I don't know why he doesn't just admit to all the murders and have done with it," Robert Lyle told DS Rankin and Josephine.

"Because he didn't kill Annette O'Connor!" Josephine announced.

"How can you sound so positive? He could easily be lying," the chief replied.

"But why should he? He's got nothing to lose. He's admitted to the other murders—what difference can this one make? He hated men, not women. It was a man who raped him and infected him with the virus that killed his family. Elizabeth Gunter was a mistake. He doesn't hate women— he saved my life!"

"So you now feel in his debt?" Rankin suggested.

"Not at all, I believe he saved me for his own salvation as much as mine. He couldn't save Anna, or do anything to help her. In saving me he saw some kind of redemption for himself."

"We are talking about a serial killer, or have you forgotten that," Lyle said, with a note of sarcasm.

"Look, forget about him dragging me out of the canal. He made a genuine mistake—Beth looked more like a man than most men I know," she said, giving a sidelong glance to Rankin, with his highlighted hair and false tan. "There was no way he'd mistake Annette for a man, she was far too pretty and feminine. Apart from which, according to Doctor Mortimer's report, a different weapon was used to kill Annette. McCallum used a hammer on all of the rest of his victims—why would he change for one killing?"

"Well, there's the cufflink she was holding. The initial matches," Lyle said.

"I know that, but he reckons he's never worn a shirt in his life, apart from the day he got married, and that was a button cuff. The cufflink is twenty-two carat gold. I doubt if he could afford one, never mind about two."

"You've become too involved, you're letting your emotions get the better of you. According to Chief Cunningham back in Devon, that's always been your weakness," the chief told her.

Josephine was livid and her face became red.

"Look, just because I can understand what motivated this once innocent young man to kill, nevertheless he did still murder four people. Perhaps Reid and Melchett deserved to die; still, I'm not God, who am I to say? I personally don't think that Terry Ryan and Elizabeth Gunter did, but that's beside the point. He had nothing to gain by saving my life; in fact if he'd have let me drown he may have escaped. Just as he has nothing to gain by telling us he didn't kill Annette O'Connor. We have a second murderer on our hands.

Later that day, Josephine phoned Andrew to tell him about her encounter with McCallum on the boat.

"For God's sake Jo, I didn't save you from a maniac so you could get yourself in the same position again."

"I'm fine," she assured him. She didn't feel like going through the details of how her life flashed before her as she was drowning.

"Well, I'm bloody worried about you. In fact, if you weren't coming back home shortly, I'd be in Birmingham with you now."

"I won't be coming back," she told him.

Andrew's heart pounded.

Oh no, surely she's not going to stay there? I've lost her!

"What do you mean?" he asked, dreading her answer.

"There's a few loose ends I need to tie up first," she explained.

"That's just an excuse, you don't want me do you?"

"Andrew, if only you knew, I desperately want to come home to you. I've missed Jessica, and even Bill, would you believe."

"In that case there's nothing to stop you. Surely you can hand over the investigation to Sergeant Rankin, and he can wrap up the case. You've caught your man, now it's just a case of going through the procedure and paperwork?"

"It's not as simple as that," she told Andrew.

"It never is with you, is it Josephine?"

"What do you mean by that remark?" she asked angrily.

"You always seem to look for further complications, even when things are straightforward," he announced.

"That's rubbish, there's one murder we haven't solved, Annette O'Connor the last victim. McCallum's insisting he didn't kill her, and yet he's admitted to all the other murders."

"Perhaps he doesn't want to face up to the fact she was a girl and he had made a mistake again," Andrew suggested.

"I don't think that's the case—he confessed to thinking Elizabeth Gunter was a man. I mean, why on earth should he lie about one victim, he has nothing to lose or gain by doing so, what do you think?"

"It's difficult to say, unless I'd spoken to him and done a professional profile. He could just be messing you about for the hell of it, and you believe him. The location was the same, and he murdered her in the same way."

"Well that's not strictly true," she began. "A hammer wasn't used in this particular instance, but an implement with a more rounded edge."

"Murderers don't always use the same weapon, as I told you before certain circumstances can change their method of killing."

"Well, there is one other thing—" Josephine began.

"Oh, go on then, what is it?" he asked sarcastically.

Shall I tell him? Will he worry, and jump in his car, and come here insisting I go back to Torquay with him. He's saved my life once, maybe, he feels I should have taken more care. Oh what the hell!

"Look Andrew, there was a bit of an incident," she started a little vaguely.

"An incident?"

Here goes, just tell him straight!

"I fell into the canal, and I was drowning; Ian McCallum saved my life," she announced.

Andrew was silent. She decided to omit the details about how her life flashed before her, and how the medical symptoms that a drowning person experiences, that Doctor Mortimer had told her, were ringing in her ears.

"So I saved your life, and you felt indebted to me, and now he's taken my place and you feel an obligation to this murderer, and consequently believe everything he says is true," Andrew said in an aggrieved manner.

"There were certain tragic circumstances that started him on a murder spree," Josephine began to explain.

"There always are, that's no bloody excuse. I would always support you in the past to chief Cunningham, as I felt a certain involvement and soft approach, that has always been your way of operating, has got you results in the past, but I really do believe you've lost it this time. We're talking

283

about a bloody serial killer Jo, or had you forgotten!"

"Look Andrew, in a nutshell, he was raped and contracted AIDS. Unbeknown to him, he infected the only two people he ever cared for, his wife and young baby, and they both died. So that's what triggered him off. I'm not making excuses for the man, he's a killer. But he could have let me drown, and he might have stood a good chance of escaping, Who knows? But he's adamant he doesn't kill women. Elizabeth Gunter was a mistake. He's admitted to all the other murders and has signed a statement to that effect. As far as him saving my life, I think as I was losing the battle he had a flashback to when his wife died. He couldn't save her... Oh... I don't know... As for being indebted to him, that's rubbish, don't compare it to when you saved me from the Ripper. I was in love with you *before* you saved my life. I feel no obligation at all towards McCallum. I just happen to believe him when he says he didn't kill Annette O'Connor. Therefore her killer is walking around free, and I don't approve of murder."

"Well, the rape would have triggered him off— it's rather tragic—but he's still a dangerous serial killer," he remarked.

"I can assure you I have never forgotten that fact, Andrew."

"It must have been a terrible experience for you, almost drowning, why didn't you phone me as soon as you had recovered?" he asked.

"What, and worry you even more? You've been

through enough with me Andrew," she told him.

"That's the way I want it to be, and I had hoped you felt the same."

"I do, and when I get back, we'll start working on our relationship, and spending more time together, but in the meantime, I've got a killer to catch!"

Chapter 24

JOSEPHINE AND RANKIN were in her office.

"So if we assume he's telling the truth," Rankin began.

"Which he is," Josephine intervened.

"It's odd, so many other factors about Annette O'Connor's' death match up to the other murders, apart from the weapon," Rankin remarked.

"Unless the killer wanted it that way," Josephine stated.

"What do you mean?" Rankin asked.

"Let's assume the murderer wanted it to look like the others."

"A copycat killer, you mean?"

"Well not exactly, as they usually commit several murders, and there's been no more deaths since we arrested McCallum. No, what I mean is, it's possible some homicidal maniac killed Annette, but if that was the case it would be highly unlikely that she would be found in the same vicinity and murdered in a similar way to the others. But how about if it was premeditated, and someone planned to get rid of her? Say, as an example, she owed money to a drug dealer. He might decide to bump her off in the same way as the other murders, hoping that the police would assume it was another victim of the Canal Killer. Whoever it was had obviously read all the details in the newspaper," Josephine explained."

"But there's the cufflink. I mean, the initial 'I'. If

it doesn't belong to him it's a bloody big coincidence."

"He's adamant he'd never owned a pair of cufflinks in his life, and if he did I doubt they'd be solid gold ones," Josephine replied.

"So what we have to do is find out as much as we can about her. It's obvious someone wanted Annette O'Connor out of the way, we just need to know why," Rankin stated.

"I've got the address of the hostel where Mark found her, so we can go and speak to the people there, whether they'll be very communicative is another matter."

"I suppose we could talk to her brother to see if he knows of anyone who might want to harm her," Rankin suggested.

"I can't see us gaining much from that. Don't forget, he hasn't seen or heard anything from her in the last four years. He wouldn't know anything about the seedy characters she'd been associating with," Josephine added.

"I think she was a bit of a loner, I mean no-one came forward to identify her, if it hadn't been for your cousin recognising her, we'd have had a problem," Rankin observed.

"Perhaps the down and outs at the hostel did recognise her but just didn't want to get involved. I don't need to tell you most of them are anti the police to say the least."

Josephine and Rankin decided they needed to speak to all the people at the hostel. They'd use the angle that Annette was killed because she was a vagrant of sorts, and not for some personal vendetta. They'd suggest that other vagrants and homeless people could become victims if they didn't co-operate with them.

"Surely, we're okay? You've caught the killer. I read it in the newspaper," one rather bedraggled young man said.

"Surely, you don't believe everything the papers say," Josephine began.

"Well—I—thought you'd caught him. Are you telling us we're still not safe?"

"It's possible," Rankin told him.

"Well then, your bloody lot ought to get your finger out, if you haven't got the right man. You get paid enough bloody money!" the young man said.

"How well did you know Annette?" Josephine asked.

"Spoke to her once or twice, pretty little thing she used to be, though she d'aint look so good lately, could've been the drugs I suppose."

"Are you a user?" Josephine asked him.

"No, I ain't got the money, what bit of cash I do get goes on food, not drugs."

"I'm glad to hear it," Rankin added.

"Do you know anyone who might want to harm her?" Josephine enquired.

"No, we don't harm our own kind, we try and

help each other out when we can," he told them.

I doubt that's true. I reckon you'd rob your own mother for money, Josephine thought.

"Have you spoken to Smelly Kath yet?"

"I don't believe so," Josephine said.

He smelt foul himself, so Josephine dreaded to think what sort of odour Smelly Kath would transmit.

"Her and Annette used to knock around together sometimes. I don't know her room number, you'd have to check with the warden."

Smelly Kath was in her early thirties, and she told Josephine and Rankin she'd slept rough for the past five years, and had only been at the hostel for eight months. Josephine was tempted to ask what circumstances had led this woman to such a sorry state, but she decided against it.

"Yeah, me and Annette were good pals, she could have been a model you know, she was a pretty thing."

"I don't suppose you know of anyone who would want to harm her, had she upset or crossed anybody?"

"Nah, no more than any of us do. There was her supplier, she had one or two run-ins with him, but I can't see him wanting to harm her, he'd lose a good customer."

"Do you know his name?" Rankin asked her.

"No—well—we all call him Doctor Doom, but I can tell you where he hangs out. It'll cost you though."

Josephine took a ten pound note out of her purse and handed it to her.

"Kebble Street in Aston. You'll find him on the corner by the scrap car place, he's there most nights around eight o'clock. He calls it his clinic, fucking bastard. *He's* a bloody murderer, in my opinion."

"I take it you don't use drugs then," Rankin remarked.

"I did once, screwed me up, and I nearly died, no—I ain't touched the stuff—ooh—must be three years now. I tried to talk to Annette and told her she could kick the habit if she really wanted to, but the kid wouldn't listen to me."

"I'm surprised you didn't recognise her picture in the paper," Josephine said.

"What paper was that?"

"Well, it was in the Evening Mail amongst others," she told her.

"I never read the Mail, can't say I've picked one up in years. If I had seen her photo, I would have told the filth."

"Are you sure?"

"Yeah, I don't like your lot, but if it meant helping you to find who killed Annette—poor little mite," she said, as she blew into her dirty handkerchief.

Josephine was amazed she even possessed such a thing.

"Anyway," Kath said, "I thought you'd caught the bastard."

"We're not sure he was responsible for Annette's death," Josephine informed her.

"I don't know why she ever left home. Her family had a bob or two. She could have had a good life, married some posh bloke and been sorted."

"Did she ever talk to you about her family?" Josephine asked.

"No, every time I mentioned them she'd clam up. I reckon something happened, but she'd never discuss it."

"Her father employed an investigator to find her, when he was very ill. Did she ever mention meeting him?"

"No and I'm sure she would have, I mean, I was the only mate she had."

"Right, thanks Kath, here's my card. If you can think of anything please contact me, I know we're the filth, but we want to find out who's responsible for Annette's death, and I'll pay you for any information you give me."

She took the card with her dirty, nail-bitten, scabby hand.

"Okay, I will, I'll do anything if it helps you to find who killed Annette."

They spoke to the warden of the hostel before leaving, but he was unable to give them any information. He seemed the sort that just did his job, but never got involved with the residents, which looking at some of their characters was understandable.

Chapter 25

THE FOLLOWING DAY, while Rankin was arranging back-up to go and speak to the dealer who supplied Annette, Josephine phoned her cousin Mark Hitchen.

"It's good to hear from you, Jo. Perhaps we can finally get round to having that drink now, I seem to have got the majority of my work out of the way," he said.

"Well, I'm afraid *I'm* up to my neck in it again," she told him.

"Really? I'd have thought things were easing up for you, now you'd caught the killer," he replied.

"They should be in normal circumstances but I'm afraid things are a little more complicated," she told him.

"Are things ever simple in our professions?"

"Ian McCallum is adamant he didn't murder Annette O'Connor, even though he has signed a statement confessing to killing all the others," Josephine told him.

"That's odd, I don't suppose there's any reason—"

"None that I can see. What's he got to lose? No Mark, I'm convinced he's telling the truth. Due to the fact he was raped by a vagrant, his hatred and revenge was directed towards males, Elizabeth Gunter was a mistake, he thought she was a man."

"So in that case, Annette's killer is still free?" Mark said.

"Precisely, and I'd like your help—well—any information you can give me that might be of use."

"I'd like to be able to give you something, but I really didn't know the girl or who her friends or enemies were. I managed to find her at the hostel, and then let her father know where she was, but I never even spoke to her."

"I do appreciate that Mark, but just rack your brains, anything might help. There's a possibility it could be drug related, as she owed money to her supplier, but we're looking into that angle at the moment."

"The location, everything, pointed to it being the Canal Killer," Mark said.

"Exactly. Whoever murdered her purposely made it look like she was the victim of the serial killer. She was murdered for a particular reason, unlike the others, which were revenge killings, by McCallum. If they were gay, vagrant or lived by the canal, they were vulnerable."

"I'll go through her file again to see if I can find anything, though it's doubtful, but I'll do my best," he told her.

"Thanks Mark, I'd appreciate it," she said, before putting down the receiver.

The following day the chief and Josephine issued a press release that stated that the Canal Killer, as the papers had called him had been caught. The proprietors of the various businesses along the canal could now no longer moan about it affecting trade, or blame the West Midlands Police for incompetence.

Although most of them would never admit to it, the notoriety of the area had actually attracted visitors. One café owner was taking people on a conducted tour of the canal for a small fee, showing them the various locations of the murders, just as they still did with the Ripper in the Whitechapel area of London. They decided not to let the press know that it was possible that one victim could have been killed by someone else, as it would come out soon enough at the trial.

The piece in the Evening Mail was as complimentary as the press could be to the police, although it said that Detective Inspector Josephine Blake from the Torbay Police Department, who had led the investigation, had played a major part in securing an arrest.

Many people would have thought it was a feather in Josephine's cap, but she felt differently. When the Ripper was caught in Devon, she felt a real monster had been apprehended and the streets were now far safer, whereas she felt the circumstances that had led Ian McCallum to kill were tragic. Until Annette O'Connor's murderer was found, she felt she couldn't return to Devon, even though in her heart she yearned to leave.

She could have handed over to Rankin and returned home, even though her secondment time wasn't completed, but she had never been one to shirk her responsibilities. She would see it through to the bitter end.

Chapter 26

JOSEPHINE AND RANKIN arranged to see James O'Connor, as they had to inform him that the man they had in custody had denied murdering Annette.

A very attractive blonde woman in her thirties answered the door to them.

"Oh hello, James is expecting you, he's in the garden."

"And may I ask who you are?" Josephine enquired.

"I'm sorry, I should have said, I'm Isabella Benning, a friend of James."

It was a warm sunny day, and they sat in the garden. Isabella offered them refreshments, and they accepted, so she went into the house to fetch them.

"A very attractive woman, if I might say, sir," Rankin noticed.

"Yes—Isabella and I have been seeing one another for some time. I suppose we would have been married by now, if I hadn't had to look after father. Anyway, she's moved in here now and it's good to have the company," James replied.

"I can't recall you mentioning her before," Josephine said.

"Oh—didn't I? It was probably all the stress of father's death and then Annette's—" he said looking rather distressed.

"Well that's understandable. The reason we've come to see you is that we have cause to believe that Ian McCallum didn't kill your sister," Josephine began.

"But—I thought— Surely he's admitted to the murders, the papers said—" he looked dismayed.

"He's confessed to all the other murders, but not Annette's."

"But why ever shouldn't he—?. What can he possibly gain by denying responsibility for her death?" James asked.

"Nothing, and since he readily gave us the details of his other murders, we see no reason for him to lie about this one," Rankin informed him.

"It seems he didn't intend his victims to be women," Josephine added.

"What—!" he looked aghast.

"His first three victims were men, supposedly gay, although one was straight."

"But I read somewhere—" James began, "About a girl—not Annette—"

"Yes, Elizabeth Gunter; he thought she was a man. Mind you, it was a mistake anyone could have made. Her hair was close cut to her head and she was sturdily built, and dressed in men's clothing. Whereas, your late sister was very feminine even though bedraggled and dirty, if you don't mind me saying," Rankin informed him.

"Err—no—not at all."

Just at that moment, his girlfriend brought four glasses of iced lemon cordial and placed them on the garden table.

She picked up her own glass and said,

"If you'd like me to leave you to talk in private—"

"No Isabella, stay," James said as he grabbed her hand. "That's if you don't mind—" he said looking towards Josephine.

"No— please take a seat, Miss Benning. I know it's a long shot, since you hadn't seen your sister for some time, but is there anyone you can think of that might have killed her?" Josephine asked him.

"God, no. I didn't even know where she was, but apparently since the people she hung round with in the Birmingham were mostly down and outs and drug dealers, I suppose she was mixing with a dangerous bunch. The only people I know of are the friends that she had here, before she left home, and as far as I know, she's not been in contact with any of them since the day she left," James told them.

"To think she left all this," Isabella observed as she looked round the magnificent garden. "She had some decent friends who came from good families, and she deserted them to go off with a load of ruffians. She must have been mad!"

"One or two people in the hostel where she was staying did look out for her. Sometimes the poorer people tend to help each other. The middle classes and the rich don't always make the best friends," Josephine remarked.

"Well, at least she wouldn't have been on the drugs," Isabella said rather haughtily.

"The drug problem is not exclusive to the poor you know, in fact, most of the users and dealers that I've arrested in the past, have come from quite good families," Josephine corrected her.

"Well, if she'd remained at home she wouldn't have been murdered," James declared.

"That's may be true. The fact is, she is dead, and if McCallum didn't kill her we need to find who did," Josephine replied.

"Oh by the way, I meant to ask you," Rankin began "The private investigator, Mark Hitchen, told your father where your sister was staying. How come neither of you decided to contact her?"

"My father was obviously too ill, and when I did find the letter in his personal effects, I decided to go and speak to Annette after the funeral, but then you came and informed me that she was dead," James explained.

"Bit of alright, wasn't she?" Rankin observed as they drove back.

"Mm, she's attractive, I'll give her that, but a bit of a snob in my opinion," Josephine replied.

"I like my women with a bit of class," Rankin told her.

"Yes, knowing you, I'm sure you do," she said sarcastically. "By the way, any luck with the drug dealer who supplied Annette?"

"We've had him in for questioning, but couldn't get much out of him. I don't think he's involved in her murder. The only good thing is that we've arrested him for possession, as he did have a lot of drugs on him at the time," Rankin told her.

"Oh well, not all bad then," Josephine stated.

"Jan, can you get me Annette O'Connor's file? I just want to look through it," Mark Hitchen said to his secretary.

A few minutes later she placed the folder on his desk. He opened it and examined the contents carefully. Inside was the original photo the father had given him of Annette when she was eighteen, and all the reports and details of the case. He sat and read his notes as he thought of the weeks he'd spent looking for her. If only he had discovered her sooner, she might still be alive. He sat back in his chair and meditated. After a time he got up and said to Jan who was sitting at the desk opposite, "Have we got any correspondence on the file, or the bill I sent Mr O'Connor?"

"Yes, I have actually," she went to a cabinet as she looked through the sections, which were in alphabetical order.

"Let's see, O'Neill—Owen—Here we are— O'Connor," she pulled out the paperwork. "I've even kept the letter he sent you, though obviously we cashed the cheque some time ago."

He read through the copy of the bill and the letter that Mr O'Connor had returned to him.

"Mm—I wonder," he said thoughtfully.

"Everything alright?" Jan asked.

He jumped up and kissed her on the cheek.

"Whatever was that for?" she said slightly taken aback.

"I apologise for having a go at you the other day about keeping too much old paperwork, but I thought I'd told you to throw it out."

"I know you did, but I'm the secretary and I do things my way, I had no intention of throwing anything away."

"Well, thank God you didn't," Mark told her.

It was Sunday afternoon, Mark and Josephine sat in a small pub restaurant in Lapworth, eating roast beef and drinking red wine.

"I'm glad you brought me out here, it's lovely countryside, and I needed a break from the city," Josephine told him.

"Well apart from the get-together at Auntie Win's, we haven't really seen much of one another though we've spoken on the phone," he said as he put a large piece of Yorkshire Pudding in his mouth.

"What I meant to ask you was, have you ever met Annette's brother, James O'Connor?"

"No, when I went to see the father James was at work. I did speak to him on the phone when I located Annette, but as his father was too ill to talk to me, I didn't give him any information. I sent a letter to Raymond O'Connor the following day," he told Josephine.

"Don't you think it's odd that the father never told his son he was trying to trace Annette?"

Josephine asked him.

"When I first went to visit the father he said 'We've been so worried about her', and I just assumed he was referring to his son as well as himself," he replied. "I did think it was strange that neither of them contacted Annette as soon as they knew where she was, but I suppose with him being so ill there was no chance. Still if they had, Raymond O'Connor would have had his dying wish granted to see his long lost daughter."

"Anyway, what was the reason for this meeting?" Josephine asked him.

"Can't I ring up my cousin and take her out for a meal then?" he teased. "No actually, it may be nothing, but all the father's correspondence sent to me at the beginning was hand written, but the last letter that I received was typed on a word processor, and he signed it. I've brought a copy to show you."

He put down his knife and fork and reached into his pocket, producing a sheet of paper.

Josephine read it for a minute or so and then said,

"It seems okay to me. Do you doubt it's the father's signature?"

"No, I'm sure it's the same as on all the other letters. It's just that I didn't realise he had a computer in the house, as in the past he'd always written everything by hand. Apart from that, I'd have thought he would have been too ill to use the computer, unless someone set it up for him. If his

301

son hadn't denied any knowledge of a private investigator being employed, I'd have thought he perhaps could have typed the letter for his father to sign. There was a nurse attending to him, so I suppose it's possible Raymond O'Connor asked her to type the letter. We could ask the son the address of the agency that employed her."

"If there is a computer in the house, it's quite feasible the father typed the letter himself. He may have felt a little better one day and had the strength to do it, but if there isn't, someone must have typed it for him. The son could have done it at his workplace for instance," Josephine suggested.

"Yes, but he's denied any knowledge of his father employing me," Mark added.

"Well, I don't know why he should lie, unless he's got something to hide. Maybe he knows more about his sister's death than he's letting on. Still, there's no point jumping to any conclusions at this stage. He's been asking about funeral arrangements for his sister. But I've explained we can't release the body while it's still being examined for forensic evidence. I'll get Rankin to go back and see him, he can make more enquiries and check if he's got a computer in the house."

"Wouldn't it be easier to ask him outright?" Mark suggested.

"No, I don't want him to think we're suspicious," Josephine told him.

"Do you think he may be involved in his sister's death?" he asked her.

"I don't think so, he seemed genuinely shocked and upset when we told him of her death. It's just that he may know more than he's letting on, it could be information we need to find her killer," she told him.

Rankin rang the doorbell and after a minute or so Isabella Benning answered the door.

"Good morning, ma'am, is Mr O'Connor at home?" Rankin asked, knowing full well he wouldn't be there.

"No he's at work. Can I help you?" she asked.

"It's just to let him know we won't be able to release his sister's body for some time. Well, at least not until we find who's responsible for her murder."

"I can give you his works telephone number," she offered.

"Well, it's not the sort of thing you really want to discuss on the phone," Rankin replied.

"Oh yes—of course—I can see that now. Well since you're here, would you like a coffee?"

"Yes, that would be nice," Rankin replied. She showed him into the lounge before going to the kitchen.

Adjoining the lounge was a small study area. On the polished U-desk stood a Pentium III, a top of the range computer. *Well, the father must have typed his letter here, so perhaps the son is in the clear*, Rankin thought to himself.

On the desk next to the computer stood several

very colourful paperweights. One had small dolphins inside, there was a multi-coloured crystal and another with a real butterfly inside; they were exquisite, and Rankin examined them carefully.

Isabella returned with their coffee.

"Oh, you're in here," she observed.

"You must forgive me, I was rather taken with these beautiful paperweights," Rankin told her.

"Yes, they are nice; James collects them you know."

As they sat drinking their coffee Rankin asked,

"What do you do for a living Miss Benning?"

"Oh please call me Isabella— Well this and that you know, a bit of modelling, and some promotion work, but I'm not in employment at the moment, I've moved in here to live with James and keep house for him."

A nice little number, I bet this place never gets messy with just her at home all day, it must be a doddle, Rankin thought.

"Somedays it's a bit boring, but won't be for very long," she said as she offered him a plate of chocolate biscuits.

"Oh, why's that?"

"We're selling up and going abroad," she told him.

"Has Mr O'Connor got a job lined up overseas?" Rankin asked.

"No, I think we'll just bum around for a few weeks and see a bit of the world."

I bet this house must be worth at least two hundred

and fifty thousand. I suppose they'll sell up and use the money, Rankin thought.

After he had finished his coffee he said "Thank you, that was lovely, but I must get on."

"It's been good to have some company," she said squeezing his arm. "It's a pity you have to rush away."

Rankin knew she was giving him the come-on, and for a split second he was tempted, but decided not to take up her offer.

"Unless, you don't fancy me of course."

"You're a very attractive woman, but I am investigating the death of your friend's sister."

"Fiancé," she corrected him flashing a huge diamond and emerald engagement ring. "Well, run along then, before I drag you upstairs," she said teasingly.

"Oh by the way, that's a great computer, the latest model; I'd love one myself but they're a bit pricey."

"According to James, it's got all the mod cons, DVD drive, internet capabilities, but it's all foreign to me. James only had it delivered last week and he's like a kid with a new toy."

Rankin arrived back at the station and went into Josephine's office.

"How did you get on?" she asked.

"Would you believe she made a pass at me" he told her.

"I bet that gave your male ego a boost," she said smiling.

"I do have women after me, quite a few in fact," he boasted.

"Right, so she had the hots for you, but did you find out anything else?"

"I did actually; he's selling up and they are moving abroad, but he hasn't got another job, so I suppose they will sell the house, which I assume is paid for, and live off the proceeds," he replied.

"Mm I suppose it's worth what—a quarter of a million," Josephine suggested.

"Yes, at least that amount I'd say."

"Isabella Benning has certainly landed on her feet. While she was making me coffee I went into the study, and there was a top of the range Pentium III computer on the desk."

"Oh, so it must have belonged to the father; so it's feasible he did type the letter to Mark," Josephine observed.

"Well, according to her James only bought it last week, until then there was no computer in the house," Rankin informed her.

"In that case, it's possible James did send the letter back, perhaps he typed it up at work," Josephine suggested.

"I can understand that, if his father said he needed a letter written, as his hands were too shaky for him to write, he would ask his son to do it for him."

"Yes, but he denies ever having any knowledge of it. That is, if he's telling the truth."

"I wonder why he should lie?" Rankin said

thoughtfully.

"We will have to get hold of the family solicitor and find out the contents of Raymond O'Connor's will," Josephine said.

"There's one other thing, although it may not be relevant. He had a collection of paperweights on his desk, lovely things; they were quite heavy, I should imagine he paid a lot of money for them. Didn't Mortimer say something similar to a paperweight in shape was used to kill Annette? It may be nothing but—"

"Let's see what the solicitor has to say before we jump the gun," Josephine told him.

Chapter 27

THEY ENTERED the offices of J. Edward and Sons Solicitors, and were shown up to Mr Edward Senior's office.

"It's rather irregular discussing the personal financial affairs of my clients," he began. "But since this is a police enquiry, I don't suppose I have any option."

"It's a murder enquiry," Josephine corrected him.

"Er—yes—I appreciate that, but since I have been the late Mr Raymond O'Connor's solicitor for the past thirty years and am now acting on behalf of his son, I feel a certain loyalty is needed to protect the family affairs."

"I am sure, if Mr O'Connor had was alive today, his only wish would be to try and find who murdered his daughter," Rankin told him.

"Yes I agree, but I can't see how you prying into their financial situation will help," he replied.

"That's our job and our concern sir," Josephine stated. "I know you're a very busy man, so if we can get on."

Mr Edwards opened the file as he glanced at his watch.

"Right, let's see, the last will and testament. The family home, which is valued at an estimated three hundred thousand pounds, was to be left jointly to James and Annette O'Connor. Also the remaining assets, bonds, investments, shares and the money in the building society and various bank accounts would be split fifty-fifty."

"So how much did they total?" Rankin asked.

Mr Edwards looked a little hesitant to part with the information, but answered,

"Approximately five hundred thousand pounds."

"Phew! I wonder what he did to accumulate that sort of money," Rankin said a little suspiciously.

The solicitor became rather annoyed.

"I can assure you sir, Mr O'Connor was a very shrewd business man who invested wisely, and I hope you're not suggesting otherwise."

"Not at all, it's just that, compared to a policeman's salary, it's a vast amount."

"It's a considerable sum to a solicitor," Mr Edwards added.

"So total assets including the house, total eight hundred thousand pounds. So if Annette had lived, they would have received four hundred thousand each. Is that correct?" Josephine said.

"Yes, if the house was sold that's how much money they would receive," the solicitor told her. "Since the mother passed away, the children were the sole beneficiaries, so when Annette died the entire estate went to James O'Connor."

As they drove back to the station, Rankin said,

"Four hundred thousand is a fortune by anybody's standards, but with his sister out of the way he stood to inherit her share. Eight hundred thousand pounds, he's now a very rich man to say the least. I've known people murder for a fraction of that amount."

"There's definitely a motive, but we still can't assume it was him. Her murderer was either some sort of maniac who just struck or it was pre-meditated. Even though McCallum didn't kill her, if it wasn't James O'Connor, the man who did finish her off certainly did him a favour and made him a very rich man," Josephine stated.

"There's a thought. Do you think it's possible he paid a hitman to kill her?" Rankin suggested.

"I never thought of that, it's feasible. Anyway, let's recap. He denies knowledge of his father employing a private detective. Why should he do that? When Mark phoned the house, he told him his father was too ill to speak on the phone. Mark says he didn't tell him what he wanted to speak to his father about and he wrote to him the following day. Now the father replied and sent a cheque to settle his bill. But it's odd he used a personal computer to type the letter, since he originally wrote to Mark by hand. That is understandable, most older people don't like computers, and feel a hand-written letter is far more personal, even though nowadays many firms find them unprofessional. So what we have to ask ourselves is, how did he get access to a computer if there wasn't one in the house at the time?"

"Perhaps James O'Connor suggested to his father he replied to the letter and offered to type it on his computer at work. Remember, Mark said at the time the cheque was made out neatly, but he recognised Raymond O'Connor's shaky signature."

"But why should he deny knowledge of his father's reply, what would he gain by it," Rankin said.

"Well, if he knew Annette might be found and return home, and he knew his father was dying, perhaps he didn't want her to get half of the money. Let's face it, she hadn't bothered with her father for the past four years. Whereas James had lived at home and cared for him, perhaps he thought he had a right to all the money. I suppose it's possible that, unbeknown to his father, James opened Mark's letter, which contained Annette's address at the hostel. He could have kept the information from his father, written back to Mark and wrote out a cheque setting the account. He could easily have forged his father's signature," Josephine suggested.

"So what you're saying is, he knew her whereabouts, but didn't tell his father."

"Precisely," she replied.

"But wouldn't the father have contacted the investigator asking him if he had made any progress in finding his daughter?" Rankin suggested.

"Maybe, as he deteriorated, and with the drugs he was taking he just became confused. And remember Mark assumed the letter he received was from the father. As far as he was concerned, the case was closed," Josephine told him.

"So James gets his sister's address and goes to bump her off. He's read about the serial killer that's

311

taking the lives of vagrants along the canal and decides to kill her in a similar fashion. And we would think it was just another of the Canal Killer's victims. But remember a different weapon was used."

"All the papers said was that the victims head's were badly beaten. If I remember correctly, the fact a hammer was used was information that was never passed on to the press," she said.

"It sounds very nicely worked out. He had the motive and the opportunity, but we have no proof, and it's pure conjecture. We could be barking up the wrong tree," Rankin told her.

"We could be wrong, but I've got a feeling we're not. Just call it female intuition?"

The following day, James O'Connor was brought into the station for questioning. They could have visited his home, but decided that would have been too informal, and they didn't want him to feel relaxed and think it was just a casual interview.

"We have spoken to your solicitor Mr Edwards and he has told us the contents of your father's will. Due to your sister's death, you've inherited the entire estate, which is in the region of eight hundred thousand pounds."

"How dare you contact my solicitor without permission," he began, "It's my business what money he left me. I stayed with my father and looked after him, I earned that money," he

312

announced.

"A nice little earner then, wouldn't you say, almost a million pounds," Rankin observed. "Especially with your sister's share going to you. Let's face it, you were the only person who would benefit from her death."

"What are you suggesting?"

"That it was very much to your advantage when she was murdered," Rankin replied.

"Even if Annette had been alive, I would have got four hundred thousand, that would have been ample," James said.

"But since you're giving up your job and going abroad with Miss Benning, surely the extra half a million would come in handy?" Josephine added.

"What you're suggesting is preposterous. I didn't kill my sister, and I'm not saying anything else until I've spoken to my solicitor."

Josephine pushed a sheet of paper over the desk to him.

"Do you recognise this Mr O'Connor?" she asked.

He sat for a minute or so as he read the typewritten letter that was addressed to Mark Hitchen.

"I haven't seen this before, but it's the letter my father must have sent to the private investigator, look, there's his signature," he said pointing to the bottom of the page.

"Your father's first correspondence was written by hand. Don't you think it's strange this one was

313

done on a computer. You didn't have one in your house at the time, so how did he type this letter?"

"I don't know, maybe he got someone to do it for him."

"Whoever would that be? He only saw you and his nurse."

"Well, perhaps she typed it for him," James suggested.

"The lady in question can't type," Josephine lied.

"Well, maybe she got someone to do it for her," was his second suggestion.

"Not according to her."

"Well, she is lying."

"Why ever should she? She has nothing to gain by doing so. You typed that letter. There's nothing wrong in that, it just means you knew where Annette was living and wrote back to the investigator on your fathers behalf. It's not a crime, so why deny it?"

"You can't prove I sent that letter, my fingerprints aren't on it."

"Well they are now, because you've just touched the page."

"Now look here… You can't do that!"

"Don't worry, this is just a copy of the original. Though funnily enough, there were no fingerprints at all on the paper, which I find very odd. It was as if whoever handled it wore gloves."

"Look, I don't know what the hell you're talking about. I didn't kill Annette and I didn't send that letter. You can't prove I did, so I'm not saying another word until I get legal advice."

"Perhaps you could just tell us where you were on the fourteenth of April, say from six o'clock in the evening onwards."

"That was weeks ago, I'd have to check my diary."

"Well, you do that Mr O'Connor, I want to know what you did and who you were with on that evening," Josephine told him.

"Do you reckon he's our man?" Rankin asked.

"Yes I do, but it's all circumstantial evidence, it wouldn't hold up in court. We've got to get something else on him," Josephine said.

"I mean, it's possible he used one of those paperweights on his desk to kill her, but if he did, he'd have washed it thoroughly, and since they are smooth glass, there most probably wouldn't be a trace of blood or skin on them. Then again, he may have disposed of whatever he used to kill her with," Rankin added.

"We'll get Mortimer to check her over again, for fibres or anything he can find. Oh, I don't know, there must be something on her, some clue," Josephine said half-heartedly.

"Well, there's only the cufflink with the initial I engraved on in the broken heart. It didn't belong to Ian McCallum even though the initial was the same. He says the only time he's ever worn a shirt was the day he got married and that was a button cuff. It obviously doesn't belong to James O'Connor, so perhaps she just stole it from someone," Rankin remarked.

"Yes, but why should she be clutching it in her hand? It was as though she had taken it off her assailant. No, there's got to be something else."

Kath, the young woman at the hostel, phoned Josephine saying she had some information for her and they arranged to meet at a café in the city centre.

"I was talking to someone at the hostel the other day," Kathy began "who said he can remember a posh chap with dark hair poking around asking for Annette. I told him to come to you with the information, but he hates the police, and anyway, he's left there now."

"Do you think he'd be able to identify him if we traced him?" Josephine asked.

"I don't know, Joe-Boy, that's what they call him, is a user, so he's not that reliable," Kath told her.

"His evidence may not hold up in court, but we'll try and trace him, thanks Kath," she said as she pushed a ten pound note into her hand.

Five days later, Joe-Boy returned to the hostel and Kath contacted the police. He identified James O'Connor as the man he'd seen at the hostel. After the identification parade, O'Connor was taken into the interview room.

"I suggest for your own good, you start telling us the truth," Josephine said.

"Okay. I did type that letter for my father at his request and sent it to the investigator with a cheque," he admitted.

"Then why deny it?" Josephine asked him.

"I knew it would look bad, especially when Annette was found dead."

"How did you know where she was living?" Rankin enquired.

"My father told me the address of the hostel and asked me to go and see her to persuade her to come home, if only for one day, to see him before he died. The callous bitch wasn't having any of it. Told me to go to hell and said she didn't give a damn that father was dying, and that she wouldn't set foot inside the house again. I pleaded with her, but she didn't want to know."

"I'm amazed she wouldn't go back home, if only to get the money," Josephine remarked.

"I didn't tell her father had left her half of everything in his will. If she'd have had the decency and compassion to visit him, she would have found out herself. She was a hateful little bitch. Oh, she looked pretty enough, that angelic little face with her long red hair, but underneath that sweet exterior, she was an evil cow! Why should she have half of father's money, she didn't deserve any of it. I'm glad she's dead, but I didn't kill her."

"Do you think he's telling the truth?" Rankin asked Josephine.

"He seemed bitter when he was talking about Annette, and in a way I can understand his anger, if he pleaded with her to see her father and she refused, especially since it was his dying wish. He had cared for him; maybe he genuinely thought she was entitled to none of the money. Then again, we only have his word about her reaction when he asked her to return. Since she's dead, we don't have her side of the story."

The following day they called at the house to see Isabella while James was at work. She opened the door looking a little dishevelled.

"Oh hello, come in," she said showing them into the lounge, which was strewn with clothes. All the chairs and sofas were covered in shirts, dresses, trousers and other articles of clothing.

"Please excuse the mess, only we're going away at the end of next week, and I'm trying to sort this lot out. Although James has told me to throw most of mine away, and buy all new gear. He is a sweetie, still, I'll have to keep some of these designer dresses," she said holding up a very classy looking dress in deep green velvet.

"We just need to confirm your fiancés statement that you were with him on the evening of April the fourteenth from six o'clock onwards," Rankin told her.

"I'll just check my diary," she removed a small black book from her handbag and opened it.

318

"Yes, that's right, we were originally booked to go to a restaurant, but I cooked for James instead."

"When did he arrive home?" Rankin asked.

"Oh, about six thirty."

"And he was in all evening with you?"

"Yes, we went to bed about midnight, if I remember; we did consume rather a lot of red wine, so I can't be precise about the time."

"It's a pity, in a way, you didn't go to a restaurant, at least then we'd have the confirmation of the staff and the details of the booking would be on their records," Josephine told her.

"I know, but I'm telling you the truth, why should I lie?" Isabella said.

Josephine looked round at all the trappings and the luxurious life this woman was about to have. Isabella would never have to work again or worry about where the money was coming from to pay a bill. She could think of loads of reasons why the woman should lie.

Rankin was standing at a nearby table looking at several pairs of very expensive cufflinks, some in gold and others in silver. There was a pair that looked like miniature golf clubs and some diamond cut ones.

"These are very classy," Rankin noticed. "I like designer cufflinks myself, but it's not often I can afford to buy them."

"I know, he's got loads of them. I was just sorting out his shirts to go to the laundry and he's left the cufflinks in all of them. Mind you, he's lost one of the best pair, that I bought him as a birthday present last year," Isabella told him.

"Oh really, that's a pity."

"Yes, they were really lovely, half a broken heart on each cufflink with a J engraved on one and an I on the other. I think it was a nice idea of mine, James and Isabella, two parts of one heart, romantic don't you think? He's only got the one left now, the one with the J on—see—" she said picking it up off the table. It was identical to the one found at the scene of the murder; the only difference was the letter.

Rankin signalled to Josephine and she walked over to the table.

"Yes!" she said out loud "I think we've got him!"

Isabella Benning looked at them in amazement.

Chapter 28

Later that day they arrested James O'Connor for the murder of his sister. For several days he concocted several excuses and stories, even though his cufflink was found on her body.

Eventually, even Isabella suspected the man she loved was responsible, and she made a statement to the effect that she wasn't with James on that particular evening. He had made up some sort of excuse and persuaded her to lie to the police.

Josephine and Rankin weren't far off with their ideas on how he'd committed the murder.

When the letter arrived from Mark Hitchen saying he'd found Annette, James didn't even show it to his father, he just typed a letter and sent it back, he wore gloves when he was handling the paper, his only mistake was to use a computer. He wrote a cheque out, it was easy enough to forge his father's signature. Mark didn't suspect anything at the time; he had no reason to believe that Raymond O'Connor hadn't sent the letter he'd received. His account had been paid, and as far as he was concerned, the file on Annette was closed.

The father died thinking that his daughter hadn't been found. As his health deteriorated, he became confused with all the drugs, and didn't contact Mark Hitchen again.

Once he knew where she was living James went to see his sister with the intention of murdering her. It was unlikely he ever asked her to return home, if she had done so, who knows, Raymond O'Connor may have changed his will and left her everything. He couldn't take the chance that one day Annette would get fed up with living rough and decide to return home. He had read in the newspapers about the 'canal killer' taking the lives of vagrants in Birmingham, and that gave him the idea to dispose of his sister in a similar fashion. He hoped that the police would think she was just another victim of the serial killer. When he'd read of Elizabeth Gunter's death he'd assumed that both men and women were being killed at random.

A friend of the family came forward when they read in the paper that James had been charged with her murder. He told the police Annette had loved her father, and left home because of her brother's cruelty. He would often physically and mentally abuse her.

"God, her life at home must have been hell if she left a luxurious house to live in squalor," Rankin observed.

"Maybe things were so bad, she'd rather have been poor, cold, hungry and on the streets than being abused at home," Josephine stated.

"She should have told her father what was happening," Rankin said.

"Perhaps her brother had so much power over her, the only option was to leave. You know, in a way, even though James O'Connor has only killed once, his was a very cruel pre-meditated murder for money. I truly believe him to be a far more evil and devious man than Ian McCallum. Even though he killed four people, his circumstances were so tragic."

Josephine was shown into the cell where McCallum was held awaiting trial.

"We now know who killed Annette O'Connor, it was her brother," Josephine told him. "Since he'd read about a serial killer dumping bodies in the canal, he decided to dispose of his sister, in the hope that everyone would think she was one of your victims."

"I told you at the start I didn't kill her," Ian announced.

"I know, and I believed you, the problem I had was if you didn't, who did?" Josephine replied.

"It's a pity we don't have the death penalty, they should never have abolished hanging. Still, I'll die with AIDS anyway. I don't want to live without Anna and the baby. I shall refuse all drugs, as I want to suffer in death like Anna suffered, that will give me some sort satisfaction," he stated.

"You endured a dreadful loss, but killing others wasn't the answer. You should have reported Charlie Reid and then he would have been imprisoned," she told him.

"Yeah, and for how long? He'd soon be released to do it again to some other poor bastard. I don't regret anything I've done. My only fault was not realising he'd infected me with AIDS and not taking any precautions when I made love to Anna, although I don't expect you to understand."

Josephine left his cell with a certain comprehension as to why he'd taken the path he had, but she would never admit it to him, or anyone else for that matter.

"Well, you've done us proud. You, Sergeant Rankin and the team, wrapped it all up nicely. I suppose you'll be leaving us now," the chief said.

"Yes, I suppose I will," she replied as she turned to Rankin. "Don't forget, if you're ever down in Torquay, I'll give you a tour of our clubs, you'll probably be pleasantly surprised, and may not need your solarium if you have a day sunbathing on the beach," Josephine told him.

"I might take you up on that offer," he said smiling. "Keep in touch, it's been good working with you," he said kissing her on the lips, rather passionately for a colleague.

Mm, perhaps now I can see why all his girlfriends are so attracted to him, she thought.

EPILOGUE

EPILOGUE

AUNTIE WIN stood on the platform crying, "Come on now, luv," Arthur said, handing her his hankie.

"You'll come back and see us, won't you Jo?" she said.

"Of course, and you and Arthur must come and stay with me at Babbacombe."

"Don't worry, I'll get her down there if it's the last thing I do," Arthur told her.

After a few more hugs and tearful farewells, Josephine boarded the train. As she sat and looked out of the window, her eyes filled with tears. Not because of Auntie Win's emotional send-off, but because of all the grief and death she had encountered over the last few weeks. Her emotions were mixed, she desperately wanted to go back home to see Jessica, Bill and most of all Andrew, and yet—

As she looked out of the window, she noticed Auntie Win telling Arthur off about something or other and a smile crept through her tear-filled eyes as she began to laugh.

THE END

If you have enjoyed this book you will be certain to enjoy these other titles by Janet Harward

THE TEDDY BEAR MURDERS

IN THE EVENT YOU FIND IT DIFFICULT TO OBTAIN THIS TITLE YOU CAN ORDER IT DIRECT FROM THE PUBLISHERS AT THE ADDRESS BELOW. ENCLOSE £4.99 PER BOOK (P&P FREE).

PLEASE MAKE CHEQUES PAYABLE TO J O'NEILL

O'NEILL PUBLISHING

34 ROMFORD CLOSE, SHELDON, BIRMINGHAM B26 3TR

IN MEMORY
OF
MURDER

A tranquil Spanish church is thrown into chaos when Andrew Markham's face and hair become a blazing mass of flames and molten wax... In Devon, Detective Inspector Josephine Blake and her Team are searching for a perverted serial killer, as young girls are being held hostage for days, enduring horrible torture before being murdered...

Meanwhile across the country members of the literary establishment are dying in what seem to be a series of gruesome accidents...

Can these events possibly be related?

"The plot is gripping to the end, with Blake under scrutiny from those above her, who doubt that the roles of woman and copper can be combined."

— *Crime Time*

AVAILABLE AT ALL GOOD
BOOKSHOPS

IN MEMORY
OF
MURDER

**IN THE EVENT YOU FIND IT
DIFFICULT TO OBTAIN THIS
TITLE YOU CAN ORDER IT
DIRECT FROM THE PUBLISHERS
AT THE ADDRESS BELOW.
ENCLOSE £4.99 PER BOOK (P&P
FREE).**

*PLEASE MAKE CHEQUES
PAYABLE TO J O'NEILL*

O'NEILL PUBLISHING

34 ROMFORD CLOSE,
SHELDON,
BIRMINGHAM B26 3TR

ECHOES OF DEATH

Investigating a series of horrific murders in the quiet Devon town of Torquay, Detective Inspector Josephine Blake becomes convinced that the killer is deliberately imitating the crimes of one of the earliest serial killers—Jack The Ripper!

When the killer starts to taunt her by email, and threatens the lives of her family, her investigation becomes a terrifying battle of wits that will tax the full extent of Josephine's resources to their limit.

As the killings continue it becomes clear that the killer may have a specific person in mind for his final victim…

—Josephine!

"A brilliant murder mystery—the book grips and excites to the last twist!"

"A riveting and ingenious plot!"

"Her best yet!"

—Crime Time

AVAILABLE AT ALL GOOD BOOKSHOPS